REVENGE
OF THE
SLUTS

NATALIE WALTON

JUN 16 2021

REVENGE OF THE SLUTS

wattpad books

MORE LOVE

wattpad books **W**

Copyright © 2021 Natalie Walton. All rights reserved.
Published in Canada by Wattpad Books, a division of Wattpad Corp.
36 Wellington Street E., Toronto, ON M5E 1C7

www.wattpad.com

First Wattpad Books edition: February 2021
ISBN 978-1-98936-551-9 (Trade Paper original)
ISBN 978-1-98936-552-6 (eBook edition)

Library and Archives Canada Cataloguing in Publication information is available upon request.

Printed and bound in Canada

1 3 5 7 9 10 8 6 4 2

Cover design by Laura Mensinga
Images © AdobeStock and iStock
Typesetting by Sarah Salomon

Dedicated to the survivors who see themselves in the pages of this book.

You are brave. You are loved. Your stories are the momentum for change.

CHAPTER ONE

It had all started with a pair of boobs. More specifically, a photo of Sloane Mayer's.

I looked at the email that I had just opened, sent directly to me but not only to me. It had been forwarded, in a way that could only be described as unfortunate, to the entire student body via a LISTSERV. Regardless of whether or not the original sender had sent it to everyone on the student email directory—which, they had—it would have made its way around the student body with record speed. St. Joseph's High School wasn't so tiny that everyone knew everything, but it was small enough that gossip spread rapidly without consideration for the truth.

The facts in this case, however, were fairly apparent. It was Sloane, known for her effortlessly pretty dark hair and reputation for owning her sexuality. She was the person on campus

1

who hiked her uniform skirt up a little bit higher or undid that one extra button. I couldn't blame her; if I had boobs like hers, I'd probably show them off too.

"Holy shit." The guy next to me laughed. I knew we were looking at the same email; it had been a perfectly average Tuesday during a perfectly average week up until now. The email would undoubtedly fuel the rumor mill for at least a few days.

Phones around the room vibrated and let off sharp *dings* accompanied by students rotating in their seats to look at each other. A girl a few rows over leaned over to her friend to ask, "Did you get it too?"

The first picture was of Sloane, showing off a significant amount of her smooth, nearly flawless skin. There was talk that she got spray tans, or at least visited tanning booths regularly— she had an impeccable year-round tan that was entirely unfitting for Massachusetts winters—but there was a lot of talk about Sloane in general.

The sender hadn't been bold enough to use a personal email. Both the name and the email address were a scrambled list of numbers and letters, probably generated by a website rather than a person. None of the information was immediately identifiable.

As I scrolled, I realized it wasn't only Sloane's picture that was attached. There were at least three different pictures of female students—all seniors, like Sloane and me—in various stages of undress. The photos were flattering but not something I'd imagine were meant for public consumption. They were intimate, revealing faces free of makeup and poor lighting from bedrooms rather than photo studios.

The scroll bar on the side of the screen told me that there were even more images, but I couldn't bring myself to look any further. Even though I'd held the title of executive editor for St. Joe's student newspaper for only about a month, I'd been on staff long enough to know the email was going to be the sole topic of our meeting today. My fingers quickly pressed Delete, pushing away the curiosity that welled inside of me and choosing to, just this once, not act like a reporter.

"Class, please," Mrs. Thompson tried fruitlessly from the front of the class. Getting us to focus on economics was hard enough already but the email was going to make it impossible. "Does anyone remember from last class what the purpose of a tight monetary policy is?"

She looked exhausted and had seemingly aged five years since starting here as a teacher. Mrs. Thompson was young and probably already thinking about how there was enough time left in her life to find a new career. She was used to everyone in class looking at our phones, so it never occurred to her that what had grabbed our attention might be a concern. Part of me wished she would ask, so I could comfortably know that at least someone other than the students was aware.

At least that would be one microscopic thing working in favor of the girls involved.

"Can you believe Alice is on here?" a voice said. "Isn't that Louis's girlfriend?"

They were talking about Alice Huey. She was quiet and generally kept to herself and had been dating Louis Sanford for what would be a year in March. They were a sweet couple and both seniors. Alice wasn't well-known or particularly notable since she wasn't involved in any extracurriculars. Louis did marching band but didn't seem to hang out with many people other than Alice.

I found myself hoping that Louis hadn't been the person

who'd leaked Alice's picture—we were lab partners last year and he seemed like he really cared about her—but I couldn't come up with an alternative explanation. The only other possibility was that Alice had sent pictures to someone else. Neither option was a particularly good one.

The whispers and phone vibrations continued. My phone lit up with rapid-fire messages in the *Warrior Weekly* newsroom group, mostly staffers wanting to know who'd sent the email and why. I was wondering the same thing.

Generally, gossip moved through the mill with impressive speed. During my junior year, a rumor spread about a senior who'd gotten involved with a married assistant football coach, but it eventually faded when people got bored. The same thing happened when it was said that a teacher was selling weed to students, that Sloane got an STD from a college boy, that soph-omore Tina Rooney was sent away after crashing her car while driving drunk. But none of those had real proof.

The email, however—and the photos—were indisputable.

There were limitless possibilities of who the sender could be considering the number of pictures. The gossip and drama could easily live on until at least graduation. Whether the person who had done this had anticipated a massive impact was uncertain, but it was clear they had wanted to create news. And, without a doubt, they had achieved that.

My phone buzzed and I dreaded the potential that there was another email waiting for me. Instead, it was my editor in chief, Ronnie Greer.

Ronnie was, essentially, my boss at the newspaper and despite us being the same age, it genuinely felt like she was my superior. I liked journalism, but Ronnie lived and breathed it. She had a knack for calling a good story angle and was constantly pushing school-set boundaries with the stories she wanted to publish. She could be stubborn and had high expectations for herself and the newspaper, but she was also fair and almost always right. I was her right-hand woman and didn't mind being told what exactly was expected of me.

> Ronnie: Did you get the email?

I had a pretty good idea of where the text was leading. She was going to ask if I could send out an email and ask everyone on staff to work together to build a story about the photos. While Ronnie was most likely sympathetic to the people who had had their photos leaked, I knew she also saw potential for this story to be her big break.

I sent her a quick *yes* as a response, the flutter of excitement and nerves building in my chest. It was a feeling I didn't get often, since we rarely had major news at St. Joe's. We mostly wrote about food waste or budget cuts, which was important but didn't exactly light a fire in the *Warrior Weekly* staff.

> Ronnie: I want you to be the person to cover this story—I'll talk to you about it later.

Surprise overpowered my usually cool demeanor and I read the message twice to make sure I understood. Ronnie, the person who had been waiting for *that* story—the one that would make her stand out to colleges and would solidify her as a rising star—was handing off easily the biggest news our campus had probably seen in years. This could potentially beat out the time our wrestling team had been kicked out of the state champion-ship for getting caught drinking in the hotel. It was capital-*B* Big news.

The situation was too complicated to talk about over text but I kept my phone in my hand, lightly tapping my fingers against the screen in thought. The idea of tackling something so huge, so exciting, was nerve-wracking.

Mrs. Thompson was still talking about the differences between loose and tight economic policies at the front of the room, but I wasn't retaining any of the information. My mind was cycling through the images from the email, particularly Sloane Mayer with her chest on full display for one intended recipient. I'd never seen her break, even when the rumor about her having an STD spread, but I could imagine seeing the pho-tos might shatter her laid-back persona. I'd imagine the email followed by inevitable student commentary would be enough to justify transferring schools. If it had happened to me, that's what I'd do. While the picture of her was admittedly incredibly flatter-ing, the idea of something so private being seen by so many peo-ple, presumably without permission, was horrifying.

The loudspeaker crackled to life, shocking everyone out of their chit-chat.

"Students," Principal Yanick said in her familiar soft tone. It had to be serious for her—and not the secretary, Mr. Winters—to be the one speaking. "We have been informed of an incident and we are calling an assembly at the end of this class block. All students are to report to the auditorium and the only exceptions to this rule have to be granted through me personally."

The watch on my wrist said *9:36*, and I was almost impressed by how quickly word had reached the administration. It had to have been a student office assistant who reported it since there were no teachers on the email list.

Some comfort washed over me, hoping that maybe something could be done now. The only thing worse than the situation happening itself was the situation happening and having the school turn a blind eye to it.

The minute the announcements were over, Margot Hampton—also a senior but we weren't close—stood up in the middle of the room and exited quickly, not looking back or gathering her books. The boys behind me snorted with poorly stifled laughter and, even though I hadn't seen her photo before deleting the email, it was obvious she was one of the girls featured.

My fingernails were raw from where I'd picked at them, but the pain didn't stop my nervous tick. Months earlier, before my boyfriend, Nick Haskell, had become my ex, I'd sent him photos of myself during spring break. At the time it didn't mean much, since I'd never considered the possibility of him sharing the photos with the entire student body. All I could hope was that I wasn't one of the attachments on that email—I didn't have the courage to look.

Eventually, the bell rang, and students piled their notebooks into their backpacks, resuming conversations with each other in normal speaking tones instead of whispers. A group of kids I recognized from the basketball team were showing each other their phone screens. A pair of girls I'd interviewed about a local nonprofit they worked with chatted loudly, throwing around names of girls presumably on the email. *Alice. Claire. Sloane. Violeta.* I wasn't directly friends with anyone in the classroom or anyone involved in the email; most of them were only familiar to me because I'd interviewed them for a story or because we'd been going to the same schools since kindergarten. The same was true for most of St. Joe's student population, outside of the few people from the football team that I'd met personally through Nick. I had a tight-knit group on the paper, and that's all I wanted in terms of a friend group; the dynamics of a high school social hierarchy didn't appeal to me much.

"I *literally* cannot believe she was stupid enough to show her face in a nude like this!" a girl I recognized from the school's debate team said. It wasn't clear which girl on the email she was referring to; it could've been any of them. "I always make sure my face isn't in them when I send pictures to Eric."

Nudes, like any form of sexual expression, were messy business at St. Joe's. On the one hand, there was some inherent popularity in being someone who not only had the options to get laid but would also put out. But, on the other, female students could only go so far before they were deemed a slut. The line was thin and the rules weren't clear.

After throwing my backpack over my shoulder, I walked over to Margot's desk to gather her things. No one else seemed inclined to help, including a girl I'd seen Margot occasionally chat with before and after class.

Even though Margot and I had gone to middle school together, we hadn't spoken much then or now. But, when I saw her books still on her desk, I felt an urge to help her. I zipped up her backpack, stuffed her books and papers inside, and headed for the closest bathroom, hoping she was there. If not, I wasn't sure how I was going to explain basically stealing her things.

It was fairly short walk since St. Joe's was not a particularly large or complicated building. It was clear a lot of money had gone into the school, but no more than the roughly five hundred kids in the student population were meant to fit inside. The exterior was beautiful and imposing, inspired by Gothic architecture and built with old money, but the interior was mostly modernized except for a few small corners, like the front office and the auditorium.

After opening the bathroom door, I checked to see if there were any feet visible under the cream-colored stall crack. These were the first-choice bathrooms to go to on campus— they were significantly cleaner and newer, having been renovated my freshman year. The newly painted beige walls and tiled countertops lost their sparkle only months after installation, but they were a better option than the decrepit ones that hadn't been touched since the school's inception.

When I spotted shoes, I knocked on the door lightly. "Hey, it's Eden."

"Who?" I heard her on the other side, sniffling after the words left her mouth. I assumed I had the right girl.

"Eden Jeong, from economics," I said. "Margot?"

"Yeah," she responded. The air hung heavily between us for a second, waiting on my response.

"I have your things," I said. "You left them in the classroom."

"Oh," she responded, her voice echoing in the otherwise silent room. After a beat, she unlocked the door. She had opted for the wheelchair-accessible stall, allowing her more space and a private sink and mirror. It saved her the discomfort of having to pull herself together at the communal taps as people walked in and out of the bathroom. I stayed silent as a pair of girls took their time at the sink, gossiping probably to avoid leaving for the assembly.

"Who do you think did it?" the blond asked, most likely not a senior since I didn't recognize her.

"I don't know, but those girls must've done something really awful for someone to retaliate like this," her friend responded. I repressed a wince, knowing Margot could hear them.

When the girls left, Margot finally stuck her hand out weakly to take her backpack. She was a little bit shorter than my five foot eight, and curvy. Margot gripped a wad of toilet paper in her other hand with trembling fingers. Her skin had taken on a sickly pale overtone. I desperately wanted to give her a hug and tell it would be okay but I knew lying wasn't going to help. Maybe eventually it would be okay, but for now it would suck.

"Thank you," she said.

The door creaked open, turning our heads in that direction. Mrs. Thompson's round face peeked around the partially opened door. "Hey. Just a reminder that the assembly is happening in three minutes. I am begging you to please show up. Principal Yanick is talking serious consequences for the students who skip."

We responded with quiet *okay*s even though it didn't seem like Margot intended to move any time soon.

"I'm sorry," I said after Mrs. Thompson closed the door, the words tumbling out of my mouth before I could stop them.

"You don't have to be sorry. I did this to myself, right? Just a slut getting what she deserves," she said.

"You didn't deserve this," I said. "No one did."

Margot let out a halfhearted laugh that turned into a pained guffaw. "Yeah. Let's see how many people have *that* mentality."

Her eyes turned down and welled up. My cue to leave. It was a situation that deserved an ugly, awful, self-pitying cry; at the very least, I owed her the chance to do that alone.

Exiting the bathroom, I readjusted my backpack and tried to brace myself for the shitstorm that was about to come.

CHAPTER TWO

Ronnie spotted me within seconds of walking into the auditorium. It was an impressive feat considering all of St. Joe's was using the same entrance and I was surrounded by bodies.

"Eden!" She waved from her seat in the third row from the back.

Grateful, I walked over to sit next to her. I didn't have a plan prior to walking in and it was absolute chaos. Students were lining the walls, waiting to file into seats. The room buzzed with anticipation and nervous energy; all we needed was a spark and it would explode. Principal Yanick, Mr. Winters, and Father McGlynn, our school's priest, tried to contain the crowd. I surveyed the room, knowing almost everyone who attended St. Joe's was going to be there, including Nick, who was seated a few rows ahead of me.

"Wild, huh?" Ronnie asked, picking up her bag from the seat she'd reserved for me and letting me slide past.

"It's definitely something," I said. "Fast turnaround on organizing an assembly. I wonder how much the St. Joe's administration could really have to say since the email was sent out only about an hour ago."

"I think they're panicking." Ronnie looked at the crowd. "I think a lot of people are."

Ronnie and I had a tendency to view the student body from an observational standpoint, something that was probably rooted in having spent so much time writing about them. Or maybe our disconnection from the people around us, our tendency to view the student body as potential sources and subjects, made us want to write about them. My parents sometimes joked that I was born ready to be a young professional, entirely focused on my work and my personal goals rather than making friends—or, in reality, actually going out and living. But it was easy when I didn't dwell on what I might've been missing. I'd had Nick, that was enough then. But since we'd broken up, most of my social interactions had taken place between the school's four walls.

"So." Ronnie pushed her dark-brown spiral curls out of her face. She had a number of glasses she liked to switch between and that day she had decided on massive round ones, making her hazel eyes seem even larger than they were. "I was thinking you would tackle this story."

"Don't you want to take this one on?" I asked. "There's a lot of potential here."

"There is, but I feel too connected to the problem to write about it."

"We're both seniors," I said.

"But I don't think I can present a balanced perspective." She placed a hand on my arm. "You know me and so do most other people here. I'm not exactly quiet about my feelings toward social issues and I don't want it to impact the story's credibility."

She had a point. Both of us were pretty politically aware, but Ronnie was more open about it than I was. She'd gone to every Washington DC Women's March with her mom since the first year it had started, and she frequently posted online about being pro-choice. Last year, her post online about increasing taxes to support public programming for single moms had led to full-fledged virtual arguments with nearly half of St. Joe's. It was her M.O. to stir up debates and it garnered a lot of attention, usually from the wealthy, white, and male crowd that populated St. Joe's. She never let a social studies or history class go to waste and would frequently end up causing in-class arguments about topics like the war on drugs or housing discrimination. Usually, it would end with Ronnie fending for herself against a group of boys who were no more intelligent than she was but were louder and part of a bigger pack.

"It's not going to," I insisted. "Everyone here is going to have an opinion on this issue; it's hard to stay balanced or even remotely neutral. You being openly political isn't going to impact that."

"Sources aren't going to want to talk to me, Eden," Ronnie said. "You know it and I know it."

Ronnie stood out at St. Joe's, both for her opinions and her physical appearance. She was one of four Black girls attending the school and, although wealthy and born into a successful family like most of St. Joe's, Ronnie was expected to work twice as hard as anyone else to prove herself. Ronnie and I weren't the kind of people to openly share personal feelings, but sometimes Ronnie would mention the ways students and faculty talked about her, how students were often reluctant to work with her on group projects and then would later say how eloquent and articulate she was as if it was a surprise or a compliment.

One of the first stories she'd pitched to the *Weekly* freshman year was related to the lack of racial diversity at St. Joe's, how insular the community was, and how difficult it could be to find footing. Since Ronnie had moved here from New York the summer before freshman year, she was one of the few people at St. Joe's who had an honest outsider's perspective.

The pitch hadn't been picked up and it hadn't made her popular, but it meant something to me that it'd even been suggested. She opened my eyes to the experiences I'd had with my own classmates and people I'd called my friends, made me realize I could be critical of my hometown and school. I trusted her immediately and we stuck by each other as two people who felt like they didn't belong at St. Joe's except in the newsroom that they helped run.

I knew what Ronnie was saying; students were already skeptical of her, and her running an investigation—especially one that would probably lead to those who bullied her the most—would be hard on her. The unfairness of it all made my skin itch.

"You'll do a great job," Ronnie said. "I'll still contribute where I can and I'll make sure everyone else on staff does too. This is an *opportunity*, Eden. Seriously. You can't pass this up."

The underlying tension in her voice wasn't lost on me; taking herself off this story was going to be impossible for her. But I also had known her long enough to know she wasn't going to change her mind. She had made her decision and there was no way around that, even if I was feeling cautious. And, reasonably, I was, since the story was going to be a huge undertaking. I was already having a difficult time balancing college applications, schoolwork, and executive editor duties.

"What if I conducted interviews and you helped write it?" I offered, trying to find a way to make this work. "We could split the interviews, at the very least. I'll take the douche-y guys."

"You know the girls feel the same way about me," she said.

The female population of St. Joe's was stuck between wanting to make their own path and wanting to make their families proud. It was a familiar pressure to me.

Being a student population raised by some of the wealthiest and most successful families in the area, we had more than enough female role models to aspire to. Most of the students were raised by empowered, intelligent women: the first female CEO of a massive locally based business, a district attorney, a chemical engineer. My mom was the head of trauma surgery at the biggest hospital in the state. But many of the women were also public figures in some sense who kept a watchful eye over their family and their reputation. Even with upper-level jobs and progressive attitudes about female leadership, their values were old school and often not so different from those of their male spouses or coworkers. The chance that students here would want to risk the wrath of their parents by being quoted on the record about nude photographs was minimal.

Before I could respond, Principal Yanick spoke up from the front of the room. She looked composed as usual, her gray hair up in a tight bun that accented her high cheekbones and intense green eyes that caught even the smallest details. She was one of the most intimidating women I had ever known, her intensity punctuated by her severe wardrobe of muted pencil skirts and impeccably tailored blouses. During the meeting where she initiated

Ronnie and me into our new positions as editors, I barely said a word to her and I'd managed to avoid any in-depth conversations a month into my position. Thankfully, Yanick kept herself and the entire St. Joe's faculty removed from the day-to-day business of the newspaper—unless we were reporting on something that made the school look bad.

"Hello, students."

The hum of voices slowly decreased in volume as she looked out over the sea of faces. "You must be well aware of the email that was sent out earlier to the entire student body. This kind of communication is expressly and wholly banned, and the consequences for the sender will be swift and far-reaching. The faculty and I have reason to believe that the person who sent it is a student at this school."

None of this was surprising. It was assumed that, in order to access the student directory, the person who had sent the email needed a St. Joe's student login. There were probably ways around this, but why anyone would try that hard was uncertain.

The microphone in Principal Yanick's hand squeaked. "If you are found to have any connection to distributing this email, you will be punished. This is final. No argument. St. Joseph's has a hard zero-tolerance stance on the distribution of pornography on school servers."

The idea of categorizing what had been distributed as pornography almost took the breath out of me. She wasn't entirely wrong from a technical standpoint, but it felt harsh.

A *whoop* was let out from a back row, followed by scattered laughter from students at our esteemed principal having to say the word *pornography* in front of us.

"Enough, Luke," Yanick said into the microphone, directly

naming Luke Anderson, also a senior like me, who had been a relentless pain in her side since arriving at St. Joe's. He'd also been a pain in my side for the roughly seven years I'd known him.

Ronnie had set up her phone on a small pullout desk attached to the auditorium chair and was recording every word said during this assembly. The room was sometimes used as an AP testing center or a space for guest speakers, activities that required writing space, which worked in our favor.

Later, we would work on transcribing the recording and write a quick article for publication that Thursday morning, meaning our deadline was technically Wednesday night and about thirty-six hours away. It would be tight, but if we weren't quick with a story like this, it would evolve and the assembly would immediately be deemed old news.

Muffled laughter carried from a group of soccer players who were huddled together, still snorting at Luke's comment. The sound echoed off the walls, but none of the teachers said anything.

The soccer team was infamous on campus for being as rowdy and loud as they were good-looking, and I wouldn't be surprised if they had received their own fair share of nude photos. It wouldn't surprise me, either, if one of them was behind this.

The source of the sound was primarily Luke and Ricky DiMarco. They'd ducked behind the people in front of them slightly, laughing to each other, probably with their phones out. Next to them was Atticus Roth, also on the soccer team. There are two local middle schools that feed into St. Joe's and he'd gone to a different one than Luke and me. I knew Atticus only because I'd edited a profile about him, but his lack of laughter suggested he was different from the guys he was socially adjacent to.

His first name was John, but he went by Atticus—his middle name and maternal-grandfather's name—because he refused to share a name with his father, a recognized genius but also an ass-hole with barely any relationship with his family. His father had been caught up in multiple sexual harassment lawsuits and, in an article about his new tech company, had been quoted saying he didn't have women on the board because *females* couldn't handle it. Atticus refused to answer any questions about his family in his profile as a soccer captain, but everyone at St. Joe's seemed to know either way. Atticus had shut down the line of question-ing pretty quickly, apparently telling our reporter that the only thing his father was good for was passing on the genes that made Atticus tall—nearly six foot six—and athletic.

Despite rarely getting wrapped up in Luke's antics, Atticus was well-known in school probably due to the uniqueness of his name, his dad's infamy, and his role as cocaptain of the soccer team alongside Luke. Mostly, he was known for having been close with Sloane since childhood, which might've explained his sour attitude toward his teammates' laughter.

"St. Joe's is going to do everything it can to help those involved in this situation. Dr. Patterson, the guidance counselor, will be taking walk-ins all day for anyone who needs to talk to her," Yanick said. "The local police have been notified and hope-fully this situation will be resolved *quickly*, and we'll find, and punish, the perpetrator.

"While we would like to answer your questions, we are not sure how much information we can provide at this time," Yanick continued, "but we will keep the student body updated as more information becomes available."

Ronnie snorted. "Can you believe they're trying to pass this off as a statement?" she whispered. "Like, okay, we get it, you're trying to do something but don't know anything and won't share what you do know. Perfect."

"They probably should've waited before holding an entire school assembly," I responded, also keeping my tone low.

"The assembly's a show," Ronnie said. "Now they're going to pat themselves on the back for doing something while the person who sent the email is hanging out, waiting to get caught."

Ronnie was, more than most, a skeptic of the system. I could see myself morphing into one too. Constantly hitting a wall while trying to get quotes from administration could do that. They didn't even want to comment on our more positive stories; it would be nearly impossible to get anything from them when it came to a scandal.

"How long do you think it'll take them to figure this one out?" I asked.

"Entirely too long," Ronnie said, and I could only agree. "Can't wait to discuss this at the staff meeting tonight."

The somber mood that had fallen over the student body followed us out of the auditorium. It would be a challenge for me, or anyone else, to concentrate on classes and the day had just started.

CHAPTER THREE

St. Joe's buzzed with gossip and theories the entire day. Most teachers gave up on trying to teach lessons effectively, turning the day into basically one long study hall. The collective student body was anxious to get out of the building. The halls were empty on the walk to the *Warrior Weekly* office, a very rare occurrence since meetings were directly after the last class of the day.

"Okay, so," Ronnie's mouth was partially full, and she placed her slice of cheese pizza back onto a paper napkin, "here's what we know: An email was sent out at 9:23 this morning, which is toward the end of first period. The assembly was announced at 9:36 and then started around 9:50, near the start of second period."

My computer was open on my lap in front of me. Nearly the entire staff was in the newsroom, a group of about fifteen of us, lounging in rolling chairs and on an unfortunate-looking leather couch with uncertain origins. The newsroom was a surprisingly cozy place that felt more like a former-classroom-turned-lounge than anything else. It was a second home and one of my favorite places to be, both for *Warrior Weekly* meetings and for when I needed a quiet place to study.

Ronnie and I spent more hours in this office than anywhere else in the school, but I didn't mind that much. It was nice to be out of my house and Ronnie and I worked well together, making our seemingly endless hours of writing and editing genuinely productive. I would still make it home by five or six, which was the same as the theater kids or athletes with after-school practices.

It was one of the few spaces on campus that felt like ours; the only place on campus where Ronnie's intelligence and leadership abilities weren't questioned, where I wasn't told I was basically white.

It wasn't built that way, though. Based on previous staff pictures, *Warrior Weekly* had been primarily white for decades. It wasn't until last year when Naira Bhatti took over that we had an editor in chief of color. She'd worked with Ronnie, who was then executive editor, to diversify the staff the best they could and introduce discussions of social issues—like the social gap between scholarship and nonscholarship students or the school's "suggestion" that a student who was a lesbian shouldn't bring her girlfriend to St. Joe's homecoming—at St. Joe's and beyond.

Naira had a gift for writing about social issues without really writing about them, doing her best to inform without ruffling feathers. In a way, it worked, but I could also tell Ronnie was frustrated with skirting around the truth to make others comfortable. She ran for editor in chief unopposed, clearly the most passionate and best-suited on staff to take on the role. Even then, there were students and teachers who assumed Kolton was higher ranked than Ronnie.

And, despite our efforts, we were a somewhat underutilized and underfunded part of the St. Joe's campus. Unless we were an editor or reporter with social pull, like how our sports editor was close with most of the athletes on campus, we weren't inherently popular. The bylines were never as important as the subject of the stories.

Recruitment was difficult, too, since students rarely wanted more writing assignments on top of the assignments they already had for school. Articles weren't taken seriously by either St. Joe's students or faculty; the only pull we had was that, if people talked to us, they could see their name in print. It was surprisingly effective, but it meant we overindexed on fluff pieces like student profiles. Other than that, it was a lot of events, like covering school plays or football games.

But part of the thrill of the paper was that we were entirely independent in the office. Technically, we had a faculty supervisor, Ms. Polaski, but her involvement was limited at best. She taught chemistry and had little interest or background in journalism other than a brief stint as a science writer at her college newspaper.

Despite it being just past four, the sun was starting to set, casting only shadows and fading light into our already dim room. It was late October in eastern Massachusetts, and we were bracing for what was expected to be a cold winter. Temperatures had already started dropping and it could be felt in the office. As it got increasingly dark outside, the linoleum floors and large windows made the room cave-like and almost icy.

I logged onto my school mail account, making the decision

to drag the message out of my deleted folder. It was an action that I didn't want to do, but I knew for the sake of producing an article, it had to happen.

Ronnie's voice hummed in the background as I read through, not pausing to examine the faces of the girls, but scrolling to the bottom. There was a small message there, probably in a font size no larger than 10 pt.:

This is just the beginning. —Eros

"Who's Eros?" I asked, temporarily forgetting there was a meeting going on around me. Ronnie stopped talking immediately and the room focused its attention on me, making my skin feel hot.

"Greek god associated with sex and desire," said Jeremy Wexler, a lead editor from the sports section. We'd first met during freshman year and had stuck together since. I liked him because of his cool demeanor; he didn't mind carrying a conversation and would always say hello to me, even when I grumbled at him about deadlines. He wiped his hands on a napkin and leaned forward in his seat, making the base creak. "Did you catch the note at the bottom of the email too?"

I nodded. "Definitely a little ominous."

"I'd say more than a little," he said. "He's considered disobedient, only loyal to his mother, Aphrodite. At least in the versions where he is Aphrodite's son. It gets kind of weird since there's a couple of variations of his origin story."

"Interesting choice to use Eros instead of Aphrodite," I said. "Considering she's the goddess of sex, right?"

"She's more romantic love, I think," Jeremy said. "Eros does kind of make sense in this case. Some texts about him make him out to be this really handsome, superbuilt guy who got a kick out of stirring up shit."

My mind immediately pictured Luke.

"You make a good point," Ronnie said. She leaned back against the whiteboard, rolling the dry-erase marker between her palms. "It had to have been intentional to use Eros, then, if we use that interpretation."

"Makes you wonder if there's an Aphrodite somewhere too." Julia Roswitha, from the news section, leaned into the old gray office couch in thought. I didn't know her personally since, at my place in the hierarchy, I needed to directly communicate only with editors.

"Not to go all Oedipus, but maybe the girls in the pictures are supposed to represent Aphrodite? You know, they're the goddesses of sexuality and he's loyal to them?" Jeremy said.

"I don't know if I'd consider spreading pictures of them naked or in their underwear to be loyal," I said.

Jeremy shrugged. "I wouldn't either, but this doesn't exactly strike me as someone who is thinking from a reasonable perspective."

"But it *could* be someone who is acting reasonably," Ronnie said. "I mean, this was a calculated decision. This so-called Eros would have had to gather these pictures one way or another and rationalize why they sent them."

"Do you think it was calculated enough for them to cover their trail?" Jeremy asked. "I'm not a tech guy, but there must be ways of tracking where an email came from and narrowing it down from there. It would take skill to be able to hide completely after doing something like this online."

"I don't know if St. Joe's would have the ability to do something like that," Ronnie said.

"The police might, though," I said.

"What if all that effort is for something that ends up being a practical joke?" Jeremy said. "Eros might not even realize the repercussions of what they've done."

"That's true," I said. "And using a fake name doesn't necessarily mean they're trying to hide their identity from the people they did this to. They might only be hiding to avoid getting into trouble. And there could very well be multiple people who worked together on this. There's really no way to know."

Ronnie gathered her curls in thought. "Even if it is a joke, it still hurts people so it must count for something. In this case, lack of intent might not make up for the fact that Eros is clearly harassing the girls."

"I wouldn't exactly put it past anyone we go to school with," Bree Osborne offered. She was a reporter from the arts and culture section, and I mostly knew her because I helped edit a piece she wrote about LGBTQ+ history in Greenville. "They could've meant it to be a genuine attack, especially based on the message attached to the email. It seems threatening."

"We're going to assume for now that whoever did this attends St. Joe's?" Julia asked.

"Assume is a strong word," said Ronnie. "We should follow the school's general statement about how they have reason to believe it's someone from St. Joe's. This would be an incredibly difficult undertaking for someone who didn't go to this school. It's not like these were pictures available online for anyone to steal. They would've somehow been connected to the school."

"Maybe not," I said. "All they need is a person who can

get them into the student directory. It could be someone who doesn't go here but goes to St. Joe's parties, regularly interacts with students. It's not far-fetched."

"They don't get to see any of the backlash, though," Ronnie insisted. "If they don't go here, what would they get out of this? What's the motive?"

Jeremy asked, "Maybe it was a recent graduate? Like, their last hurrah is a big fuck-you to St. Joe's?"

"But why specifically these girls?" Ronnie responded. "Why not a message directly to the faculty here? Why use intimate photos of current students? And did this person really have this many girls they wanted to personally attack? For most of these theories, it seems like they would want to be in school watching the shit hit the fan. We all know St. Joe's is going to do everything it can to keep this under lock and key, so there's a chance it might not even make it into the local news. What would an outsider gain from that?"

"Are you thinking maybe it was someone other than a student? Like a faculty member?" Bree asked.

"No, it's just a theory," Ronnie said. "I don't know who would do this. At this point, no one is off the table."

"As awful as that is," I said.

"It makes it even harder to predict what their next move will be," Jeremy sighed. "Is Nudegate going to be a one-off or are the hits going to keep coming?"

Ronnie snapped her head in Jeremy's direction. "Nudegate?"

"That's what some of the guys have been calling it," he said.

"Interesting," Ronnie said and, to my surprise, wrote Nudegate in huge block letters on the whiteboard, right above the time the email was sent out. With her marker posed to write, she said, "Okay, what else do we have so far?"

"Other than the email time," Julia said, "we know the sender is going by Eros."

Ronnie wrote the information down in shorthand on the board, as we called out the series of events.

Bree spoke up again. "Seven girls had their pictures leaked."

Ronnie stopped. "Seven?"

"Seven," Bree confirmed. "I triple-checked."

Ronnie wrote *seven* on the board, circled it, and tapped her marker against it. "Whether we know who did it or not, this email has effectively changed seven girls' lives, probably forever. This article and the St. Joe's gossip, for better or for worse, will be about them. Keep them in mind during everything that you do, say, and write about the email. Going in order, can someone tell me the names that we have confirmed?"

"Sloane Mayer," someone said, and the names started rolling. It wasn't difficult since a large chunk of the staff was composed of seniors, and all of the girls who had photos leaked were in our grade. There was Sloane and her close friend Vera Porfirio, and then Alice and Margot. Claire Leon, who was best known for being the lead in nearly every St. Joe's theater production. In a couple of weeks, she would be performing as Laurey, opposite theater-stud Jason McDonough as Curly, in *Oklahoma!*.

I also recognized Violeta Ordonez, a clarinet player from the school marching band, on the list too. The last on the email was Angela Ainsley, a pretty volleyball player I was partnered with on a psychology project last year. I'd assumed she'd graduated since she was a volleyball captain at the time we worked on the project, but maybe I only thought that because captains were typically seniors.

There was no obvious social connection between any of the girls; they all had different friends and ran in different social circles. The only two who were close were Sloane and Vera. Otherwise, before the email, the girls didn't seem to have anything in common.

"Why these girls?" I asked, echoing Ronnie's earlier sentiment and not speaking to anyone in particular. No one responded, either not feeling brave enough to guess or not having a clue whatsoever. I was betting on the latter.

The photos of each of the girls were so intimate they were uncomfortable to look at. All of the pictures varied in quality and angle, but they clearly showed the faces of the girls.

When we finished identifying everyone, we all sat quietly, looking at the names of the girls on the whiteboard. It all felt so clinical. My stomach knotted and it required genuine effort to not immediately delete the email from my inbox again.

"I'm still stuck on this whole Greek name thing," Jeremy said. "It seems so weird to me."

"Any junior who took non–AP English last year had a full unit on Greek tragedy," Ronnie said. "It hardly limits our pool."

Jeremy seemed skeptical, but he didn't try to change Ronnie's mind. All of us had been on the paper long enough to know our EIC was not one to bend. Ronnie put the cap back on the marker, satisfied with the product of our meeting and ready to move on to the next topic.

"Eden will lead the investigative team for this story, so if you want to help out talk to her. And make sure to get your other stories in on time, or at least give the story to someone else if you can't cover it anymore."

She looked at me to see if I had anything else to say. With her announcing that I was officially leading the team, my heart rate increased.

"If you want to help out, hang around for a few minutes after the meeting and we'll talk game plan," I said, addressing the entire room. "All I ask is that if this is going to be a conflict of interest, be cautious and know exactly what we're working on here."

"All right, meeting officially adjourned," Ronnie said.

People stood up and shifted their papers and laptops, preparing for their section meetings with their specific editors.

"Wait," Bree said, and everyone stopped. "What about the police?"

"St. Joe's will probably update us once the investigation is underway," Jeremy said.

"You're being optimistic," Ronnie said and grew quiet, thoughtfully looking at the board. "It'll depend on if everyone involved is over eighteen or not."

"Why?" Julia asked.

"Under eighteen turns this into a child pornography case," Ronnie said. "Over eighteen the police can't do much. Or they might not decide to do much."

"What do you mean?" I asked.

"Technically, I don't think there are any laws against the email and sharing people's nude photos without permission. I'll have to check again, but I read an article a few months ago about revenge porn, and Massachusetts doesn't formally prohibit it."

"Eros could get away with it?" Bree asked.

"I never said that. And most seniors at this point in the school year aren't eighteen yet, so there shouldn't be any problem prosecuting. I think the biggest step right now is figuring out the girls' ages." Although Ronnie seemed confident in the statement, it was obvious the thought Eros having a possible loophole troubled her. She immediately switched gears to keep us focused on the newspaper. "Section meetings. And section editors, please move your articles through the editing chain. Everything should be to me and Eden already, so if it's not, it's officially late."

Since Ronnie and I were the editor in chief and executive editor respectively, we weren't in charge of individual sections. We supervised the other editors and made sure the final product of the paper looked good. Because of that, I knew the names and faces of a lot of the reporters, but not much more. It was odd to know little things, like that Bree used excessive em dashes in her articles, but not know what they did outside the office.

Sections met briefly as a check-in to pick up pitches for the upcoming issue and to check in about deadlines and editing notes. Editors, and Ronnie and I, usually stayed behind even after the rest of the staff left just to talk. Sometimes it was about the newspaper, sometimes it was to socialize.

I glanced at the board in thought, my mind wandering and the chatter of the newsroom turning into white noise. Ronnie had the right idea—the perpetrator would *have* to be at school to get the full impact. The person who had done this most likely wanted to see this happen; it was hard to believe that they hadn't, hard to believe they didn't want to get off on the emotional devastation in some sick way.

Jeremy looked up from his laptop, turning to me. "Does Kolton know?"

Kolton Glover was our news editor. He had been out of school for two days with a cold, so he wasn't able to make it to the meeting.

"I called him earlier about it. He's pissed he missed the assembly," Ronnie said from across the room, always listening.

"Eden?" Bree was standing next to Julia, both of them

it wasn't okay that the girls were expected to carry this burden on top of everything else while covering the story was optional for me. It was a privilege to be able to prioritize my grades, to be able to pick a side on the issue at all.

My mom reached out and grabbed my hand across the island. "You can always talk to us, okay? High school is hard sometimes, whether you're the person being bullied or not."

"Thanks, Mom."

"I'm just glad you're not one of the girls involved. Our very responsible daughter." As soon as she said it, my mind flashed back to Nick, all the times we'd snuck around, made out in his car. The fact that I'd sent pictures too. I didn't say anything in response.

My dad handed me a bowl of stir-fry, the vegetables and *dangmyeon* visibly steaming. Food was one of my family's most obvious connections to our Korean heritage. Being second-generation Korean with parents who'd both moved to the United States as children meant that both my parents and I had been mostly raised in American culture. I'd gone to Korean Saturday School with my cousins for most of my childhood and we tried to go to the local Korean Church at least once a month, but it was hard with my mom's schedule. Mostly, we watched a lot of K-dramas.

But Korean food was a source of comfort, the smells bringing me back to my grandparents' houses and family get-togethers and holidays. Some of my favorite memories included learning how to make *mandu* with my mom and grandma.

"Do you have any homework to get done?" He looked at me through his reading glasses.

"A little bit," I said. "I have an article to edit too."

"Eat first, you look exhausted."

"Yeah, yeah," I said, but still appreciating their support. I leaned over to kiss my dad on the cheek, taking the bowl of food with me. "Goodnight."

"Goodnight, sweetie," Mom said.

~

Despite having said goodnight, I knew actually going to bed was still hours away. As high school had progressed, I'd added the additional pressure of writing articles and editing other people's onto my yearly-increasing homework load. The submission deadline was coming up for college applications, too, and I still had to finalize those. What had once been my bedtime was now the time I'd start my homework.

Despite having my statistics textbook out and ready, my mind focused on Nudegate, the different possibilities churning. There were so many people to talk to, so many angles to take into consideration. And we still had to deal with the biggest question mark of all: the actual identity of Eros. It was overwhelming, but I was excited.

As if able to hear my thoughts, Ronnie texted me to say that Kolton had reviewed the article and, after a final look-over, we could submit it to Ms. Polaski for print. It wasn't a long article and Kolton hadn't left many notes, meaning we'd have it finished pretty quickly. The harder part was focusing on editing and approving the other, non-Nudegate-related articles for the week; my thoughts kept drifting toward the email and Eros, distracting me.

None of the girls were close friends of mine, so it'd require strategy to talk to them, especially about such a touchy subject. I'd have to plan it right so they'd be interested in talking to me; sometimes, enticing a source to cooperate required different tactics and approaches. There were sources who were more open to interviews with others, and even with my interest in journalism, being rejected by a source stung, especially when it was a fellow classmate.

After running through the names again, there was one person who stood out the most in my mind as a starting point: Alice Huey.

Alice was known, generally, for being nice. She was a passing, almost forgettable kind of nice that would've felt forced on anyone else. I knew her through her boyfriend, Louis, who talked about her in an enviably sweet way. Other than that, and her scattered social media presence that was almost entirely about Louis, I knew very little about her.

Her shy demeanor and the mutual connection made me hopeful she'd want to open up to me. At the very least, I didn't think she would be mean if she didn't want to be interviewed. I tracked down her email, took a deep breath, and typed out my first Nudegate interview request, hopeful we'd meet the next day.

CHAPTER FOUR

I woke up the next morning still thinking about Alice. My sleep wasn't terrific, the night filled with tossing and turning and anxious thoughts about what was to come. The day after the shock of the email was poised to be even harder than the day of—now the girls had to go to school and face everyone.

Even though I hadn't wanted to get my hopes up, I immediately checked my phone to see if Alice had responded. It was a simple *yes* agreement to being interviewed during lunch, nothing particularly enthusiastic, but it was better than nothing. The plan was to use her quotes for a follow-up article about specifically the girls from the email, if anyone other than Alice ever responded.

To prepare for school, I put on a coat of mascara before grabbing my backpack from my bedroom floor. The room was spotless, a trait, I was sure, rooted from my parents being equally as neat. It used to drive Nick up the wall. It wasn't that he was a messy person, he just wasn't as tidy or as organized as I am.

Where are all of your things? Do you really keep all *of your clothes hung up all the time?* He'd asked the first time he came over, invited without my parents' knowledge while they were at work. It made me nervous, but it was also thrilling to do something just a little bit reckless. That's what Nick was for me. He was my chance to be a teenager, to be Edy instead of Eden. To be Nick's girlfriend instead of the intense editor, to pretend I wasn't someone who preferred time alone to going out to parties with friends.

And to be fair, Nick did have a point about my more minimalistic living. I'd never really liked *things*. I wasn't much of a collector and I didn't have any sort of trophies or participation ribbons or posters. My hobbies were limited to journalism, something I hadn't been sensitive about until Nick and I broke up and I felt genuinely lonely for the first time. While Nick had football and a genuine interest in environmental studies and a desire to go out with friends, I wasn't sure I knew what I liked or what I wanted outside of the newspaper.

The differences between Nick and me was what had originally drawn me to him, but then later made us end things. I knew when we met that I'd fall for him, regardless of whether he felt the same way or not. We'd met entirely by chance during a school-sanctioned college fair late sophomore year. We'd been standing at the same booth, both looking at a university neither of us had any real interest in attending. All it took was him talking about how he wanted to go to school near the mountains and we spent the entire rest of the event openly talking about our interests and our goals and what we hoped to do with the rest of our lives.

On my way out of the house, I spotted a sticky note from my mother—*Love you 24/7*—pressed against the refrigerator. The thought behind it made me happy, even if it was a reminder that I might not see her for more than a few minutes over the next few days.

Dad was still sleeping, so it was quiet in the house. The sun was just beginning to rise, a harsh telltale sign of how early I had to get up for school. I sipped orange juice and broke a piece off a blueberry Pop-Tart, trying not to dwell too much on Alice or the reality of what today might look like for her and the other girls.

It was hard to come up with an idea of what to expect with the interview and the day in general. There could be calm as easily as there could be chaos. The school could quietly make this go away, or it could be a months-long whodunnit. The only way to know was to actually go to school, something I didn't really want to do.

I carried my breakfast with me as I exited my house and locked the front door. My neighborhood was peaceful, an upper-class suburbanite's paradise as usual, entirely unaware of what was brewing only fifteen minutes down the road.

~

Alice Huey did not look like the beautiful, shiny, happy girl I had seen walking the halls of St. Joe's weeks prior to the email. She was still lovely, but in a sad way. Her face drooped and frowned; her red hair acted as a shield, and her freckles popped against her pale, nearly translucent skin. It looked like she hadn't slept.

As I walked into the cafeteria for lunch, I noticed her sitting alone at a table, backlit by the gigantic windows that face the football and track fields behind St. Joe's. She had opted for baggy uniform khakis, the closest thing we could wear to sweatpants. The way they hung off her small frame in addition to her slumped shoulders radiated with the misery that Alice was carrying around with her.

"Hi, Alice?" I asked, doing everything I could to keep my voice level. Even when I wasn't nervous, my voice would sometimes give me away and quiver without permission. "Eden Jeong," I said, introducing myself. "Are you still interested in being interviewed about the email?" Using the word *Nudegate* around her felt dirty and invasive so I tried to steer away from it. "And is it okay if I record this?" I asked and put my phone on the table between us, making sure she knew that I wasn't going to pull any cards on her.

Alice kept her face down, her chin almost touching her chest. Her blue eyes followed my every move as I pressed the button on my phone to record.

"All right," I said, mentally checking myself to make sure I remembered my backup interview questions in case she froze up. I glanced at her quickly before pressing the record button. "I—"

"Has Louis said anything to you?" Alice asked. Her voice dropped when she said his name.

"Louis? Why?"

"He talked about you. Sometimes," Alice said and, upon seeing my face, reconsidered her words. "He thinks you're nice. Back when you were lab partners. I remember you."

"Oh." My cheeks burned. It had never occurred to me that someone might talk about me to their significant other. Or anyone, really. "No, he hasn't said anything. We didn't really keep in touch after the semester finished."

"Okay." Alice exhaled, but her shoulders were still tight.

I waited to see if she was going to say anything else. Journalism was as much about listening as asking the questions. When she didn't, I said, "I wanted to check in and see what this experience has been like for you."

"I'm miserable," Alice said. "I didn't sleep last night. People keep texting me and messaging me. Guys I've never even spoken to before are asking me for more pictures. I feel like nothing I ever did mattered until now. No one ever saw me."

She had allowed herself to get personal earlier than I had anticipated, and it threw me off my game. Usually, sources weren't willing to share their deepest feelings with a stranger, particularly a journalist, within minutes. Clearing my throat, I asked, "Do you have any idea how the picture could have gotten into Eros's hands?"

I wanted to avoid framing it as either hers or Louis's faults. It was hard since it seemed like a fairly obvious choice that one of them had to have leaked the photo, somehow, some way.

"No. Louis broke up with me over it." Her voice choked on the words. "He thought I was sending pictures to other people. Cheating on him. I don't know how he could ever think that. I want to say he was the person who sent it around but I . . . I can't bring myself to believe it. He's a terrible liar and when I asked him, he swore he hadn't done it."

I wanted to have that much faith in Louis, too, but I wasn't sure who to believe. Maybe it was none of my business to decide who was right. Journalists are impartial. Or we're supposed to be, at least.

Either way, Alice hadn't deserved getting a picture sent out to everyone. None of the girls did.

"Has St. Joe's offered anything to support you or the other girls?"

"Not really. They offered free drop-in times for the counselor, but I've been too embarrassed to go. They're offered only during the school day, too, so I'd either have to miss class or miss lunch to go."

"Have you told your parents?" I asked, somewhat out of concern because it didn't seem like Alice had much of a support system.

"No, I haven't told them. They got the same phone call from the principal everyone else did, but they don't know that I was one of the girls."

"Have you been updated about anything happening with the police? Have they contacted you?" I asked.

"No. I was sent an email from the school telling they're doing everything they can, and the police might bring me in for questioning. I think a lot of the investigation is external," Alice said. "Hopefully the police will at least be able to figure it out. I don't think I'll have anything helpful to tell them, but St. Joe's is small. Secrets don't stay secret for long."

I thought it was interesting that the school had contacted Alice only by email instead of directly speaking to her in person. It seemed impersonal. Dismissive, almost.

"Have you been told if St. Joe's is going to do anything else to support you?"

"The email said they were keeping their options open to requests from us, so it sounds like maybe they'll do more in the future if we want it."

Alice's voice softened through the course of her sentence, so openly sad in a way I hadn't seen by anyone. I knew it was time to wrap things up. If anything, I'd get more from her later. I also still had at least six other sources to speak to, plus a possible interview with Yanick.

"Is there anything else you want to share?" I asked. "Either about your personal experience or how you're feeling right now?"

Alice was quiet for so long that I assumed the interview was over until she started speaking again, her voice taking on a renewed sense of confidence. "This isn't something I'm going to forget. We can all graduate and move on, but I will never, ever forget that this happened. And I will never, ever forgive who did this." Although her voice was quiet and level, it was angry.

"Thanks, Alice." I pressed the button on my phone to end the recording.

"If you see Louis, please tell him I didn't have anything to do with this. I really didn't. I don't know what's going on, I just know that I love him, and this all hurts so much. Even if he doesn't get back together with me, I can't have him thinking I would do something like this."

I hesitated before asking the next question, knowing it wasn't my place to ask, but curiosity had gotten the best of me. "Do you have any idea who might've sent the email? This won't be recorded or printed, I—"

"Want to know if I did cheat on Louis? No. I didn't. He was the only person I sent the photo to. I don't know if he sent the email but thinking about him having photos of all those girls makes me physically sick with jealousy."

"Do you think Louis is behind the email?" I asked, getting right to the point.

"I don't think he'd do something like that," she said. "Louis is a good guy. He never would've shared my photo with anyone. Ever."

As I was about to leave, I remembered what Ronnie had said about the difference between how the case would be handled if it involved minors rather than adults. "Alice, how old are you?"

"Eighteen. My birthday was at the end of September," Alice said. "Louis took me to the Public Garden to celebrate."

I thanked her again. She wasn't a minor, which avoided a potential underage situation. But I picked up on what could've easily been denial about Louis. She seemed insistent it wasn't him, but she was equally clear it wasn't her. My best next option was speaking to Louis; at the very least I had Alice's interview, which was leverage to get a statement from him. I convinced myself it was for the sake of journalistic integrity and balance, but I knew it was also out of curiosity.

After exiting the cafeteria, I noticed a familiar head of black hair at a locker.

"Sloane!" I called.

The casual tone of my voice surprised me. We had never interacted one-on-one and hadn't had a class together. I'd been well aware of who she was during our time at St. Joe's, but I doubt she knew me. The *Warrior Weekly* staff didn't have a reason to interact with her since she didn't play sports or act or go to academic competitions. But we all knew her because she was pretty and partied and had the attitude of someone entirely untouchable—such was the way with the popular kids.

She turned to face me, and I approached her. "Hey," she said, her voice cool and level and deeper than I'd expected it to be.

She had on her distinctive deep purple lipstick that I rarely saw her without. School dress code generally prevented any sort of makeup that wasn't deemed natural but they usually used that against the ones they believed were deviant—people who wanted blue hair, Goths, those with a love of non-nude eyeshadow. But despite Sloane's loose attitude toward sex, at least in St. Joe's terms, the school let her pass because she was Sloane: wealthy, white, presumably normal by their standards. She could get away with pushing buttons because, at the end of the day, her parents were friendly with school administrators, sending yearly holiday cards and regularly donating to support the school.

"I'm Eden, an editor for the *Warrior Weekly*. I was hoping to ask you about the email," I said, and she went from intrigued to annoyed with impressive speed.

"Perfect," she said. "Exactly what I wanted. My name plastered all over print and online associated with nude photographs."

"I want to ask about possible motives—"

"You're not the only one who wants to know that. I'd like some fucking answers too," she said and closed her locker. Her long nude nails tapped against the metal. "No comment."

She brushed past me, her hair swinging as she walked.

I was irritated, but I understood. Not all sources were going to open up immediately; sometimes, they needed time to warm up to the idea. I'd have to save interviewing Sloane, and maybe her friends, for later.

~

To my surprise, the rest of the day flew by without anything out of the ordinary happening. The gossip levels were still high, I'm sure, just not in my circle of friends because we were so focused on the paper, the story itself.

The teachers kept a tight rein on all of us, strictly enforcing the antiphone school policy and shushing students acting out of line, so no one was spending class time giggling and whispering. For a brief moment, I let myself believe the email itself might be the most dramatic Nudegate would get.

It wasn't until I was walking back to my car at the end of the day that I realized I'd underestimated St. Joe's. I'd assumed that the type of people who would leak nudes to the school would wait until the other side retaliated, that we had to wait for someone like Sloane to turn this into a war. But we didn't need someone like Sloane to escalate the situation. We just needed someone who hated people like Sloane. And based on the yelling I heard a few parking spots down from mine, it seemed like the second move had been made.

It didn't take much investigating to realize Vera Porfirio was the source of the noise.

Vera and Sloane had been friends for years, the kind of attached-at-the-hip dynamic duo that no one had really seen coming all throughout elementary and middle school. Despite Sloane's affinity for dark lipstick and rumored drunk rendezvous with guys, she had never been a chatty or loud person. Vera was the better known of the pair for being naturally outgoing. She had a distinctive voice, heavily influenced by her family's Boston origins, and an even more distinctive laugh. Vera and I had been close in elementary school, but it was mostly artificial; we went to each other's birthday parties and sometimes hung out during recess. By middle school, we had completely lost touch and, by senior year of high school, it was hard to believe we'd ever had anything in common.

Sloane and Vera were known for being targets of the Freshman Hunt, where senior guys would try to spy out the "easy" younger girls. The girls became friends not long after a rumor spread that Vera and senior Seth Franklin—a well-known advocate for the Hunt—had hooked up at prom. Around the same time, Sloane had been dealing with rumors about herself with a similar theme about her and Andre Parker from the baseball team.

"What the fuck is this?" Vera's voice was shrill. I knew she had become progressively less outgoing, less shiny and fun, the closer we got to graduation. Her most recent social media posts frequently expressed a desire to get out of Massachusetts once school was done. But, even with that, I had never seen her genuinely angry. Danica James, a close friend of both Vera and Sloane, approached her, seemingly trying to calm her down.

They were too far away for me to hear them, but she held Vera gently by the arm and talked to her with a stoic expression. Vera turned to point at her car, her hands moving rapidly between being crossed in front of her to waving in the air to pulling at the hem of her school-sanctioned sweater. I wouldn't be surprised if she was crying based on her body language.

I stepped forward and realized, finally, what she was so upset about: someone had graffitied her car.

"Eden?" Kolton said from behind me. He was shorter than I was, with a round baby face that didn't fit his intense personality. He had no interest in being a writer professionally; he was hoping to go to MIT for nuclear engineering, which was somewhat heartbreaking since he was so gifted with running the news section. "What's going on?"

"It's Vera," I said and nodded my head in her direction.

I spotted a crooked S on her windshield and my heart skipped a beat. Someone had scrawled *slut* across the glass in rough, choppy letters. It didn't look like spray paint and I hoped it wasn't, for Vera's sake. The only thing worse than getting a car graffitied was having to pay to get said vehicle repainted.

"Who the *fuck* did this?" Vera raged. Her face was shiny and damp. I couldn't tell if the tears were from anger, frustration, sadness, or a combination of them all. "Anyone want to confess?

Huh? Who's the dickhead that's going to take credit for this great job?"

Kolton cleared his throat and readjusted his backpack uncomfortably. "I should talk to them," he said.

"Now?" I asked.

"Not them," he said, referring to Vera and Danica. "Her friends. Witnesses. This could easily turn into a criminal or civil situation, depending on what Vera plans to do with the perpetrator. We should get an article going. Take some quick pictures with our phones."

Before I could stop him, he moved past me and left me alone in the crowd.

A boyish laugh erupted, turning the crowd's heads toward Luke Anderson in all his glory. He was everything that Ronnie and I didn't like pre-, and now post-, Nudegate. He was powerful by blood—the son of a successful former federal prosecutor and current judge—and arrogant. He wasn't my type, but there was something about him that people found appealing. It might've had something to do with the parties he would throw, or it might've been related to his indescribable, almost magnetic sex appeal.

Luke leaned against his car, his lean but muscular arms folded across his chest like a cheap James Dean impersonator. The St. Joe's uniform made the whole show almost comical.

"Jesus Christ, calm down." He laughed the words, widening his eyes to his friends as if to say *women are crazy*.

"Did you do it, asshole?" Vera shouted. "This seems like some shit you'd pull. What? You miss hooking up? You upset I found someone with a dick bigger and better than yours?"

Confrontation made me uncomfortable to begin with, but

Luke could easily go from joking to deadly serious in seconds, which put me on edge. Last year, he had almost been kicked off the soccer team for getting into a physical fight during a game with one of his own teammates. He was allowed to stay, and be named captain, only because of his undeniably impressive stats, and threats his dad had made against the school. Luke didn't seem to have any qualms starting something and Vera was ready.

"Come on, babe, you know that isn't possible," he said, letting the comment slide right off.

She made long strides over to him. They were about the same height, probably somewhere around five foot ten. I wasn't much shorter than Vera myself, but she was long and lean in a way that made her look much taller than I was.

"What's going on?" Atticus asked, startling me. I hadn't realized how close I was standing to him; I'd been too caught up in the show in front of me.

"Vera thinks Luke vandalized her car," I said.

"Fucking dick," Atticus said. It was mumbled and not directed to anyone in particular, but it was validating to hear someone vocalize what I'd also been thinking.

Vera kept her voice low, out of earshot from where I was standing. My instincts told me to run, but I knew I had to stay. Articles were rarely independent work; if Kolton was working on something, I'd need to contribute or at least verify the events.

Vera's friends were standing near her car, talking and picking at the paint. One was taking pictures of the damage. As I looked closer, the graffiti consisted of different words that had been written all over her silver Lexus. It wasn't particularly creative, just variations of *slut* and *whore*, but, obviously, it still hurt Vera. It would hurt anyone.

Vera's hands flailed again while she spoke as Luke remained cool and collected, providing justification for the line I'm sure he would use while relaying the story later: *She was crazy, bro. I had no idea what she was talking about.*

"I wouldn't be surprised if you had some involvement in that stupid email," she shouted, loud enough for everyone in the parking lot to hear. "Seems like something you and your moronic bunch would do."

"No way. We wouldn't *want* nudes from a majority of the chicks on that list," Luke said, looking genuinely disgusted. Some of his friends laughed, others didn't respond. But they were all complicit. "Did you see the fat bitch? Whoever asked for that must've been one desperate dude."

I indulged in a moment of wondering what it would be like to run across the parking lot and throw a fist into Luke's face.

"You're disgusting," Vera said, the only person around willing to be the voice for us all.

Sloane forced her way through the crowd, meeting Vera and Danica. She exchanged quiet words with Vera and they both started walking away. Sloane turned her head over her shoulder and said, "Watch your fucking mouth, Anderson."

"Oh, I'm so scared," he said, mocking her. "I didn't vandalize your car. Leave me out of your personal bullshit."

Vera said, "Our personal bullshit is public now. Everyone knows way more than they need to. I have nothing left to hide."

I knew exactly what she was saying: This wasn't going to end quietly.

Sloane half pulled Vera into her car, and Luke climbed into his own. I turned to Atticus briefly and he looked at me, his brown eyes meeting mine. My heart thudded in my chest, mostly because of the fight. But also, embarrassingly, because Atticus was far better looking than I'd previously noticed.

I redirected my attention to find Kolton, but it was impossible in the crowded parking lot. Eventually, I gave up and got into my car, ready to leave the scene behind.

CHAPTER FIVE

By the next morning, rumors were swirling that Vera was going to push for pressing charges, both criminal and civil. She had the means and motivation for both, and I couldn't blame her. At least her car had returned shiny as ever the next day; the paint that had been used was washable and nontoxic, not even a streak left behind after cleaning.

As I entered the building, the first thing I noticed were the papers. It wasn't uncommon for flyers to be posted throughout hallways promoting school plays or group meetings. But this was different.

The time for change is now —NG

The bold font stared right at me. The posters were thrown up on the wall in a crooked, rushed way, half of it covering the school's advertisement for the upcoming performances of

Oklahoma!. I didn't know what it meant, or who NG was. I considered checking the student directory until I realized there was someone who would most likely know.

The first warning bell rang, but the students around me were distracted. A number of them had ripped the letter-sized papers off the wall. The poster looked like something someone had printed on a home computer. My best guess was that it was speaking out against whoever had vandalized Vera's car. It looked like two could play the game.

I texted a picture to the editor's group chat despite the guarantee most of them had already seen it. I was mostly curious what their responses to the situation were.

Under one of the loose papers I found a stack of *Warrior Weekly* newspapers, the headline *Criminal Charges Being Considered After Pornography Shared on School Server* taking up the entire front of the cover. Kolton had won out in the end, although I knew Nudegate had been used in the body text.

Regardless of the actual text of the headline, I felt a small amount of pride. One of the reasons I'd stuck with the newspaper for so long was being able to see my name on the front page. It made all of the interviewing and writing and editing, especially the night before publication, worth it.

Sloane entered the hallway, her posture perfectly balanced with my own renewed sense of confidence. I moved through the crowd with impressive speed to meet her, but she didn't throw a glance in my direction. Setting aside my pride, I pretended to be a journalist tracking a source instead of a high school student desperate to talk to her peers.

"Sloane," I said, matching her pace.

"Yes?" she asked, though it didn't seem like much of a question or an invitation to continue speaking.

"Maybe you, or someone you know, is behind these posters? Who's NG? Or *what* is NG?" I asked.

She continued down the hallway, easily brushing past students. I struggled to keep up, weaving past groups of students and forcing my way through to keep Sloane within reach. Refusing to let the issue be put to bed so soon, I followed her.

"What makes you say that?"

"You had a friend who was specifically targeted."

"Lots of people have been specifically targeted as of late, if you think about it."

"Getting their cars graffitied?"

"We're all being called sluts, anyway. What difference does it make when someone writes it on the hood of a car?"

"It wasn't only the hood of the car," I said, still maneuvering around other students to keep up with Sloane. "It had been the windshield, the doors, the hood." Sloane's jaw visibly tightened in response. "You can't deny it was a public and personal attack."

"Something about calling it public and personal seems almost contradictory," she said, still not looking at me. "Aren't you an editor? Shouldn't you understand how words work?"

"I do understand words, that's why I'm taking this so seriously," I said. "Anyone can *say* anything. But writing it is different. It gives it power."

"Straight from the mouth of someone who writes all the time."

I refrained from groaning in frustration. She was even more resistant to talking than I thought she'd be.

"Do you think there was a reason why you were the first

picture on the email?" I said, and she finally stopped walking. That caught her attention.

"God, I hope you know you're in a profession that people despise," she said, turning to face me. We were at a full stop in the direct path of students walking, but Sloane didn't seem to care. "Even if it is *only* a high school paper."

"It's an honest question, Sloane. Did it raise any flags with you? Is there anyone in your life who seems like they have something to prove? What do the posters mean by *change*?"

"How am I supposed to know?" she said. "And you're not a detective, Eden. I don't know what you're hoping to gain from this."

"Knowing where you stand on the issue."

"Where I stand on the *issue*? Don't make this sound like a choice. I was forced into the position I'm in. This isn't hopping party lines or changing my values," she said. "I might've made the choice to send pictures to someone, but I didn't realize it would lead to me being pigeonholed."

"I get it," I said, even though I didn't really. And Sloane saw right through that.

"You don't, actually. You what, sent a picture to your boyfriend one night? He was away, missed you, wanted to see you? Or was it that he was having a bad day and made you believe the only possible way to make it all better was by sending a picture? Or, wait, my favorite—did you send one because he wouldn't stop asking, so you finally did it to get him to be quiet?"

She had hit the nail on the head, not only with the reasons, but with why I had said I understood. It was embarrassing to be so transparent and I didn't know how to respond.

"Look, I don't know how else to explain it," she said. "You

sending a picture one night to one person is not the same thing as getting your photo leaked to the entire school. You might think you understand how I feel, but we're not in some club because we've both sent nudes to people."

She walked away just as I found the ability to speak again.

"Why did you do it?" I asked, hoping for some clarity about the posters.

"Because it's time, that's fucking why," she said, raising her voice over the hum of noise. "And you can attribute that quote to me."

~

Later, I was picking at my fries during lunch, entirely uninterested in eating. I was trying, and failing, to shake off the shame of Sloane brushing me off and then calling me out within a mere two-day period. My earlier confidence had deflated into near nothingness. Sloane was important to the story, but I couldn't figure out an angle to make her open up to me. I was rapidly losing her trust, not that there seemed to be much there to begin with.

Sitting alone at a lunch table in a crowded cafeteria didn't make me feel any better. Usually, I sat with Ronnie, Kolton, and Jeremy, but none of them had arrived yet. After a few minutes of messing around on my phone to look busy, I looked up to see Ronnie.

"Damn, who hurt you?" she asked, sliding onto the bench next to me. She pulled a bag of pretzels out of her backpack.

"I'm not feeling it today," I said, my head immobile in my hands. Ronnie waited, using the psych trick of silence to get me to speak. It worked. "I talked to Sloane."

"How did it go?"

She was testing me. She knew the ups and downs of writing. Most of the time, I was able to keep pretty even-keeled, but there was nothing that increased my stress levels like an article, or a source, that I couldn't get a handle on. In addition to the walls I was already hitting with the Nudegate story, Kolton told us in the group chat the night before that he'd struggled to get quotes for his article about Vera's car, so the story would have to be dropped for the time being. It turned out that when students were asked about vandalism, the most they had to say was *yeah, that sucks.*

While I knew it was too early into Nudegate to be this stressed about it, I couldn't help but feel like I was already doing it wrong. I didn't want to disappoint the staff and I definitely did not want to hurt the seven girls even more than they were already hurting.

"Okay, fine, we won't talk about it yet," Ronnie said, her hands up in front of her in an I-surrender motion. We sat in silence for what couldn't have been more than ten seconds before Ronnie's curiosity got the best of her. "How is she?"

I wasn't sure how to respond. She seemed normal by Sloane standards, but I also didn't know her all that well. She seemed cross with me and was, as predicted, upset by the situation.

"She basically admitted to making the flyers," I said. "She didn't say who or what NG is, but it obviously means something to her. When I asked her why she did it, she was cryptic, 'Because it's fucking time, that's why.' Her words."

"Can we quote her 'on it? With the *F*-word taken out, at least."

"She made that clear," I said. "I typed it up in my phone notes, so I'll remember it for later. I'm hoping to get more from her soon."

"I mean, there still is time to talk to her. And you still have five other girls to talk to."

"I had just been hoping she would . . . talk to me. She always seems so open about her sexuality. Even when I was talking to her, she had no shame about sending photos. Does that strike you as someone who would be shy about being interviewed for a newspaper?"

"She might be. You can be confident sexually and still be shy; the two aren't necessarily correlated," she said. "And it's different when you know the words will be in print."

"That's what she said to me when I asked her about it," I sighed. "All of this feels so surreal. If you'd asked me a week ago what I thought I'd be doing right now, I would've said editing the same event coverage and student spotlight pieces we always have. Nothing to this degree."

Ronnie dug into her pretzel bag. "I think things overall are weird right now."

"Tell me about it," I said and tried eating another fry, which had gone cold. The hum of voices in the cafeteria—a combination of talking, laughing, clattering trays—filled the empty air between Ronnie and me. I thought about my interview with Alice. "Do you think Eros could be an ex?"

"An ex of all of those girls?" Ronnie snorted. "I don't think so. It might be someone who hooked up with them casually, but I don't know who that could be. I feel like that would be so obvious. And all of the girls are so different. I don't know if there's a common denominator for a theater kid, an athlete, a band girl, a girl who seems to only talk to her boyfriend . . . I could go on."

"But it would give us motive."

"Not guaranteed it will. Like, yeah, okay exes. But someone wanting to hurt seven different girls to this degree? And at the same time, in the same way?"

"Weirder things have happened," I responded. It felt like a passive, almost hopeful, thing to say but I wanted to believe it. It would be so easy if it was someone directly and clearly connected to the girls.

Maybe Eros was someone so obvious they were in front of us the entire time. Or it was someone effectively hidden from plain view; someone who seemed so unreasonable that they're not even on the potential suspect list. Either way, the suspect list might as well be everyone at St. Joe's, if not everyone in the state of Massachusetts.

"I hope St. Joe's is actually helping the girls. Alice told me that, so far, they've only offered time with the guidance counselor. But I guess they're taking suggestions from the girls on what they want too."

"Meaning St. Joe's will probably take their emails and calls and then not do anything with them," she told me. "Right now, their priority is avoiding a PR nightmare."

The bell rang, signaling the end of lunch, and I stood up to toss out my half-eaten fries.

"Let me know how everything goes," Ronnie said and waved, our version of a goodbye.

As I was walking to statistics, Louis was standing next to his locker. Even though I was feeling a little rejected and down on my journalism skills from my conversation with Sloane, I knew I couldn't pass up the opportunity to speak to him.

"Hey, Louis," I said. He dug through his locker, refusing to make eye contact with me. "How's everything been going?"

"You know exactly how it's been, Eden." His tone was more aggressive than I'd anticipated, but it only made me want to dig in deeper.

"How are things with Alice?"

Louis slammed his locker shut, making me jump. "Besides the fact she cheated on me?"

"That's funny since she's denying she cheated on you."

"Of course she is. Why would she own up to that?"

I took a deep breath, refusing to let two sources bully me out of the story in one day. "Maybe you might know something you're not telling either of us. Maybe she didn't cheat, and you sent the photo around. Did you have anything to do with the email?"

"Why would you say that?"

"Both you and Alice are equally believable. One of you had to have done something, but you're both denying any wrongdoing."

"Because she doesn't want to be labeled a cheater."

"Or because she didn't actually cheat, and you know something you're not telling me or Alice."

Louis hesitated. The wheels turned in his head, but he refused to elaborate. "I have to get to class," he mumbled before quickly disappearing into the crowd.

~

Mr. Monroe, my statistics teacher, stopped me as I entered the classroom, "Hey, Eden." He leaned closer to me and kept his voice low. "Principal Yanick would like to see you. She told me to tell you to go to the office when you arrived."

"Now?" I asked, my stomach knotting immediately.

"Yes," he said. "I'll mark you as present and on time for the class, so don't worry about that."

The walk to the principal's office was painfully short and I thought I might be sick the entire time I was moving. The last time I'd been there was when Ronnie and I were sworn into our new positions as lead editors last year. Yanick had droned on about how important it was for us to understand each other and to work well together. She'd also promised to try her best to keep us in the loop with the administration, a lie if I had ever heard one.

"What's going on?" Ronnie asked as she entered the office, only about a minute after I'd arrived, and sat down next to me.

"I have no idea," I said, the only truly confident statement I'd said all day.

"Maybe she called us in about the Nudegate story?" Ronnie responded. We were sitting in chairs that were side by side, facing the rest of the office. It was a huge space, old and dark, filled with heavy wood and no windows. There were a few administrators' desks but only one person was in. Office phones were ringing on a seemingly endless loop, which eerily echoed through the high ceiling. It was just after lunch so some of the office assistants still weren't back, but it still felt strange and almost neglectful, especially in a time of crisis, like Nudegate.

"Girls." We looked up in tandem, a Pavlovian response to hearing Yanick's voice.

Guiding us into her office, she glided behind her desk and gestured to the seats in front of her. Her office was clean and traditional-looking, featuring almost exclusively dark wood like the front office. The only source of light was through the large window to her right, showing off a view of woods where the cross-country team practiced. On the wall, I spotted her

REVENGE OF THE SLUTS 69

degrees, undergraduate and Master's, then her PhD in Education from the University of Pennsylvania. She had other certifications, too, most of them related to teaching. I wondered briefly how she'd ended up here.

Principal Yanick calmly folded her reading glasses, placing them gingerly on her desk. "The faculty and I have some concerns about your coverage of the recent events on campus."

Neither Ronnie nor I were feeling audacious enough to play dumb. "We believe we're handling it—"

Yanick put up an index finger to silence us. "Let me finish, Ronnie. We have concerns and would like to lay some ground rules so we don't run into any problems," she said. "We've managed to keep the local media away from St. Joseph's and we would like to keep it that way."

Ronnie made a sound of agreement. They both had the same goal but for two different reasons. Yanick didn't want the bad press and Ronnie didn't want the competition.

"I understand what you're trying to do, ladies, I do. But you are not the *New York Times* and there is no reason to pretend that you are. I want this to be covered with a light touch."

I inhaled, feeling somewhat offended even though she was right. We were a high school paper and not a major nationally recognized news organization, but it didn't make our coverage any less valuable. "We're covering what's happening on campus. It's important that students know the truth. That's our *job*."

"Tread carefully, Eden," Yanick said, her voice unchanged despite the obvious irritation in my tone.

"Why are we here?" Ronnie said. "And the real reason, not that you're *concerned* about local news."

Either Yanick was used to student outbursts or she had an

excellent poker face. "To remind you that high schools have the right to censor what their students publish."

"But that's not fair," Ronnie said, leaning forward in her chair. "It's not. I don't care what the Supreme Court said in *Hazelwood v. Kuhlmeier*. Or what you have to say, for that matter."

"The *Weekly* is a school-sponsored newspaper," Yanick said, brushing off Ronnie's impassioned argument. "We have a right to be represented accurately in the news. If we don't want it printed, it doesn't have to be."

Ronnie kept quiet, but fumed beside me, steam practically pouring out of her ears.

"Why would you want to limit our coverage?" I tried to keep my voice even. "Would you prefer the local newspaper covers it?"

"We want *no one* to cover this—the faculty and the student body already know about the events and we've alerted all of the families, and that's as far as our obligation goes."

"The email is a big deal," Ronnie said. "You can't just wish it away. It's already led to a student getting her car graffitied."

"There's no proof the two events are related," Principal Yanick said, ignoring the words that had been written and the fact that essentially everyone knew that it *was* related. Confirmation wasn't necessary; it was clear why someone would feel emboldened enough to suddenly graffiti someone's car with derogatory language.

"It's important to talk about it. These girls, your students, have had their privacy violated, their bodies violated," I said.

"Taking this further will cause more problems than it will solve," she told us. "For now, I would like all articles related to significant events on campus to go through my office first. They will need my seal of approval."

"Ms. Polaski already goes through them," Ronnie argued. "That's the point of us having a faculty adviser."

We both knew that Ms. Polaski had been attentive for the first week or two of classes and then left us alone to do our own thing. She hadn't given Ronnie or me feedback in weeks. We sent her the articles as a matter of course, but we no longer waited for her approval before setting the articles for print. She trusted us.

"She can go through them first, then forward them to me. I have already spoken to her about this and we agreed it's the right course of action. And, frankly, St. Joseph's is not feeling confident in Ms. Polaski's ability to lead after she allowed your first article to be published," Yanick said. "End of discussion."

"This is going to push back our editing timeline," I responded, which, although a somewhat minor point, was true. The editing chain was already tight, after having to go from the writer to their section editor to a copy editor, then another copy editor, onto me, and then Ronnie. Adding in two more people would make things increasingly difficult, especially considering most articles came in dangerously close to our weekly print deadlines anyway.

But Yanick was probably trying to do exactly that; if publishing cut too close, the school wouldn't have time to print. It was all a domino effect. If Yanick played her cards right, she could delay her approval process so long that by the time she approved it, the story would already be old news.

"We care about the reputation of the school," Yanick said. "If that means pushing deadlines or publishing less frequently, then so be it."

"We care about providing students with the truth," Ronnie said. "Unedited."

"Your dedication to journalistic integrity is admirable,"

Yanick said, putting up her entire hand this time in a *stop* motion. "But this can*not* continue. Today's article never should have been printed. All forthcoming articles *will* require my approval. Consider this your first strike."

Ronnie and I stayed silent, eyes in our laps.

"Am I understood?" Yanick said.

We mumbled weak-hearted yeses and stood up to grab our backpacks. Principal Yanick unfolded her reading glasses and placed them back onto the bridge of her nose. She was already looking at her desktop screen again when she said, "Have a nice rest of your day, girls."

We didn't respond.

Once we had walked a comfortable distance from the main office, Ronnie exploded, "Why is she doing this?" She stopped in the middle of the hall nearby one of the newly installed and donor-funded Rehydration Systems and started pacing. "We're a student newspaper, we *have* to cover this."

Both Ronnie and Principal Yanick were right. I didn't like it, but Yanick had the power to halt publication at any time. It wasn't fair, especially on a story like this, but I wasn't sure I had the same fire in me that Ronnie did. There wasn't a single part of the system on our side, since the administration, our advisor, and the American judiciary were all working against us.

"Are we actually going to send the articles through her?" I asked, my eyes ironically landing on the stack of newspapers in the front lobby. I no longer felt that warm feeling looking at the papers. Yanick might as well have physically ripped the last of my enthusiasm over this story out of my chest with her bare hands.

"We'll see how it goes." Ronnie shrugged. "We probably

should, but if things keep happening at the pace they have been, we won't be able to afford to stop for her."

"Do you think her concerns about local media are reasonable?" I asked.

"I've heard they've already had to kick reporters off school property."

"You're kidding."

Ronnie wasn't one to gossip. In true newspaper spirit, she confirmed no less than twice before spreading any piece of information.

"One of those local Fox station vans was outside earlier," she said. "I think they're realizing something big is going on and it won't be long until the full story is revealed and everyone, including donors, is fully aware of what's happening. Yanick's not even concerned for the girls—it's all faculty and administration bullshit."

"It sucks," I said. *Understatement of the year.* "There's really no way around this either."

"Don't worry. If I have to, I'll find one," she said. "No way we're letting this story die along with the paper."

The valiant effort was something to appreciate, but I wasn't confident she'd find a way to execute it. Ronnie was capable of nearly anything, but this seemed bigger than both of us.

"I wonder what would happen if we continued to publish," I said absentmindedly.

"The consequences would be harsh, I'd expect, but I'm not so obsessed with journalism that I want to find out," Ronnie said, mainly trying to convince herself that following the rules was actually what was going to happen—we both knew it wasn't.

"Maybe we can talk to Ms. P—?" I said, but immediately cut off my thought as footsteps echoed in our direction.

Atticus. He had a reusable water bottle in his hand and was wearing the usual uniform of khaki pants and a button-down shirt, both fitting him ridiculously well. Ronnie's eyebrows shot up, the universal symbol for us to pause the conversation. Going dead quiet seemed equally suspicious, but it felt strange to continue while he was within earshot. We probably should have picked a far less conspicuous spot to talk in the first place.

Atticus filled his water bottle, the only sound in the hallway a soft whirring from the machine and the sound of water hitting plastic. These stations were a school treasure and a huge step up from the coppery water we used to get from the old water fountains. We had done an article on it last year, where Principal Yanick was more than happy to talk about how exciting the fountains were, but not willing to release how much the school had actually spent on them. We should have known then that she'd never put up with any kind of real investigative journalism that might tarnish the school's "brand."

Eventually, his bottle was full, and the silence had gone on so long it was making me squirm.

I hadn't realized I was watching him tighten the lid back on until he spoke to me. "Nice article," he said, his voice deep and slow.

"Thanks," I said, and he lifted one side of his mouth in a semismile before walking away. Ronnie looked at me and I did my best to ignore the burning sensation in my cheeks.

What was that? she mouthed at me, and I shrugged one of my shoulders. She raised an eyebrow, an amused smirk playing at her full lips.

"Boy's got good taste," she said to me after he was far enough away. "And not just in articles."

I tried to laugh, but it came across as more of an uncomfortable breath. "I have no idea what you're talking about."

"He's cute. I liked him better with his long hair from last summer, but this school can't even let me enjoy that," Ronnie said.

Atticus had posted a few random pictures online here and there over the three months, revealing hair nearly down to his shoulders that I had tried to play off as not being as sexy as it was. It was back to being short because of school dress code, but he still kept it long enough to run fingers through.

Not that I was thinking about that.

"Let's get moving, ladies," said Mr. Rennison, a faculty member who was forced to play hall monitor. It was an unfortunate job that usually led to wandering around for hours looking for stragglers.

"Yes, sir," Ronnie said. When Mr. Rennison was out of earshot, Ronnie said, "You should investigate *that*," she joked, giving Atticus the up-and-down as he walked away.

But we knew that Atticus was only a temporary distraction. Within minutes, Ronnie would have a tight jaw and the same look in her eye that showed she had something to prove. She wasn't going to forget Yanick's actions. I had a feeling I wouldn't either.

CHAPTER SIX

Despite the fact I was late to statistics, Mr. Monroe's lecture on normal distributions felt never-ending. I was grateful when my phone vibrated with a text from Ronnie.

> Ronnie: I know you mentioned talking to Ms. Polaski off-handedly, but I think we should do it.

Even though statistics is not a strong subject of mine and I should have been paying attention, I couldn't resist responding. Ms. Polaski was pretty much our last hope in being able to have any sort of freedom of press at St. Joe's. Even though Yanick had said she'd already spoken to her, there was a chance that maybe Ms. Polaski was still on our side.

The thought of going behind Yanick's back made my heart pound, but I was more excited than nervous.

Eden: I'm in.

I didn't know if Ms. Polaski would be helpful at all, but I didn't want to write her off completely. Between my conversations with Sloane and Yanick, and Kolton's article not working out, luck was not our side.

But the interview with Alice had gone fairly well and had given me good quotes. And I'd managed to confront Louis, something I'd never done previously in my role as a journalist. Maybe the feeling of piecing together a story, working alongside Ronnie with both of us buzzing from the high of a good headline and lede, could be worth the trouble.

Feeling cautiously optimistic, we figured out a game plan through text over the next couple periods. Ms. Polaski usually graded papers—another perk of being newspaper advisor was having a private office, which most teachers at St. Joe's didn't get—at the end of the day. There were weeks when she was here later than Ronnie and me doing exactly that, but mostly she'd leave before us, sometimes poking her head into the newsroom to say goodbye.

We decided to explain why *Warrior Weekly* was so important and to try to talk her into persuading Yanick to cut us some slack on editing. We could handle the additional pressure of Ms. Polaski scrutinizing our work more closely, but we knew Yanick would not be kind if given the power to edit.

We just had to hope Ms. Polaski would listen to us. We owed it to the girls to get to the bottom of this, regardless of what damage Yanick was worried about it doing to the school. A decrease in donations would be bad for the school, but the stigma of being a Nudegate girl would shadow everything else these girls had done at St. Joe's. It would follow them the rest of the year and probably into college—possibly for the rest of their lives. And it seemed like Yanick didn't even care.

~

Ronnie and I met up at her locker after the final bell of the day, ready to walk to Ms. Polaski's office together. As the rest of the students poured out of their classrooms, slamming lockers and loudly talking to their friends, we stayed put and braced ourselves.

"I think we got this," Ronnie said. Thinking optimistically, I knew it was not the end of the world if it didn't work out. Technically, Yanick had never banned us from working on Nudegate articles; she just said she'd have to edit them. And while not ideal, it didn't fully take away our ability to act as journalists. But, at the same time, it didn't seem worth it to be working on an article that would never be published in its authentic form. And whatever voice we could give to the girls would be lost, the school sweeping their feelings under the rug—that didn't sit well with either of us.

Students rushed past, catching my eye. Danica was with her boyfriend, Rolland Pike, who was on the football team with Nick. Nick and Rolland were pretty close, and so Rolland and I had always been friendly. I found him more approachable than most of the other guys on the team, who tended to look right through me.

Ronnie had also spotted them. "Have you spoken to Danica or Vera yet?"

"I haven't had the chance to yet."

"Okay. Try to talk to them soon, since they're good sources," Ronnie said. "And how are interviews with other students going?"

She meant well, but it grated me to hear her talk about the article like it would be a breeze. Julia and Bree had gotten a few interviews done with sophomore classmates, which was some good news. But I already knew I had to talk to Vera and Danica, in the same way I knew Sloane was a great source; I didn't need to be reminded. It just sometimes wasn't that easy. It wasn't obvious if Vera and Danica would be interested in an interview, especially considering how irritated Sloane was with me.

Luke and his goons had their smirks firmly planted on their faces as they headed in our direction, like they were in on a joke no one else could understand. They looked like they were pulled straight out of a teen drama—handsome, but questionable, potentially a little dangerous. A living cliché.

Luke's eyes were on me as he approached, but I was unable to read his expression even though we'd known each other for years. We flirted in middle school—as much as twelve-year-olds can flirt with each other—before his personality soured and his head became too big for his body. I didn't know if he was the person behind Nudegate, but I was suspicious of him, probably with good reason. He always seemed to be up to something, whether it was slinging his arm around an unsuspecting girl or picking a fight with someone who breathed the wrong way around him.

"Eden," he dipped his head.

My expression didn't change. I had no interest in playing his game.

After middle school, Luke and I had lost all real reason to

interact. And despite running in similar circles, Nick had always told me he wasn't interested in being friends with Luke. Partially because Luke was a dick, but mainly the reason was he never gave Nick the time of day. But, considering Nick's desire to be friends with the cool guys like Luke was one of the reasons we broke up, I assumed Nick's supposed disinterest was meant to appease me more than anything.

Even with Luke being the person he was, I wasn't sure if he was capable of something like Nudegate. He seemed cold, but not necessarily calculating. More like the kind of person who would do some spur-of-the-moment thing to cause physical pain, or throw in a one-liner, rather than someone who would go the whole psychological scarring and isolation route. But then again, maybe he hadn't realized how traumatic Nudegate was going to be. Either way, there was no way I'd get him to sit down for an interview unless it benefited him, and that would require effort to plan on my part.

"Ready?" Ronnie asked. Luke's group had already disappeared from the hallway completely by then, already outside.

"I think so."

"Love the confidence," Ronnie said and then quickly barged in, knocking on her way through the door. "Hi, Ms. Polaski."

"Ronnie, Eden. Hi."

Students at St. Joe's generally liked Ms. Polaski, and even though I hadn't had her for chemistry, I wished I had. She kept the cards students gave her and lined them on her office bookshelves alongside photos of her family. It looked like she had two sons; both were toddlers in the photo, but it was hard to tell how old the picture was and if the boys were the same age now.

She put the cap back on her purple pen and leaned back in

her chair, away from the pile of midterm exams it looked like she had been grading. "How can I help you girls?"

"We were hoping to talk to you about Principal Yanick's warning," Ronnie said. "About the articles we're writing. We had a meeting with her today."

"Yes, she told me she was going to call you into the office," she said, her blond bangs bobbing.

"What should we do?" I asked.

"Sit down," Ms. Polaski said gently. We took the seats in front of her desk. "Principal Yanick is taking this very seriously. She made it clear she doesn't want student press covering it and, even if I want to help, I don't know if I can. I really don't have much leverage in this situation."

"Is there anything that we can do?" Ronnie asked. "Like, at all? Can't you promise to Principal Yanick that you'll oversee us more intimately in future?"

Ms. Polaski chuckled, revealing a small gap between her front teeth. "I don't think she'll trust me to do much editing or supervising on my own from here on out. I broke some sort of unspoken rule by publishing the first Nudegate article. At this point we have to be glad the paper can still run, and you can still write about news on campus."

"But you know she's going to censor the articles. They're not going to have integrity in them anymore. They might as well be school propaganda," Ronnie said.

"You don't know that," Ms. Polaski offered. "Maybe the review won't be that intensive. You won't know until she does it." Her face softened and her approach changed when she saw our expressions. "I'm sorry. I wish I could do more, but Principal Yanick isn't interested in listening to me right now. Try to cooperate with her. I know it's not an ideal situation, but it's something. Maybe it won't be all bad."

"Thanks, Ms. Polaski," I said and stood up. Ronnie reluctantly followed, not ready to give in as easily.

We exited the office feeling dejected and not speaking to one another. Ronnie was upset, but I didn't know how to make her feel better when I could barely help myself.

Another entirely unideal outcome. We were going to lose both the paper *and* the story.

CHAPTER SEVEN

Despite my downright pessimistic attitude after the week's events, I reached out to Vera to secure an interview. My expectations were low since things weren't going well with the other Nudegate Girls. Margot said yes but, since she had a debate club competition coming up, she had limited time and our schedules weren't compatible. Claire said straight up no, and Violeta and Angela hadn't responded. I wasn't feeling confident Sloane would ever get back to me.

Vera still hadn't responded by the time lunch rolled around the next day. I felt close to giving up, even though I knew I couldn't.

"Are you going to the party tomorrow night?" Jeremy asked, digging into his bag of chips. We were sitting at the usual, unofficially assigned, *Warrior Weekly* lunch table with Kolton.

"What party?" I asked, having never been someone at the center of our school's social events. My weekends were spent staying in, editing articles and watching TV. On the rare occasion that I'd go out, it was Nick dragging me to a party, and even then I'd still make it home pretty early in the night. It was fun sometimes, but outings with Nick's friends could be loud and unpredictable, two things that made me antsy.

"Ricky DiMarco's. From the soccer team." Kolton swallowed the bite of sandwich he was eating, "He's having a Halloween party."

Halloween didn't do much for me, but it was a big deal at St. Joe's. Any opportunity to drink was. Meanwhile, I'd almost completely forgotten it was the end of October.

"It's not really my scene," I said.

"You should think about it," Jeremy said. "Come with Victor and me if you want." Victor was Jeremy's boyfriend of a few months. "It might be kind of fun."

"Jeremy," I said, trying my best to not outright say *no*.

"Look, you might be our responsible editor," Jeremy said, waving his hand passively. "But after the stress of this week, I think you deserve it."

"I think after the luck everyone is having, going to that party will end up causing more problems than solving them," I said.

"Or it might help you relax. Plus, I heard about what happened with Yanick. Lame shit."

"Yeah," I responded with a shrug. "I have a hard time imagining a party would be any fun this weekend."

"I get that," Kolton said.

"Imagine seeing that email and thinking you have the right to get mad at the *girls*," Jeremy said as he bit into a carrot. "So, what, they sent some pictures? People do it all the time. Hell, we have multiple examples in one email."

"They probably should have at least known to keep their faces out of it," Kolton said and when he saw the look I gave him he put his hands up defensively. "I'm just saying. If you're going to get into it, might as well be smart."

Jeremy gave me a look from across the table, something that told me he wasn't with what Kolton was saying.

"The pictures shouldn't have been leaked, full stop," I said.

"Especially when it's usually the guys begging girls to send them pictures in the first place," Jeremy agreed.

Kolton raised an eyebrow slightly. "No one forced them to send the pictures."

Jeremy, being the peacekeeper that he was and not wanting to get into it with Kolton, recognized it was time to change the topic. "How's the paper looking for next week?"

"Good," I said. "I think we're on track for eight stories, which is pretty good. Or, I guess, seven, since I'm not sure what the status will be for a Nudegate story. So far I only have an interview with Alice, and Ronnie and I would want to see Yanick's edits before fully agreeing to publish the article."

"I can't believe she's really pulling that card," he said. "The school let us publish freely with nearly everything else."

"There's enough scandal attached to this one that St. Joe's wants to, as much as possible, avoid it getting out. If we print it, the local media will inevitably find out about Nudegate. It sounds like they already have, based on what Ronnie has told me."

"That's not unreasonable," Kolton said. "We might be a bunch of high school kids, but we have some good insight to local stuff."

Warrior Weekly and the *Greenville Gazette* had a history of using and regurgitating each other's information. When we didn't have the pull to get to the source, we used what was published in local papers, and when they needed ideas, they took what we wrote about. We had the home-team advantage in this case, but I wasn't sure how long that would last considering how St. Joe's was limiting us.

Jeremy sighed. "This whole thing is fucked up."

"Who is this Eros guy?" Kolton said. "Is anyone closer to figuring it out?"

"The only theory I can come up with right now is one of Luke's friends." I looked at the sandwich in front of me, tentatively taking a bite. Nerves were getting the best of me and I didn't want to eat, but I knew I should. "It's not grounded in fact, but I feel like they have something to do with it. Or at least know something. They're way too . . . *them* to be innocent bystanders."

"They might be reaping the fruits of what Eros has done," Jeremy said.

"Maybe," I said and groaned. "I hope this is over soon. For our sake and the girls'."

"Knowing our school, nothing will be done until it's already too late," Kolton responded.

"Thank you for that positive outlook, Kolton," Jeremy noted and Kolton half grimaced at him. Jeremy then changed the subject to a recent date night with his boyfriend and a physics exam he had coming up. I was half listening when my phone lit up on the table.

Maybe: Vera Porfirio: Danica and I can meet during last block today. We'd prefer to do the interview together.

Even though a joint interview wasn't what I'd had in mind, it was workable. That would be quotes from Alice, Danica, Vera, and maybe one from Sloane, that I could include in an article, in addition to what Bree and Julia had collected. It was a good start. I was cautiously optimistic I could eventually schedule interviews with Claire, Margot, Violeta, and Angela too.

I'd have to skip my last class—which was, fittingly, ethics—for the interview but I refused to pass up the opportunity. There was no guarantee that Vera or Danica would want to talk to me at any point after this. And, hopefully, once I spoke to them, Sloane would be more trusting of me.

I responded with a *great!*, the exclamation mark being faux enthusiasm but sent with the hope of making them more willing to open up to me. *Let's meet in the Warrior Weekly room.*

After my response to Vera, I sent a group text to the editors' chat so they knew to avoid the office for the time being. I wanted to guarantee privacy for the girls even more than I usually do for sources. Jeremy and Kolton's phones simultaneously lit up on the table with my text.

"I'm so sorry. I have to head to the office to prepare for an interview," I said.

"All right, go off, do your thing. And let me know about the Halloween party," Jeremy said.

"Okay," I said, already knowing I had no intention of going.

~

Vera and Danica showed up to the office a full fifteen minutes late, which was enough time to make me believe they weren't coming. I had been mentally constructing my self-defeated text to Ronnie when they walked in.

Both Vera and Danica were attractive—the kind of pretty that made people really look at them and it was hard to believe they'd ever taken a bad photograph—but in different ways. Vera was tall and lean and had enviably shiny light brown hair that she kept trimmed below her collarbone. Her cheekbones were high, but not severe, and her eyes were attentive and bright.

Danica was less conventionally pretty but more striking. She had distinctive wide-set blue eyes and a tan that was fading from warmer months. She kept her blond hair long and framing her face with a middle part. She was much shorter than Vera and had curves that she had embraced now that we were older. She'd been one of the first girls in our year to get noticeable boobs and spent most of middle school trying her best to cover them up with loose-fitting tops and high collars. It seemed like Danica had gained the confidence to wear tighter-fitting clothes around the time she became friends with Sloane and Vera, during the transition from freshman to sophomore year.

"Thanks for agreeing to meet with me," I said.

"Is this going to help get the guy who did it?" Vera asked.

"Probably not," I said, a bit caught off guard, figuring I'd be the one asking the questions, "but it can help with exposure and showing people what effect revenge porn has had on their classmates. Is it okay if I record this?"

Both Danica and Vera answered with a simultaneous *yes* so I set up my phone to record.

"How would you best describe your experience after the email came out?" I asked.

"It's a lot of the same, but people are more willing to be up front now," Vera said, "People were calling me a slut behind my back, but now people are *really* calling me a slut, like, as I'm walking down the hallway. It fucking blows. And then my car . . . "

Danica made a sound of agreement. "It has been so hard watching what Vera and Sloane have gone through. I love them a lot and they're great people and definitely don't deserve the name-calling. Or getting a vehicle vandalized." Danica reached out to offer Vera her hand, but her friend brushed her off. The interaction seemed odd. "I don't know who did this but I hope they're found. They've ruined senior year for a lot of girls here."

"They've ruined more than senior year," Vera said, her tone biting. It sounded like they'd had the conversation before.

"Right," Danica added, seeming to not register Vera's words.

"Has St. Joe's done anything to support you?" I asked.

Vera snorted. "There are drop-in hours with the counselor. And the girls and I have the chance to talk to a sexual offense support counselor if we want."

The specialized counselor was a new advancement. One of the girls must have requested it. "Have you talked to the police?"

"My dad did, mostly," Vera said, which made sense since her dad was a lawyer. He was in patent law so it wasn't a perfect fit, but he at least had a legal background. "The police are being dicks about it so I don't think it's worth the effort."

"What do you mean?" I asked. "And you told your dad?"

"Of course I fucking told my dad, I think he's even angrier about this than I am. I'm not going to hide; I *will* get this asshole in court," Vera said. "And the police don't say it outright but I think they believe the case is pointless. It's not a criminal offense to share nudes of adults online in Massachusetts, and it seems like they think we brought it on ourselves. Other girls have said the same thing. So, as long as all of us were eighteen when we sent the photos, the police just aren't interested."

"Wait, when was your birthday?" I asked. I'd already known Alice was, but all of the girls being eighteen changed things. It was still early in the school year, so most of the class was still seventeen. Her comment also implied Vera was in contact with the other girls, which seemed interesting, but I didn't want to change the subject yet.

"Late September. Sloane, Margot, and Alice have early September birthdays, Violeta's is, like, three days before mine. Claire's birthday was maybe two weeks ago. The only one I don't know is Angela's, but she's made it clear she's eighteen."

Only featuring legal adults in the email must've been a calculated decision so Eros could avoid the risk of child pornography charges. Even though I trusted Vera, I'd confirm the girls' ages either with them or in the student directory to make sure I was on the right track. I didn't know enough about criminal law to say it confidently, but it seemed like picking specific girls for their age had to prove some kind of intent.

"What did the police say about your car—do they think the two events are connected? Is there anything they can do about that?"

"Yeah. We showed them pictures, but I doubt anything worthwhile would come out of a report. Since the paint was washable, they're not taking it very seriously. My dad has been talking to his lawyer friends to figure out loopholes, but it sounds like it's going to be mostly up to St. Joe's to punish the person who did it. And, like, good fucking luck with that, you know what I mean? I am *not* feeling optimistic they'll get their shit together."

"Have you spoken to any school administrators about your car?"

"Yeah, they're 'trying' to do something, whatever that means. I think they'll be checking video cameras and hoping for the best. It's whatever. High school, right?" Vera said humorlessly.

"You mentioned the other girls," I said, looping back. "Are you all keeping in contact?"

Vera sat up straighter in her seat and looked at Danica. "I mean, sort of. Like, as a way to kind of lean on each other."

"Can you talk more about that? The support aspect?"

"I think Sloane might be the best person to ask about that."

"Sloane?" I questioned.

"Sloane Mayer," Danica contributed, somewhat unhelpfully since there was only one Sloane at St. Joe's. "There's a group."

"Danica, please," Vera said and pressed her fingers to her forehead, showing off perfectly kept acrylic nails. "Stop talking. Sloane is going to be so pissed you brought this up."

"You brought it up first," Danica snapped. "It's cool what she's doing."

Knowing it was too late to backtrack, Vera sighed. "Sloane formed a support group called the Slut Squad for the Nudegate Girls or whatever the fuck we are. We weren't supposed to mention it to you and it's *off* the record."

"Why?" I asked.

"Sloane doesn't want it to turn into a big thing," Vera said.

Danica spoke up again. "If we take you to the meeting they're having tonight, do you promise not to write about any of it?"

I looked between Danica and Vera, noting Vera's tense and clearly peeved face. She looked like she wanted to strangle Danica for offering, but I knew the opportunity was too good to miss. Even though I was risking the wrath of Sloane by going, I could hopefully gain the girls' trust by going and listening to them. I was still waiting on interview responses from half of the girls. "Yes."

"The meeting is off campus since Sloane didn't want anyone to know about it," Vera said, shooting one last look at Danica. Using a pen and paper left behind on the table, she wrote out an address. "You can follow us there."

CHAPTER EIGHT

I drove behind Vera and Danica to the meeting. They stopped in front of a beautiful tan colonial-style home in an upscale residential area, with a huge wraparound porch and a garden that looked well taken care of. There were a few cars parked outside lining the sidewalk and the cul-de-sac.

As I parked, Vera and Danica stood on the sidewalk with their arms crossed against their chests, bracing against the wind. A cold front had moved in, a teaser for the quickly coming winter. When they spotted me, they led the way up to the front door of the home and I followed behind, unsure of what I was walking into. I hoped they had warned Sloane I was coming.

We stepped up to the porch together, and when Vera opened the front door, I was immediately enveloped by warmth. The inside of the home was as cozy as the outside. It looked straight out of *Better Homes and Gardens*, with coordinated furniture and professionally-taken family portraits on the walls.

"Sloane!" Vera called, her full voice nearly echoing off the walls.

Sloane appeared from the living room and I watched her eyes move from Danica to Vera to me. Her lips pursed. "What are *you* doing here?"

"Danica told her about the Slut Squad."

"You told the fucking editor of a newspaper about the one thing I told you *not* to tell other people about?" Sloane asked, directing her attention to Danica.

"It slipped out, I'm sorry. She said she wouldn't print anything about it."

"Then why did you come? What's the point?" Sloane focused her attention on me. She'd exchanged her uniform for a sweater and a flattering pair of jeans. It was jarring to see her wearing something that wasn't polo or plaid.

"I-I wanted to see what was going on." *What else could I say?*

"This is meant to be a support group. It's for the girls who have been victimized to get together and talk to each other without judgment," Sloane said. "But I'm sure that wasn't fully explained to you before you came."

"Technically, Danica shouldn't be here, either," Vera offered.

"Yeah, but I trust her," Sloane said and pointed at me. "*You* haven't earned that yet."

"She's very nice," a quiet voice said from the living room. Both Sloane and I peeked out to see who the source had been. Alice. "She interviewed me a few days ago."

"She helped me too," Margot said. She looked better than she had been that first day of Nudegate but her heavy undereye circles gave her away. I felt a hint of warmth flush through my chest at feeling vouched for.

Sloane looked back at me and pressed her lips again before speaking. "You stay quiet. This is not your space."

I nodded and, finally, she let me into the meeting.

There were a few girls lounging in the living room almost immediately to my left when I entered. I surveyed the faces and recognized all of them as Nudegate Girls—Alice, Margot, Violeta, Claire. As Vera and Sloane got settled into seats, I realized Angela was the only one missing.

I wondered if any of the girls other than Alice had a connection to Louis. At this point, he was the most promising lead—the one guy we knew without a doubt had received one of the nudes. The only other viable option who had come up was Luke, and he was being accused mostly on principle.

Sloane leaned forward in her seat. "Thank you all for coming. Angela texted me earlier about a volleyball game tonight, so she had to miss this meeting." Sloane looked between the faces of the girls in the room. "I've been talking to a friend of mine who volunteers as a victim advocate at Greenville College. I know I've texted a few of you, but she said that doing something like this in person could be cathartic for us. We might not have other opportunities to be in a space with people who can truly empathize."

"What's the point?" Claire asked. She had her highlighted blond hair back in a ponytail and was still in her St. Joe's uniform. "Just talking?"

"To say it's 'just talking' kind of simplifies the point," Sloane responded. "It *is* talking but it's a way for us to get out anything we've been thinking or feeling since Nudegate happened."

"So it's therapy." Claire's voice went flat.

"If you're not interested, you don't have to be part of it,"

Sloane said simply. "I said it *could* be beneficial to us. It doesn't mean it *will* be. We all deal with things differently."

Claire didn't respond, but she also didn't get up to leave. Sloane continued. "Does anyone have anything they want to say to start this off? It could be related to anything."

The girls sat in silence for a second, which turned into nearly a minute. I resisted the urge to check my phone to ease my discomfort. It felt suffocating.

"My ex told my parents that I was one of the girls on the email," Alice said, finally breaking the stillness of the room. "He came over to my house to explain why he'd broken up with me and that it was important to him that my parents know the kind of person that I am. We'd talked about getting married and having kids and now we're *here*. He won't even look at me."

"You were planning on marrying him?" Claire asked, trying not to sound judgmental but still coming across that way.

"I love him and I thought he loved me," Alice said. "It made sense to talk about the future. But, now, the best thing Louis has done for me is not tell anyone at our church. I wouldn't be able to handle them turning on me too." Alice's voice wavered as she spoke. "I can't believe he'd hurt me like this. I never thought he could. I'm trying to convince myself that he didn't share my picture with other people, but I know it had to have been him since it wasn't me. I just don't want to believe it."

"My parents are mad too," Claire offered. It seemed like tensions had eased now that the ice was broken. "They're so disappointed in me. I tried to keep it a secret but it was like they knew I was lying to them. They're worried I'm going to ruin my dad's chances of winning the next senatorial election."

"*You?*" Vera asked.

"Yeah, they'll blame me if he loses. Almost undoubtedly. But, like, no pressure."

"God, that is so fucked up," Vera responded and paused for a second. "My dad has been good about it. I think he's blaming himself for it more than anything and he's trying to compensate by giving me legal support. But, I don't know, I know it's my fault, so I still feel guilty for putting him through this."

"There's nothing wrong with sending photos," Sloane said. "You sent the picture to someone who consented to receiving it and you're an adult, so you didn't do anything bad or wrong. And that applies to all of you equally. The only person to blame here is the person who sent the email."

"Thanks, Sloane," Margot said, sounding genuine. "I want to believe it, but I don't know if I'm ready to yet. Maybe eventually I will, but as long as people are treating me the way that they have I'll keep feeling like I'm in the wrong."

"Do you want to talk about how people have been treating you?"

Margot sighed. "I don't know. It's like, people keeping asking me for more photos. Hitting on me. Even Luke seems to be changing his tune when it comes to 'fat bitches.'" She snorted. "I hate this school. I really do. I've never felt so popular but I'm still entirely alone."

Alice's eyes welled up with tears. "I get it."

Listening to the girls share made it increasingly obvious that there was not one type of girl who sent nudes and not one universal experience. It felt important to emphasize this fact in the article in some way. I owed it to them to not lump them together as simply the Nudegate Girls. They deserved to have their own experiences and voices represented. It was how I would've wanted to be represented, had Nick been a slightly different person and my pictures had ended up on the email.

Violeta was the only one who hadn't spoken. She was picking at the material of her St. Joe's polo, eyes down.

"Has anyone decided if they'll be talking to the police?" Sloane asked. "Other than Vera."

"They didn't do much, but my dad is out for blood and using his contacts in civil law to see what we can do," Vera said. "If anyone else is interested, I can probably forward phone numbers."

"I don't know what I want to do," Alice said. "My parents think I deserve the email happening. They view it as a punishment. There's no way they'll support me with a lawsuit."

"You're eighteen," Vera said.

"Yeah, eighteen with no job and no money. I'm still entirely owned by them. I love them so much and I'm so grateful for everything they've done, but they hold all of the cards right now. And since they're furious with me. . ."

Margot seemed to relate. "I was grounded and can't use my phone at home anymore. My parents have no idea what to do with me. And my mom just keeps *crying*, like, nonstop. They don't trust me anymore. And because of what? I sent a photo? They'd given me a sex talk and condoms but the thought of sending a *picture* of my bare boobs was too much?"

"I wish I could trust anyone right now," Violeta said, breaking her silence. "I cannot believe my photo was sent to everyone at St. Joe's. It is so unbelievable, you know? Like I send one photo to *one* fucking guy because I'm feeling a little cute and flirty and suddenly it's *everywhere*? And people won't stop *talking* about it? It's ridiculous."

"You don't deserve that, Violeta. None of you did. No one

does." Sloane kept using the language of someone who wasn't also affected by Nudegate, the only Nudegate girl who hadn't spoken about her own experience. She continued, "Is there anything else people want to talk about? Get off their chest?"

"Does anyone want to go to the police station with me to file a victim report?" Margot asked.

"I don't know if I'm going to," Alice said.

"I don't think I can either." Claire twirled her ponytail with her fingers, looking at the ground. She looked so different from the girl I was used to seeing on the posters of musicals at our school. So much smaller.

"I can go with you," Sloane said.

"Same," Vera offered.

"Is there anything we can do?" Claire asked. "Besides a criminal complaint. And I know the posters around the school were something at least, but I feel like we can do more. Go bigger."

I'd been wrong; it wasn't just Sloane behind the posters. It was an entire group.

"What do you have in mind?" Sloane asked.

"Like, maybe a way to get back for the email. Revenge. Anything. I think finding Eros would be the best chance we have at that, but I'm thinking something more realistic."

Sloane was hesitant. "I don't know if we can. I don't know what we're able to do."

"I mean, do you think this Eros fucker thought about what he was able to do? No, he just did it because he *could*," Vera said. "I like the track that Claire is on."

"I don't know," Sloane said. "I thought this meeting should be used for something different where we just focus on us. But maybe there's something we can do. I don't know." It seemed like the only time Sloane had ever been unsure of herself.

None of the girls said anything in response and Sloane looked ready to change the topic of conversation.

"Do you think our photos are going to be shared outside of the email? Is anyone outside of St. Joe's going to see it?" Violeta asked, her voice quiet.

"I hope not," was all Sloane said in response.

With that, the meeting was over. Sloane thanked everyone for coming and watched them exit, slowly and quietly. Once everyone else started to file out, I hung back, wanting to talk to Sloane.

"Thank you for letting me sit in," I said.

"Do you get it now?" Sloane asked, her brown eyes on mine. "Do you understand how you're different from us?"

"I—" I said, embarrassed to be called out and desperate for something else to talk about. "Who is NG, Sloane?"

"Nudegate Girls," Sloane said, something so obvious I couldn't believe I'd missed it. "But Margot thought we should have something that's our own, so I came up with Slut Squad." She paused, thinking over her next statement. "Thanks for listening to us, Eden."

The earnest comment caught me off guard. "Yeah, sure. It's literally what I do." She kindly half chuckled at my lame attempt at a joke.

As I was heading toward the door, Sloane stopped me.

"We might do something for Ricky DiMarco's Halloween party tomorrow night," Sloane said. "I have an idea." When I tried to get more details out of her, she brushed it off. "Just be there."

I texted Jeremy during the walk to my car, telling him I'd changed my mind and wanted to go to Ricky's party. It wasn't clear what Sloane was thinking or what to expect from her, but I knew I couldn't miss it.

CHAPTER NINE

Jeremy immediately responded with a *yes* and told me how excited he was that I was going out. It made me feel a little guilty for going only to see Sloane's plans for Ricky's party.

Since I didn't go out often, I'd forgotten what it was like to feel uncertain about what to wear. Even though I'd had Friday night—immediately after the Slut Squad meeting—and most of Saturday to figure out what to wear, I was stuck.

I eventually decided to scrap the Halloween costume idea and go for something dark and vampy. I hadn't anticipated that I would be going out at all, so I didn't bother shopping. Actual Halloween wasn't until tomorrow and I was planning on handing out candy. Most kids in the neighborhood didn't think twice about if you were wearing a costume or not.

I put on a final touch of red lipstick, feeling vaguely like I was going undercover. This wasn't my scene and it wasn't my usual attire, and I wasn't going for anything other than research purposes. At least Victor and Jeremy seemed to go out pretty often, so I'd have them to lean on.

After sliding on a pair of black boots to complete my all-black ensemble, I exited my room and waited for Jeremy to arrive.

"You look nice," Dad said from the couch. "Can I send a picture to Mom?"

"Dad, please." My cheeks glowed. "You're embarrassing me."

"I'm excited you're going out! You're young, you should be having fun."

I had fudged my way through why I was leaving, saying it was a small get-together with some friends. But based on the people Ricky knew, his house would probably be hosting one-third of the teenagers in town. I also wasn't sure where my parents stood on underage drinking, so I decided dodging that conversation for now was for the best.

I couldn't hold back a laugh as my dad pulled his cell phone out of his pocket, placing his reading glasses halfway down his nose. He held the phone nearly an arm's length away from his face. "Smile!"

"Dad," I said, partially covering my face, but I let him take the picture. This was a regular tradition, my dad taking pictures while my mom was at work and sending them to her. I knew she appreciated the effort since it was hard on her being at work all the time. She was able to get away for larger events, like school dances, birthdays, and most holidays, but it wasn't always easy. He sometimes sent pictures of day-to-day things, too, like if I got a good grade on an essay or the first time my name appeared in print in the school's newspaper. My dad's phone probably held a picture of every day of my life that held any significance whatsoever.

My phone vibrated with a text from Jeremy, so I leaned over and kissed my dad on the cheek, careful not to leave any lipstick behind. "I'll see you later."

"Have fun," Dad said. "Your old man will be sitting at home, all alone on a Saturday night. Guess I'll have to order myself some dinner and fall asleep in front of the TV because I don't have my girls to keep me in line."

"Bye, Dad," I said, laughing.

Immediately after stepping outside, I braced against the cold and did an awkward half run down my driveway to Jeremy's car. Climbing into the seat, I was somewhat out of breath and already unable to feel my fingers.

"Hey!" Jeremy turned to look at me. "Glad you could make it. This is Victor. Victor, this is Eden."

"Hey." The guy in the passenger seat turned to me, showing off sculpted cheekbones that caught the overhead car light. He had naturally tan skin and deep brown eyes, and his hair was intentionally messy in a stylish way. I could see why, during the few times Jeremy had mentioned him to me, he always got a dreamy look in his eye.

"Hey."

"You also go to St. Joe's?" Victor asked, sounding more like he was making conversation than actually confirming. I had a feeling Jeremy had mentioned me a few times, probably describing me in ways that weren't so flattering during particularly stressful weeks.

"Yeah, I'm on the newspaper staff with Jeremy."

"Cool, I'm a junior at Lakewood," he said. "About thirty minutes out."

"Yeah, I know the one. You played us in boys' soccer." I only knew that because I'd edited an article on it, but I was grateful for the conversation starter.

Victor laughed. "Yeah, great game for you guys. Not so much for us."

"Are you also a big sports fan?"

"Sort of. Jeremy is more into it than I am," he said. "I've learned a lot from him talking to me about games, though. And he's dragged me along to a few, which always end up being more fun than I think it'll be."

"Don't act like you don't spend almost the entire time complaining."

"I don't!" Victor said. He turned to me. "I promise, I really don't."

It reminded me of me and Nick—the happy banter, the content glow, the knowing looks. It was the kind of thing that couldn't be replaced by hanging out with friends or watching a romantic comedy.

For just a second, I let myself miss Nick. I missed holding his hand and the way he'd introduce me to people as his girlfriend, "Edy." I craved the simplicity of knowing I always had someone to go to about anything. But so many of those memories that start out okay end in explosive arguments over things like making curfew or me wanting to have a weekend in while Nick wanted to go out. It made it hard to figure out if I really missed him or only missed the company.

Soft synthesized pop played in the background as we drove to Ricky's. I was mostly nervous about going but still excited to have a break in my routine, a moment to be Edy again.

Ricky's gorgeous house was far enough away from neighbors to know we most likely wouldn't disrupt them. We were in the same tax bracket, as most people at St. Joe's were, but his parents were flashier than mine; they got a plot of land away from neighbors with a gate leading to a massive circular driveway. Where my parents preferred understated and suburban, Ricky's seemed to like bold and clearly expensive.

"Ready?" Jeremy said, parking his car and turning it off. I wanted to say I was, but I had no idea what was about to happen. Sloane hadn't been specific about what she and the Slut Squad were going to do.

We stepped out of the car and I realized that Jeremy and Victor were wearing what looked like normal clothes, but Jeremy had his hair done differently and both were wearing heavy face makeup. When Victor spotted me looking, he said, "We went '80s tonight: George Michael and Andrew Ridgeley from Wham!."

Jeremy grinned. "If you get Victor drunk enough, he'll sing 'Wake Me Up Before You Go-Go.'"

"It's an ideal drunk karaoke song," he said and walked around the side yard to get to the basement entrance. Now that we were closer to the house, the number of students in our line of sight increased dramatically. They were mostly lounging around, a few smoking weed and some others looking like they weren't far from throwing up.

Through the wide basement windows, I could see a pretty large number of people were gathered. There was an actual full-service bar installed in the room where people were serving themselves drinks. One guy was mixing some for his friends, a towel jokingly thrown over his shoulder like I'd seen bartenders do in movies.

We entered the basement, the music seemingly not more

than bass. It was a rap song that I didn't recognize, but there were a few people moving along to the beat, drunkenly tripping over the words.

I realized the room was even larger than what we could see from the windows. There was additional space past the bar that included a foosball table and a dartboard. I hoped for everyone's sake Ricky had put the darts away.

The costumes dramatically varied around the room, with some more fully in character than others. I knew I was under-dressed, but considering the short time frame, I was lucky I had even pulled off showing up.

"I see my friend Megan, I'm going to go say hi," Victor yelled over the music, squeezing Jeremy's hand to say a quick goodbye. He disappeared into the sea of people easily, greeting other faces he must've recognized along the way.

I looked around, picking at my nails and feeling somewhat like an adult supervisor rather than an actual attendee. I had only been to smaller parties before and was always accompanied by Nick, so something of this scale was difficult to navigate.

"Do you want a drink?" Jeremy asked, noticing my inability to figure out what to do.

"I guess so," I said, and he laughed. He probably hadn't realized that, in inviting me out, he was signing up to be my babysitter for the night.

I rarely drank—I was almost always Nick's designated driver on the rare occasion we went out together—and my parents didn't drink much aside from the occasional bottle of *soju* they'd share with Korean BBQ. Most of my knowledge of alcohol came from TV shows I'd seen rather than personal experience.

After making our way through the crowd, Jeremy gestured to

the stool in front of the bar and moved behind it. He picked up a few different options to figure out what my preference was, and I shrugged. I hadn't been out nearly enough to know what I liked and didn't like. As Jeremy was mixing a drink for me, I glanced around the room to see if I could spot Sloane. The sooner she did whatever she was planning on doing, the earlier I would be able to leave.

He handed me a Solo cup and I took a tentative sip, the bitter taste hitting me immediately. But it wasn't so bad that I felt the need to put it down. Liquid courage could get me through the night.

"Wow, okay, so you really don't go out much," Jeremy cracked up.

"Not really," I responded and laughed sheepishly. I took a longer sip and tried my best to enjoy it, but the sweetness of the juice wasn't enough to overpower the bitter taste of alcohol. My entire body winced as it went down.

He was about to respond when I saw a hand land on his arm. "Jeremy! Hi, babe! How are you? I feel like it's been forever! And Eden! Hey!"

The hand and voice belonged to Angela Ainsley, the only girl who hadn't been able to make it to the Slut Squad meeting. It entirely made sense that Angela and Jeremy would be friends since Jeremy knew most of the star athletes on campus.

Angela looked like she might've been dressed as a cat, but the makeup on her face had smeared across her cheeks. Her expression was dazed and the mostly empty water bottle in her hand, filled with some sort of pink juice, made me think she was pretty drunk. I knew there was no way I'd be able to interview her, or plan an interview with her, like that.

With Jeremy distracted, I didn't have a crutch to fall back on and was left to my devices to look like I belonged. I saw a lot of faces I recognized from St. Joe's, but none I would be able to confidently walk up to and start a conversation.

I turned to the bar again and gulped down my drink, realizing that Jeremy wasn't there anymore. He'd probably gone out to find Victor again at some point. I sighed, feeling partially defeated. Even if the Slut Squad did show up, I wasn't sure it would make up for me being reminded of how woefully bad I was at socializing.

After draining my cup, I moved closer to the bar to find more of whatever I could find to occupy the time. If I was going to be sitting alone at a party, I might as well have a drink.

I picked up a bottle, squinting at the label to try to figure out what it was that was in my hand.

"Captain Morgan," Atticus leaned down to talk to me. He was wearing a lifeguard outfit, with bright red swim trunks and a white shirt that clung to his upper body. I had to actively avert my eyes away from his chest. "It's rum."

"Recommended?" I asked.

"More of a beer guy," he said, holding up the can that was in his hand. He brushed past me to lean under the counter and dig into a cooler I hadn't noticed earlier. Popping open the lid, he pulled out another can that looked the same as the one he'd already had.

I poured myself a drink out of a random bottle, suddenly wishing I'd paid attention to what Jeremy had been doing.

"Wow." I looked over and Atticus was glancing into my cup. "Didn't think you were that much of a drinker."

"What?" I asked, putting the bottle down.

"It's a lot." Atticus nodded his head toward my cup. "I'm impressed you're willing to drink that much straight vodka."

I felt my face burn even though it didn't seem like he was mocking me; he was making an observation, probably trying to start a conversation while he was here. I wanted to make a comment of some kind, something charming or slightly snarky, but instead I looked at the cup in my hand.

"I have no idea what I'm doing," I told him and took a sip, realizing I should've picked up from Atticus's comments that the sip wouldn't be all that pleasant tastewise.

He laughed. "How was it?"

"Awful," I admitted, laughing.

He looked like he was about to say something when his eyes moved past me, back to the front door. Sloane had arrived with a few girls, all wearing a similar uniform. At first, it seemed like it might've been a character costume of some kind until my eyes focused more.

They were all wearing cut-off shirts with *slut* written on the front in black marker. When I looked even closer, I realized they were all wearing red As reminiscent of *The Scarlet Letter*.

After making their entrance, the girls dispersed, finding drinks or their friends. It looked like it was Sloane, Vera, and Margot. It wasn't the entire Slut Squad, but it still meant something. It surprised me that Claire wasn't with them considering she was the person who had seemed most interested in making a statement.

News of what they were wearing spread pretty quickly, with people commenting on their outfits. I heard some mumbled commentary about them, both good and bad.

"Yo, you can't wear that as a Halloween costume," a guy yelled over the music. "You're already a slut every day."

Laughter that rippled through the crowd.

"I know," Sloane said, smiling. "And don't I look hot while doing it?"

Sloane approached the bar. "Hey, Eden. John."

I knew Sloane and Atticus were good friends and had known each other for years but calling him John seemed to have a story behind it. I wondered, briefly, if they'd ever dated and then realized how ridiculous it was for me to be thinking about that in the midst of everything going on.

"Guess the Slut Squad really is on," I said. "I like the outfit."

"Thank you," she said, turning to show off her crop top and Daisy Dukes. The shirt was cut to above her belly button and looked even more homemade and lopsided up close. The marker had started drying out partway through writing and the A was crooked, but there was something about it—authenticity or a sense of humor—that made it work.

But as Sloane was pouring her drink, I noticed a change in her attitude. I spotted the looks from people and those who were taking pictures, some people trying to be subtle and others not so much, and I realized it wasn't all fun and games. Sloane might have had a lighthearted approach walking in the door, but there was a hard edge. Her jaw was a tight, stiff line as she surveyed the crowd.

I pressed my own drink against my lips, willing myself to take another sip. I was definitely feeling the impact of the alcohol already after downing the first drink so quickly, but I wanted to try to ease the tension I was feeling. The Slut Squad showing up was a small step forward, but it had made a statement. There was something to be said about someone who didn't mind plastering on their chest the very word people were calling them behind their back.

"Oh, it's very classy," I heard and spotted Claire not far from where Sloane and I were standing. Claire was talking to her friends, but the direction of her face and the use of her stage voice told me she had an intended target. "Nothing like having the trash self-identify themselves."

Hurt flashed across Sloane's face, but she recovered quickly. "What about you?" Sloane asked. "We're in the same boat, so I'm not sure what you're hoping to prove."

"You and I?" Claire said, looking at Sloane. She was wearing a silver skirt and crop top with metallic makeup. Her blond hair was up in two buns.

"We *both* had our nudes leaked, Claire. Or did you conveniently forget that part?"

"At least I'm not proud of having a body count higher than the population of Delaware."

"So what?" Sloane asked, stepping closer to where Claire was standing. "Since when is who I sleep with any of your business?"

"It's all our business when you walk around with it on your fucking chest. If you don't want people talking, don't do something people will talk about."

"What the fuck is your problem? Why do you act like you're so much better than I am even though you do the same exact things? We both have sex. We've both sent nudes. Why am I a slut and you're not?"

"Who gave you the right to speak to me like that?"

Atticus put a hand in the empty space between them, acting like a barrier. "Yo, cool it. No need for all that."

Claire took a second, seemingly standing up taller and sizing up Sloane. She was barely five foot two but she was fiery.

It was hard to believe that this was the same girl who had

shown up to Sloane's Slut Squad meeting. I wasn't sure what had happened, but it must've been something significant to make her go from being pro-sisterhood—and pro-revenge of the people who called them all names—to calling Sloane out publicly at a party in a little over twenty-four hours.

Sloane seemed visibly hurt but refused to break. She didn't move and instead only stood and waited to see what else Claire might throw at her. It was admirable but also seemed painful.

"Ladies, *ladies*, please. You're both hot. Don't fight," Luke said and turned to meet Sloane's eyes. "Maybe you should kiss and make up."

"Get out of here, Luke," Atticus said. "Leave her alone. You've done enough."

Luke looked at Atticus, squaring him up. The latter was taller than the former, but I was more afraid of what Luke was capable of.

"Whatever, man," Luke said, breaking the tension and gradually disappearing into the crowd to find his friends.

"You okay?" Atticus asked, looking at Sloane.

"It's fine," Sloane said. Atticus and I exchanged a look that felt like it carried more familiarity than we had. "I wish he'd stop being like that."

"Yeah, you and me both," Atticus responded, and Sloane took a long sip of her drink. Atticus lightly squeezed her upper arm as a show of support before heading off into the crowd.

I was waiting for Sloane to leave me behind, too, but she didn't.

"I get it now," I responded, and Sloane looked at me, her eyes communicating more than I could possibly begin to fully interpret.

~

Eventually, Jeremy and Victor came to find me, saying they were bored and ready to leave. I was more than happy to oblige.

"Do you want to stay?" Jeremy asked, looking at the cup in my hand and probably noticing the slightly hazy look on my face.

I shook my head. "Mostly looking forward to getting this makeup off."

Victor, Jeremy, and I walked out the same door that we had arrived through. When we finally exited the basement, the cold weather hit me almost immediately, making me shiver. I hadn't realized how hot it had been inside. My phone screen told me it was just past midnight. It was about how long I had been anticipating I would stay; any longer and I probably would've kept drinking to pass time, a decision that would not have ended well.

"Oh, shit," Victor said, his speech slurred and his cheeks a glowing pink in the dim lighting. "I forgot my phone in the bathroom. I'll be back."

He disappeared back inside, leaving Jeremy and me with only the sounds of bass thumping from inside and people talking at low volume outside. Every once in a while someone would laugh, breaking through the peaceful quiet.

"What's the real reason you came tonight?" Jeremy asked, inching over to me and nudging me with his shoulder.

"What?"

"I've given you more than a few opportunities to hang out with me and, not being bitter, stating the obvious, this is the first time you've actually come out. I hadn't asked because I didn't want to scare you away before, but now I'm curious."

I sniffled, my nose struggling in the chilly weather. It was also a pretty good stalling technique, since it was hard to admit I was there on assignment. Thankfully, Jeremy didn't need me to say it.

"I'm still glad you came out, if it means anything," he said.

It was tempting to say the same, but the things Claire and Luke had said to Sloane left a bad taste in my mouth. It hadn't been a good night and I wasn't sure if St. Joe's would ever have one again. It was clear the Nudegate drama was just getting started.

CHAPTER TEN

The following Monday moved in slow motion, my eyes frequently falling back onto the windows of my classrooms to watch the rain fall. I hadn't thought about much related to my actual classes since Nudegate had broken. Part of me was almost relieved I didn't have much of a social life to begin with outside of the newspaper staff. I would be exhausted having to balance friends with my executive editor obligations, Nudegate, and schoolwork. Even though college application deadlines were coming up, it was hard to think about the future when the present was so demanding.

As I headed into the lunchroom, I spotted Ronnie from the door frame. She was sitting at a table with other people from staff but seemed entirely uninterested in the conversation occurring. As usual, her eyes were glued to her phone, tapping with impressive speed.

"If I didn't know better, I'd assume you were playing a game," I said, sitting down in the empty spot next to her.

"I wish I was," she said, pushing hair behind her ear. "Instead, I have to respond to Principal Yanick's email about our plans for covering Nudegate."

Principal Yanick had sent an email to only Ronnie and me, asking for updates. It was a blatant attempt at either ensuring we send her the article for review, or that we drop the piece altogether.

"She doesn't give a shit about this paper. And this whole *the St. Joseph's administration hopes you understand the gravity of the situation and the consequences that will follow if you choose to not follow my orders* thing?" Ronnie asked, quoting the email directly from her phone screen. "Like, who the fuck does she think she is?"

"We didn't even say anything explicitly bad about St. Joe's in the last issue. We typed up what they ended up saying verbatim and people didn't like it. That's not our fault."

"I guess they're bitter we're actually recording and reporting on what they have to say. They're worried about losing donors. I doubt any families will want to revamp our football field if news about a campus sex scandal gets out."

St. Joe's relied heavily on donations from both alumni and parents of current students. Tuition was expensive, but it wasn't enough to cover all of the amenities offered, like a gorgeous indoor pool, well-stocked library, and advanced classroom technology. Without money, it wasn't certain how long St. Joe's would be able to continue to be St. Joe's.

"I guess it makes sense. Bad press drives away donations and potential students," I said and opened a granola bar. Ronnie opened one of her many mini candy bars, placing her elbow on the table and leaning on her hand.

"How are interviews going?" she asked, popping the Twix into her mouth. "The quotes you got from Vera and Danica were great."

I'd shared a portion of the quotes from Vera and Danica's interview with Ronnie but cut out the bits about the Slut Squad meeting. I couldn't decide if it was worth it to tell her about it or not yet. It seemed important to mention, but I also didn't want to break the trust of my sources, especially since it seemed like Sloane had just started warming up to me.

"I'm going to try to talk to more of the girls soon. I still haven't been able to get Sloane, but I think I'm close. I'm still waiting on Violeta, Margot, Angela, and Claire. I asked Jeremy if he could connect me to Angela, but I'm not sure if she'll agree or not."

"Have you talked to any potential suspects yet?"

"Just Louis, but it wasn't so much an interview as it was . . ." I trailed off, unsure of how exactly to describe my conversation with him. Thinking about it, it wasn't particularly professional or purposeful, at least for a journalist. It was, more than anything, the kind of thing someone who was trying to solve a mystery would do.

"I think you should talk to Luke soon. I'd love to hear what he has to say."

"I'm still waiting on something that actually points to him being a real suspect and not just a horrible person," I said, thinking about the Halloween party. "I don't have enough leverage to get him to listen to me."

"I think it'll be fine. I'm feeling optimistic."

"I'm glad someone is. This story is becoming a progressively larger pain in my ass."

"I'm sorry," she said, her voice genuine. "I didn't mean for this to turn into a thing, you know? I assumed the story would come more easily than this."

"It's fine. Bree and Julia have gotten good student quotes and we have at least an outline of a story," I said, thinking about the looming deadline for publication. I had only until Wednesday night to submit something and I knew it'd come faster than I was ready for. It always did. "We have enough to publish something right now, it just might not be comprehensive."

"That's all right, it doesn't seem like this case is going away any time soon. I think it'll be relevant for at least a few more editions of the *Weekly*."

"I don't know, it might progress pretty quickly," I said. "Some of the girls are talking about filing victim reports with the police, but I'm not sure if they have yet."

"Interesting. I wonder why they wouldn't want to. I feel like it'd make it easier to find Eros."

I thought about all of the limitations brought up at the Slut Squad meeting. Unsupportive parents, fear of having their name out in public associated with nudes, fear of the nudes being shared beyond the walls of St. Joe's, wanting to avoid any possible further public scrutiny. I understood why they were hesitating.

"Actually, does it seem like the police have been doing anything?" Ronnie asked. "They wouldn't get involved in civil matters and since revenge porn isn't illegal in the state . . . the police might only go this far."

"Why would they get victim statements if they weren't planning on pursuing anything?"

"Maybe to confirm the ages of the girls? It'd be immediately criminal if any of the girls were under eighteen when they sent the photos, but it's only civil otherwise. It'd be basically up to St. Joe's to find and punish whoever did it."

"Do—" My phone buzzed on the table, interrupting me.

> Jeremy: Angela is interested in doing an interview. She said she could meet briefly today between school and volleyball practice.

Ever-so thankful for Jeremy's connections, I sent back a quick *thanks* and looked back at Ronnie.

"Jeremy secured an interview with Angela Ainsley for me," I said. "Do you think Yanick is aware of what's going on with the police?"

"I have no idea. I mean, I'm almost certain she's in the loop, but it sounds like she hasn't been updating anyone else outside of the trustees."

I groaned. "Imagine how easy this could be if we went to a school that wanted to cooperate with us."

"I don't know if any schools would cooperate since they all have the legal right to limit what newspapers publish. No one would want news like this spreading about their school," Ronnie said. "What made us want to join the newspaper? Sometimes I swear I can't remember."

"So we could cover big news like Nudegate," I said, and Ronnie popped another candy bar in her mouth, looking at me in reluctant agreement.

~

I ended up meeting up with Angela in the *Warrior Weekly* newsroom like I had with Vera and Danica.

"Hey, Eden!" Angela said as she walked into the newsroom. Angela and I hadn't stayed in contact after our psychology class, but we were friendly. "I've never actually been in here before. Cool room."

"Thanks," I responded and she sat down in the chair across from me. Her long and lean limbs folded gracefully into the seat, carrying herself like a natural athlete and someone who was entirely in control of her body.

"Feels weird doing an interview not related to sports," she laughed, acting surprisingly easygoing considering the circumstances.

We went through the usual preinterview routine, confirming that she was okay with me recording the conversation. When she agreed, I pressed Record on my phone.

"It'll be quick since I know you have practice. What's life been like for you since the email?"

"I mean, pretty much the same," she said.

"Really?" I asked, feeling skeptical but not wanting to show it. It was hard to believe, especially after the meeting at Sloane's house.

"My mom doesn't seem all that bothered by it," she explained. "She learned about it the day it happened; I guess one of her mom friends told her I was on the email. I don't think she's happy, but she hasn't kicked me out or anything. She doesn't think it's worth the argument since she already knows I regret it. She's just made sure I'm doing okay." Angela stopped to think. "Teammates have been pretty sympathetic. I don't know. It's been okay."

"Some of the other girls have mentioned receiving increased attention from guys on campus, being asked for nudes and the like."

"The guys don't really mess with me like that. I'm kind of seen as one of the guys, I guess. Or maybe my height scares them," she added, lightheartedly. "They haven't acted any differently around me."

"Have the police reached out to you about filing a statement?" I asked, and she nodded.

"Yeah, I decided I didn't want to talk to them because I didn't want to turn it into a big deal. I mean, it sucks and all. But, like, it's a picture, you know? I'm on track to play at my top pick school next year on the West Coast, so I can just leave all of this stuff behind. No big deal."

"Are you worried the email will affect the scholarship?" I asked.

"I doubt it since I didn't do anything wrong."

"And you mentioned finally getting into your dream school? Congrats, by the way."

Angela looked relived for the topic change. "Yeah. This is technically my fifth year of playing here. My number one school didn't recruit me last year because they said my grades were too low to justify acceptance. My mom arranged for me to repeat senior year to improve my GPA."

That would explain why I thought she'd graduated. I wasn't sure if she was technically allowed to do that, but I didn't comment. "So . . . . you're eighteen?" I confirmed.

"Yeah, have been for a little," Angela said, as if we were having a casual conversation. Between Angela, Vera, and Alice, and none of the other girls saying differently, it seemed like all of them were eighteen. It *had* to be a pattern. The decision might explain why specifically these girls had been chosen and why it was so hard to find Eros; there was no common enemy—they just happened to be chosen because they were over eighteen and had sent nudes. But that didn't explain *why* Eros would send the email or how Eros got the photos in the first place.

I looked at her carefully, trying to read her face for any kind of tell that she was lying. It was such a stark contrast from what I'd heard at the Slut Squad meeting; it seemed like Angela wasn't affected by Nudegate at all.

"It's kind of a big deal," I said. "It's an invasion of privacy."

"It's something that happens. I made a mistake and the guy shared his photo. It was probably sent as a joke. That's what they like to do."

"What do you mean?"

"The guys will send around photos to each other sometimes," Angela explained, her tone implying this was public knowledge. "They'll talk about it when I'm around. I think they forget that some of the girls they're talking about are my friends."

"Photos as in nude pictures they've been sent?"

"Yeah."

I was caught so off guard I could barely formulate a question. "Do you know what guys are involved in this?"

Angela hesitated. "I don't really want to give them away. It's not my place."

I redirected, hoping to get some information. I wondered if Louis—who seemed to be my primary and only real suspect, since it was the only guy who'd been named—was connected to it all. "Is it a big group of guys? Two or three guys? Can you give me any information, even broadly, about who's involved?"

"There's enough for a group chat but I don't know exactly how many."

"A group chat?" I asked, my voice faltering slightly. This was the best lead we'd gotten since Nudegate started. Ronnie, and probably most people on the staff, would be thrilled. I wondered if anyone else in the Slut Squad knew this or if it was only Angela.

"Yeah. Some of the guys from different sports teams, different connections. I don't know. It's not, like, only nudes but it happens."

"Have you been able to read any of the messages?"

"No, I only know about it because I heard Rolland Pike talking about it. He made this offhand comment about how Luke was telling him about this 'wank bank' on his phone." Angela grimaced, clearly hating she even had to say the phrase *wank bank* in front of me. "I think Luke mostly calls it that as a joke, but he's also kind of a dick so it might not be."

Calling Luke "kind of a dick" was the understatement of the year, but I was mostly focused on Rolland's connection. He was Danica's boyfriend, so him being involved in the group chat in any capacity would make Danica's friendship with Vera and Sloane infinitely more complicated. That might explain why Danica and Vera's interview seemed so oddly tense.

With the interview officially derailed, I press the End button on my phone to stop recording. "Off record, can you tell me who you sent your photo to? Is he involved in the group chat?"

Angela looked at her hands in her lap. "You won't tell anyone?" It was the first time she'd shown any hesitation since walking in. "Tyson Post." A lacrosse player. He'd gotten a lot of attention from St. Joe's, and the *Warrior Weekly* sports section, in the past after carrying the team during the state championship.

"Does it seem like he's involved in the group chat?"

"It didn't seem like it. We'd been seeing each other for a while, but I guess it would look bad to talk to your almost-girlfriend about a group chat revolving other girls' nudes," Angela said. "He must've been involved in some way since my picture ended up on the email. I haven't asked to confirm, though. We haven't been on speaking terms after the email."

"Have you told any of the other girls from the email about this?"

"No, not yet," Angela said.

"I really think you should consider it," I said, fully acknowledging that a journalistic line had been crossed but not wanting to look back.

I knew I should talk to Tyson but, before that, I had to talk to Luke about this supposed wank bank.

CHAPTER ELEVEN

The first thing that went through my mind when I woke up the next morning was, to my disappointment, Luke Anderson. I didn't stop thinking about him even as I went through my usual morning routine—get dressed, brush my teeth, grab food to eat on the way—or as I got into my car to get to school.

Associating Luke with Nudegate was dangerous because the more I thought about it, the more I started to make connections. I was going off word of mouth and multiple degrees of separation from Luke, but if the wank bank was real, it would mean he probably not only had access to nudes, but also had the ability to share them with others.

And, additionally, if Luke was involved in the group chat Angela mentioned, it would mean he'd have access to pictures that hadn't been sent directly to him. But, then again, means didn't inherently suggest a motive; just because he had access to photos didn't prove he'd done anything with them.

A smaller, more rational part of myself also knew it was hard to imagine Luke as a criminal mastermind. And the likelihood of Luke being Eros was virtually the same as any other guy on campus depending on how large the group chat was.

There were no clear indicators, no obvious motives, that pointed at Luke. The best I could come up with was revenge, some sort of attempt to embarrass the girls. But for what reason? And what reason would include Margot, Alice, Violeta—girls who'd scarcely interacted with Luke or his friends? It didn't make sense.

I was running on about four hours of sleep, adrenaline the only thing keeping me standing upright. More than anything, I was a seven-or-eight-hours-of-sleep-a-night kind of girl. Trying to motivate myself to get through the day would be nearly impossible. Sugar and coffee would have to help.

I was running over the same theories, forming connections and trying to see the bigger picture. There were answers somewhere—obviously someone was behind Nudegate—but I didn't feel any closer to finding them, putting me on edge. I'd have to talk to Ronnie and maybe Kolton and Jeremy. As much as I wanted to hear Bree and Julia's input, the sources they were talking to were mostly uninvolved, easily a few years younger, and likely disconnected from the seniors. Kolton, Jeremy, and Ronnie would have clear insight into the social dynamics of the senior class. Whoever sent this email wanted to hurt these girls, needed to prove something—about them, about him—and that was the crux we were still missing.

It was appropriately rainy and dark as I walked up to the school. I hugged my raincoat closer to me, fighting against the light drizzle that was rapidly turning into a downpour.

Early November had just rolled through, meaning we had roughly eight more months of school to get through without combusting. As I entered the doors of St. Joe's, I tried to shake off the rain that had collected on my jacket and ran my fingers through my slightly damp hair. I'd expected to see Luke in his usual form, leaning against the lockers with the same slightly smug look on his face, but I realized it wasn't going to be that easy.

Sloane was there, almost immediately in the entryway, her lips bold as ever, her hair flawless despite the weather.

Trying to keep it casual, I strolled over, knowing I was close to the top of the list of people she didn't want to see, but I was feeling emboldened. Maybe it was the lack of sleep combined with the sudden, and somewhat surprising, lead provided by Angela.

"Hey," I said, and she looked at me, her hand on her locker. "Have you thought more about doing an interview for the *Warrior Weekly*? I'm trying to get quotes from all of the girls about their individual experiences. And possible leads for Eros." I knew I couldn't publish the names of rumored Nudegate suspects because the *Weekly* would be accused of libel, but I wanted to see if a possible group chat meant anything to the other girls.

"Nice try," Sloane said. "Please don't give that jackass the ability to find pride in people using that stupid pseudonym."

"What else would I call him?"

"Jerk-off," she said, closing her locker and starting to list off other words on her fingers. "Motherfucker, idiot, dickwad—"

"None of those can be printed."

"Not my fault your editors are a bunch of prudes."

"Sloane, please."

"My mind won't change. We've been over it and the stance that I've had still stands," Sloane said and looked at me. "Don't take it personally."

"I don't understand—"

She turned away from me and put a long, perfectly manicured hand up in the air as if to wave me off. "Bye, Eden."

At least Sloane seemed to acknowledge that I was, at minimum, human. Luke's general lack of empathy made me think he would have no qualms about shutting me out, not even offering a second glance in my direction.

~

Between afternoon classes, I spotted Luke for the first time that day. He was standing by his locker with a few of his friends, some with girlfriends in tow. Danica was standing with Rolland, her head leaning against his arm as she looked at her phone.

Even though my nerves were humming at the thought of approaching him, I recognized he had no real power over me. There was no harm in asking him for an interview. That confidence held strong right up until I saw him and knew it was time. Despite the warning signs my body was giving me, I readjusted my backpack and approached him.

"Eden, what a pleasant surprise," Luke said. His blue eyes flicked over me, checking me out in a way that was probably rooted in instinct more than actual desire. "What can I do for you today?"

"I wanted to talk to you about doing an interview," I said. "For the *Warrior Weekly*."

"Do you want to talk about my impressive soccer stats again, like last time?" he asked, raising a blond eyebrow. "Maybe I can show you the fruits of my labor afterward."

A few of his friends let out chuckles at the innuendo. My skin crawled, but I brushed off the comment. "It was actually about something else."

"Oh?" He turned and walked closer to me. He had his button-down shirt rolled up at the sleeves and the front was partially unbuttoned, hinting at the smooth and toned chest just under the fabric. I stood up straighter and met his eyes again, knowing he wasn't the only person who could make a power move. We eventually stepped out of earshot of his friends, our voices blending into the white noise of the hallway.

"I wanted to ask about a rumor, one about you having something called a wank bank?" I asked, keeping my voice even. I hadn't wanted to use the card that early, but I knew he would only give me the time of day if I showed my hand.

Luke's face didn't change, but his blue eyes became stormier. More dangerous. "You shouldn't believe everything you hear, Eden."

"That's why I'm confirming," I told him. There was little chance I'd ever get permission to print this information, but I thought I'd try to frame it as being for the *Weekly* anyway. "As journalists, if we don't know what is and isn't the truth, we find sources who can tell us. And who better than the person the rumor is about?"

"Jesus, give it a rest," he scoffed. "You're not a fucking journalist. And you have jack shit so you're trying to start something with me so you can attach a name to the email."

"So, I take it you're denying the rumor?"

"Yeah, I'm denying the rumor," he said. "I preferred you when you were quieter. You're annoying as fuck when you're talking."

It was a weak insult that rolled off easily and I was glad I had struck a nerve with him. There was no reason for him to be this hostile if he wasn't hiding something. I took a second, spending a beat too long being quiet so he would get frustrated.

"I don't know what you want from me," he said and ran a hand through his hair. "If you're trying to get me alone, say it. I wouldn't complain."

My jaw clenched so tightly that Luke noticed.

"It's a compliment, Jeong. Don't look so upset," he said, and I pressed my lips together. I didn't know if he could tell hitting on me made me squirm, or if he genuinely believed this was how he was supposed to talk to women.

"Should I assume you don't have any nudes saved on your phone, then?" I asked, hoping his ego would be his downfall.

"Where'd you get that idea from?" he asked, standing up taller.

"You said you didn't have a wank bank," I said. Whether he admitted to the wank bank or only admitted to having nudes on his phone, it'd still plant seeds of doubt in his innocence.

"That doesn't mean shit," he said. "I still have nudes. I get ass."

He wasn't wrong but considering he managed to fit in multiple questionable remarks in a few minutes with him, I wished he was. "Have you ever shared those nudes with anyone?"

Finally, his face changed. His jaw became a sharp, tight line so quickly and aggressively that it made my pulse quicken.

"I know what you're trying to get at and no, what's mine is mine," he said. "I don't know where you get the impression that you can accuse me of something like that, but it's not true. I wouldn't do some shit like that."

"You've never shown your nudes to anyone? Never sent them to a group chat as a joke?" I asked, unsure of where the relative confidence was rooting from. My nerves were buzzing to the point that I was worried I might throw up, but I had to stand my ground. I wouldn't allow him the privilege of scaring me off. "Are you Eros, Luke?"

He looked away for a second and then back to me. "I might show them to a few guys sometimes, but I wouldn't send them out to everyone like a fucking moron. Girls send me pics sometimes, what's the big deal?" The anger in his face melted away, leaving his usual passionless smirk in its place. "They're for my own personal enjoyment, anyway."

"Right," I said.

"If you ever want to get added to the collection, let me know," he said, meeting my eyes again and dropping his voice. "I've heard you haven't been shy about sending them in the past."

The comment nearly knocked the wind out of my chest, but I wasn't going to break in front of him. I folded my arms across my chest. "Thanks, Luke. I'll reach out again if I have any follow-up questions."

"See ya around, *Edy*," he said, his voice flat.

I had every intention of making sure he wouldn't, mostly because he was an asshole, but also because I knew I was going to cry and I refused to let him see it.

Despite my best efforts, I made a beeline to the bathroom immediately after turning away from Luke. The only thing echoing through my mind was Luke's voice implying that he knew I'd sent nudes. *I've heard you haven't been shy about sending them in the past.* The only way he would've known that was because Nick told him.

Nick.

I hadn't spoken to him in months. The last time we'd interacted was when we ran into each other in the hallway during finals and made small talk about summer plans. It was such a fleeting moment. So trivial. At the time, I wondered if he could tell I'd cried about him for the entire weekend before that, already a few weeks removed from the breakup.

Suddenly, more than ever, I wished I hadn't given him a second thought after ending things.

But, despite my best efforts, I still remembered how he'd light up whenever he saw me. And how he could be so tender when he knew I needed him to be. There were so many small things that meant so much.

They just weren't enough to make up for how badly he wanted to be someone Luke liked. Most of what I remember from our last few months together were arguing over how I wanted to watch Netflix at home with Nick rather than awkwardly drink with football players who didn't acknowledge me.

Feelings, somewhere at the intersection of betrayal and anger and regret, bubbled in me and I felt like I was going to throw up. I braced myself on the bathroom sink, unable to tell if I was going to cry or not. I was surprised by how much I wanted to. But, instead, I looked at myself, stone-faced, in the bathroom mirror.

That was when I realized, if Luke knew, there was no telling how many other people knew. Nick and Luke weren't even friends. There was no reason why Luke should've been told in the first place; there was no reason why *anyone* should've been told in the first place. The only people who should've known about the picture were me and Nick.

Realistically, the only reason why Nick would ever tell Luke was to brag. It was the only possible option. Nick told me he loved me, called me when he was having a bad day, cried into my lap once after he'd messed up an important play during a game. He'd ignored all of that to instead offer a sexualized version of me to people he barely knew. To earn brownie points with the cool guys who had never liked him in the first place.

I gagged, overwhelmed by the strongest waves of visceral anger and hurt I'd ever felt. I never would've imagined it would be because of Nick, who had not once given me a reason to believe I couldn't trust him, even during our worst moments. Who else had been talked about? Whose photos had been shared in Luke's group chat? How close had I been to being included in the email?

I took a deep breath, trying to slow down the pace of my heart and control my shaking hands. I'd gripped the sink so hard that my skin ached.

After a few more controlled breaths, I needed to act. There had to be a way that this could help me with the investigation, with continuing to help the girls.

I couldn't stop people from knowing that Nick had fucked me over. But I could maybe stop him, and other people, from doing the same in the future. I pulled out my phone and texted Nick, asking him to meet me in the *Warrior Weekly* newsroom at the beginning of lunch period.

~

Even though I'd initiated seeing Nick again, I wasn't sure I really wanted to. He responded saying he would be there, offering no indication of how he was feeling or what he thought I needed from him. It was good to know he still thought enough of me to want to show up. I didn't know how I would've reacted if he had ignored me.

While waiting for Nick in the office, I couldn't decide if I wanted to sit or stand, so I paced, moving between seats and wringing my hands, trying to come up with what I was going to say to him. I was furious, but I'd never communicated anger well and tended to be reactive and impulsive rather than in control when I was upset. I didn't like to fight, even if Nick and I had done it pretty frequently.

The door to the office opened and Nick entered, his presence still sending a shiver through me. He was kind of lanky and his hair was kept just long enough to be styled. He'd started growing in a spotty beard, something new since we'd ended things. He was wearing the same glasses I'd helped him pick out after his dog broke his other pair.

"Eden?" he closed the door behind him. "What's up?"

I immediately thought about what it had been like leading up to sending him a picture. It was a little under a year into our relationship and he was in Colorado for spring break. He hadn't outwardly begged, but he made it obvious what he wanted. I participated fully of my own volition; the only thing that had made me hesitant was being self-conscious. I'd genuinely wanted to send the photos. It felt kind of risky and sexy and new. Things I'd never really felt before. The potential risk of what Nick could do with the photos had never crossed my mind.

"Eden?" Nick said, as if he could read everything I was thinking by looking at my face. Our communication might have never been great, but Nick always had a good gauge for my moods. It was impossible to hide my feelings from him, which made it worse when I knew he was ignoring them. I still wasn't able to collect my thoughts enough to speak and I could tell it was making him impatient. He took small steps back and forth near the old office couch. "What's going on? You're worrying me."

"You know what's going on," I said.

"Actually, I don't," he said, the same tone he always had when we fought coming back into his voice. It was like an old routine, entirely natural. So little effort required.

"Do you still have my pictures?"

"What do you mean?" He messed with the buttons on his shirt, something he did when he was thinking. I tried not to fall back onto the memory of when I would have my hands on those buttons, his hands freely roaming me. If I spent too long in this room with him, it would be opening Pandora's box. All of the things I'd chosen to not remember about him had already started coming back.

I took a deep breath. "I sent you pictures. Over spring break."

I watched as he let the words sink in, his face suddenly changing. Softening. "Oh, c'mon. Please."

"No, I need to know if you ever showed them to anyone," I said. It didn't feel right to outright accuse him. I wanted a confession. I also knew that stating what Luke had implied meant I was taking Luke's word against someone I, in a small way, still loved and trusted. Luke could've been bluffing. But for some reason, even with everything Luke had done, I didn't see him as being a liar.

"I never would've shared them with anyone." He looked at me. "I know things are weird after the whole email thing, but I swear you don't have anything to worry about. I would never do something like that to you, Edy."

I flinched at the use of his old nickname for me. Looking at him then, I remembered what it was like falling in love with him. I remembered the college fair where we'd met, a memory that felt so distant and untouched it was nearly dusty.

At one point during the fair, we'd sat on the gym bleachers, both of us uncomfortable in business casual attire, when Nick had said, "I'm just hoping I'll be good. Whatever things I end up doing, I want to be good at them. I don't have to be the best, but I want to make people proud." It was something I still thought about, even after we'd broken up.

When he asked for my number at the end of the college fair, I had no doubt he would call me. We went on a date less than a week later and were exclusive within a week of that. It was so easy. It almost always was with him. Even our breakup, a decision based on individual differences and knowing we weren't a good fit, was easy. We both knew it was coming.

But, even in that closeness and trust, it took a lot for me to send pictures to him. It might not have been something all that significant on his end, but it took effort on mine. I wanted to make it feel like I looked good, despite the fact I was less than content with the size of my boobs or that my stomach wasn't as flat as I wanted it to be. We were having sex at that point, but it was different when he saw me in person; it felt so permanent to see it all in pictures. The thought of him showing them to his friends, acting like he was Luke, stung. I'd assumed I didn't need to clarify that the pictures were private, a moment of carelessness that now seemed like a mistake.

"The pictures were for you, Nick," I said. "You."

"Which is why I never shared them with anyone. I had them on my phone, obviously, but I deleted them when we ended things. I never showed them to my friends."

I exhaled out of my nose. "Your friends. Right."

"What are you talking about? What got you on this?" Nick asked, running a hand through his hair.

I crossed my arms. "I was talking to Luke."

"Oh, Jesus Christ. Really, Eden? That's what you're going to base all of this worry on? Luke? The guy's a dick. He's fucking with you."

"No, I don't think he is. I think he somehow knows I sent you pictures and the only way he could've known that was through you," I said. "You might've not *sent* my photos to anyone, but it sure as hell seems like you told people. Maybe you even showed them my pictures."

Nick was quiet, weighing his options on what to say. He refused to make eye contact. "I just . . . I told him. Luke. At one point. I wasn't specific, he'd just been making fun of me and asked if you put out."

"It's not his business if I put out." I looked at him, unable to comprehend that this person who seemed to have no concern for my personhood had once been my go-to for everything. Every bad day, every good thing, every time I was stressed. He'd turned me into an object. A conquest.

"I-I know that. Now," Nick said.

"Do you?" I responded. "Do you really get it? Do you under-stand what it does to reputations when it comes out that you sent photos? The gossip? You guys sit around sharing photos and talking about the girls you've been with like it's no big deal because it's not to you. It doesn't even cross your mind that maybe we don't want other people to know we've had sex. You're all using photos and sex as some sort of social currency. It's gross, Nick."

"I didn't know about any of that."

"I think the worst part is that you did. You heard all the jokes. You knew what other guys said about girls. But you chose to not take it seriously because it didn't affect you," I said.

Nick was quiet for a moment. Eventually, he left without another word.

And, finally, I cried.

CHAPTER TWELVE

Despite wanting to hole up in the office, or maybe go home for the day, I pulled myself together and went to lunch. This was, more than ever, a time I needed to be able to work. The rest of the interviews needed to get done. The article needed to be finished and published. I had to do it for the Slut Squad.

I was nearly halfway there, but I didn't know if any of the remaining girls would want to talk to me. Sloane was continuing to brush me off and Claire would most likely give me the runaround. Violeta had barely spoken during the Slut Squad meeting, so chances were slim she'd want to talk to a reporter. Margot was probably my best bet for the next interview, but just because she wanted to didn't mean our schedules would allow for it. It was something I'd grown familiar with while on staff.

When I entered the lunchroom, only about ten minutes after talking to Nick, I saw Ronnie sitting at the usual lunch table. Jeremy and Kolton were sitting with her, all entirely engrossed in whatever conversation they were having. Ronnie waved me over when she saw me and I tried my best to cover up all the leftover emotion on my face.

"Hey, we're talking about an article we read in *The New Yorker* last night," Ronnie said. I joined them at the table but found myself tuning them out and getting lost in my own thoughts. My brain was stuck on an endless loop of imagining Nick spilling private details about us—about *me*—to Luke. It wasn't even so much that he had done it; it was that he hadn't thought twice about my feelings when he did it. There was no consideration for how it could hurt me or damage my reputation. High school, unfortunately, came down to two things: academics and social status. Academics were good for the future, but social status was what made high school survivable. I'd managed to coast on both and had counted on doing exactly that until graduation.

"Eden?" Ronnie looked at me.

"Yeah," I responded, snapping back to attention.

"Are you all right? You seem preoccupied."

"Worried about an exam," I said, and that seemed good enough for her. I spotted Jeremy looking concerned, but he didn't verbally say anything to me. His expression seemed to read *I'm here if you need to talk.* I wasn't sure I was ready to.

I pressed my fingers to my temple, trying to slow down my thoughts. I was furious with Nick on every level, the hurt so deep I could feel it in every part of my body. But I also knew it was already done and nothing could take it back. In some ways, at least I had the reprieve of knowing it hadn't obviously changed anything when he told Luke. People weren't calling me a slut in the hall or whispering about me. I didn't get any unusual looks or proposals like the Slut Squad described. I didn't have to live with the fact that the entire student body had seen *my* body.

Kolton cleared his throat in an effort to ease the weird silence that had fallen over the table. "Everyone almost ready for deadline?"

"Ugh, don't remind me," I groaned. "I haven't started checking to see how many articles have come through for editing."

"How's the Nudegate article going?" Jeremy asked.

"It's fine, still waiting on talking to a few of the girls but otherwise, we're moving along pretty quickly. Julia and Bree have gotten a ton of student perspectives."

"I'm sure you're doing a great job. I'm excited to read it. And I hope the interview with Angela went well."

"Yeah, it did." I gave him my best attempt at a smile considering my mood. "Thanks, Jeremy."

"Are you going to publish without quotes from the last few girls?" Kolton asked, always the news editor. Since Nudegate was going under his section, I was supposed to go through him for editing, and follow his guidelines. Reporters, which I technically was for Nudegate in addition to being an editor, were supposed to frequently check in with their section editors. I could sort of bypass that if I wanted to since I was above Kolton in the hierarchy, but it made sense he'd still want to know.

"Yeah, I haven't been able to coordinate anything with them and since we're so close to publishing, it's not going to happen. But I'm hopeful I'll get them on the next article. And since it's a combination of the girls' experiences and student perspectives on campus, I think it's still pretty good."

"Yeah, definitely," Ronnie said. "We'll just have to see what Yanick thinks about it."

Now it was Kolton's turn to groan. "Thinking about all of the work that's going to go into this article only for Yanick to probably tear it apart . . . devastating."

Kolton's response was punctuated by the sound of a table collapsing from behind us—trays crashed to the ground, and the unmistakable grunts of a fight broke out. Luke and Atticus were just two tables away and were at each other's throats.

"I am so fucking tired of your bullshit, man." Atticus's voice was level and everything about him read as being physically calm, but he was agitated. "Leave Sloane alone, all right? Don't talk about her, don't talk to her, don't even fucking *look* at her."

"Who gave you the right to tell me what to do?" Luke shot back. He stood up and rounded the table to get closer to Atticus, clearly itching for there to be a physical element to this fight. Atticus stood up from his seat in response.

"I'm not getting into this with you," Atticus said. "Leave her alone. The jokes were never funny. And making them when she's not even here to defend herself? Fucking ridiculous."

"You're so sensitive, man. Get it the fuck together."

"God, get *over* yourself."

"What did you say to me?"

Ronnie whispered. "Why are none of their friends intervening? Everything Atticus is saying is true."

"You think any of those guys are going to cross Luke? I think the only guy on the team who doesn't care what Luke says or does is Atticus," Kolton said. "Everyone else just talks shit about him behind his back instead."

Atticus tried to move past him to get to the door, but Luke took it as a chance to push him. Atticus pushed him back—mostly to get Luke off him, it seemed—which set Luke off. Fists immediately went flying and the other soccer jocks jumped up from their seats to help by pulling Atticus and Luke apart. Their teammates had incentive to make sure they didn't get into any fights; Luke and Atticus were two of the best players on the team and neither would be able to play if they got suspended from school.

Eventually, school administrators came by to pull the boys apart. The fight wasn't all that physically violent, more verbal, but Luke was a little roughed up. Blood came out of Atticus's lip and nose. The boys were quickly escorted from the cafeteria, leaving the rest of the students to gossip.

While the whole scene was a lot to process, there was one thing in particular that caught my attention.

The fight was about Sloane.

CHAPTER THIRTEEN

At the very least, the fight would give me a good reason to talk to Sloane again. It made sense that Atticus would try to step up to bat for her—they'd been good friends for years—but it was interesting that it had happened so publicly. Whatever Luke said had to have been enough to set Atticus off.

After the lunch bell rang, I left the cafeteria, giving Jeremy, Ronnie and Kolton only a quick goodbye before departing. I had a short window that was going to be even shorter with Sloane, since I seemed to be on the list of people she wasn't a fan of, and I had only five minutes between lunch and class. Sloane was digging through her locker when I approached her.

"Hey," I said, trying to keep my voice casual even though we'd never once been casual.

"Hi." Sloane looked at me, making such intense eye contact that I immediately averted my eyes. "I know the boys had a little tiff, if that's what you're interested in. Danica just told me."

"Yes."

"Yeah, whatever. Two guys getting into a physical altercation to resolve their differences. Nothing new. Doesn't really mean anything to me."

"Your name was mentioned during it," I said. Sloane's cheeks pinked.

"They both know me, so . . ." she responded. Her voice was cool, but I could tell she was thrown off. It seemed like no one had mentioned that part to her.

"It seemed a little weird," I said and left it there, not sure what I was trying to get at. In a way, it was a good questioning technique. Silence could make people uncomfortable to the point that they'd start filling in the space with their own words.

Sloane closed her locker and her demeanor suddenly seemed different. Softer. "Atticus and I are good friends. He's always looked out for me, at least as far as I know. And Luke is an asshole, as I'm sure you are well aware. He's treated me like this since the first time I rejected him and every time I've rejected him since."

I thought about the Halloween party and a feeling of sympathy flooded through me. "Yeah."

"It's not much of a story. That's all it is. One good guy on a team of bad ones."

Suddenly, a realization dawned on me. "Does he still hang out with all of them?"

"Atticus? Yeah, usually. It's kind of a weird dynamic. I don't think anyone really likes each other, but they all stick it out because high school, you know?"

"Yeah," I responded. "Thanks, Sloane."

Sloane hesitated for a second before speaking again. "Thanks for checking in on me, Eden."

Any response that came to mind didn't sound genuine, and so we parted ways and went to our respective classes.

I had statistics immediately after lunch and, as had happened for the last few lectures, I couldn't focus. My mind kept wandering back to Nick and Nudegate and the Slut Squad and I was antsy to get back to the newsroom, checking the clock every few minutes as if it'd make time go faster.

But, eventually, the bell rang and I nearly sprinted to the *Warrior Weekly* office, grateful to have the office entirely to myself.

First, I emailed Tyson Post, hoping he'd be able to give me some insight into the group chat Angela was talking about. I was not optimistic since students were infamously unreliable with checking their emails. And since Tyson's name wasn't publicly associated with Nudegate, it'd be even harder to persuade him to go on record. But, even if he didn't respond, just trying to reach him was a step in the right direction.

I logged into the student directory and scrolled through student names until I found Atticus's. He was identified as John on his listing and his school picture was surprisingly charming. It looked like he had a light summer tan, making his freckles pop, and his hair was longer than it was during the school year. His expression was warm, his grin seeming genuine and casual rather than posed.

I hoped that was the kind of attitude Atticus would approach me with. Since Sloane seemed fairly confident he was still in with the soccer team, he would be the perfect source to confirm the group chat and describe it in more detail. Even if he wasn't part of it, he would most likely know something about it. Plus, Sloane trusted him, which inherently made me trust him more than any of the other guys who were involved.

I took a deep breath as I typed his number in and hoped that our very limited interactions meant he wouldn't be hostile toward me when I reached out. The very worst that could happen was that he was blatantly rude; the best was that he helped. Middle ground would be if he entirely ignored me. All of the possibilities made my stomach knot up, just for different reasons.

> Eden: Hey Atticus, it's Eden Jeong. Apologies for texting without warning, I found your number in the student directory. Would you be able to meet up sometime soon to talk about Nudegate? It'd be off the record.

I reread the message three times and didn't exhale until after I pressed Send. Eventually, I pressed the lock button on my phone and tried to get to work on the article, but I kept glancing at the screen to see if he'd responded. Reaching out to sources almost always made me a little nervous but talking to Atticus in particular for whatever reason was making me particularly jumpy.

After a few minutes passed, my phone buzzed and I saw it was a number that hadn't been saved in my phone. Atticus.

> Atticus: Hey Eden. Yeah, I'm down to chat. I was suspended so I won't be around, but I'm coming in 30 to pick up some work.

I caught myself feeling an out-of-character rush as I read the response. Everything about him seemed casual and genuinely nice. No wonder Sloane liked him.

I responded back the coolest response I could think of—*great, I'll be in the Warrior Weekly office*—and then proceeded to wait, checking the door every few minutes as if he'd just waltzed in. I knew he wouldn't show up that quickly, but I still felt nervous about having a sober, one-on-one conversation with him.

I managed to get through the entire Nudegate article during the time I was waiting and felt mostly relieved as I submitted it to Kolton so he could read through it. I focused on the aftermath of the email, combining the experiences of Vera, Angela, and Alice as victims, and various other students as witnesses to the school. It was a weak article that would've benefited from quotes from the four other Nudegate Girls, but I needed this article to prove to the girls I was someone who could be trusted. I wanted them to speak to me and I wanted to be able to share their stories. I could at least, in my own way, try to be the Atticus to their Sloane. All that mattered was that they knew I cared; it was up to them if they wanted to do anything with that or not.

As I was editing an article from Jeremy about a football game, the door opened. I was so wrapped up in my work I hadn't realized the final bell rang.

"Hey." Atticus came in and closed the door behind him. His lip was a little swollen from where Luke had hit him and a bruise was forming near his right eye.

"Hey," I said. Even though he was a little banged up, I found myself, embarrassingly, staring at him. "How are you?"

"I'm all right. What'd you want to talk about?" He took a

seat next to me, sliding in easily and rotating on the office chair to face me. His posture was relaxed and so at ease it was hard to believe he was the same guy who'd just gotten into a fight in the cafeteria. I was so close to him I could see his freckles.

"I saw the whole thing earlier. Why did Sloane come up?"

"Luke was trying to pull some shit about Sloane's sex life and then her in general. He's decided that since she won't sleep with him, she's a bitch. He's had a complex about it since freshman year. He fucking blows."

Atticus's palpable distaste triggered something. Seeing how openly he despised Luke and the way that guy treated the people around him suddenly made me realize I could hate it too. I could be angry at Nick and angry at Luke, and I was allowed to be furious for the Nudegate Girls. I gained nothing by letting Luke harass me and the people around me. If no one ever told these guys what they were doing was wrong, or if no one ever made them face consequences, they would never stop.

"I have a weird question for you," I said, and Atticus opened his palms as if to say *bring it on*. "Is there a group chat with a lot of the guys here? Like the soccer team and beyond."

Atticus looked like he was genuinely thinking about it, which I appreciated. "There are a lot of group chats with different combinations of people, I guess. There's a chat with the entire varsity soccer team and then some with smaller groups of guys with friends from the team or whatever. Or friends from other things, other schools. You know how it is."

Atticus was so casual about the number of people he regularly interacted with. My general isolation from the rest of the student body became glaringly obvious. I was part of one group chat with one small group of people with whom I regularly interacted. It only seemed like I was involved in more than that because I was always writing and reading about others.

"Sure," I said, embarrassed for some reason that I couldn't relate. "Another weird question. Are nude photos shared through any of the group chats?" My cheeks burned at saying *nude* to Atticus.

Atticus chuckled. "All right, coming out with the heavy hitters. There's not, like, one group chat in particular that I'm thinking of that's for sending nudes, if that's what you're wondering. But I know it happens. Guys will do it to prove they got photos, stuff like that. Show off the girl they've been sleeping with."

"Do you think someone in a group chat was behind Nudegate? Maybe a group of people in a chat?"

"I've been thinking about that, too, and I don't know. There are some guys I can think of that might've done it, but I don't know if any of them are behind it. There's no one obviously coming to mind, at least."

"Do you think Luke might've played a role?"

"In a way, I want it to be him. And it seems like it could've been him. But he hasn't said anything that makes me actually think he did it. I was in class with him when the email came out and he seemed as shocked as anyone else."

"Do you know anything about Louis Sanford?" I asked. I knew I'd been neglecting the Louis angle despite the obvious lead from Alice. It was easy to forget that he was even a suspect because he didn't fit my assumed profile for Eros. I imagined someone like Luke; someone who openly objectified women, someone conventionally handsome and well-connected. It was poor investigating on my part since, based on what Alice had said, Louis didn't seem to be that different from Luke, even if they weren't in the same circles.

"No, not really," Atticus said. "I think I've had some classes with him. We went to the same middle school."

I paused for a second, thinking about what I was going to say next. It was bold to assume I could trust Atticus, but he also seemed like he didn't have anything to hide. I'd never met someone who was so willing to be transparent. "Would it be ridiculous to ask you to be an inside man?"

Atticus looked at me curiously. "Like, report back to you if I hear anything?"

"I have no connection to any of the teams or guys on the teams, so I don't know what anyone talks about. They wouldn't have let me in to begin with and they definitely won't let me in on their secrets now. You could help me figure out what's going on. For the girls."

Atticus thought about it for a second and leaned forward in his seat, placing weight on his thighs. "I'm kind of into that."

"You are?"

"I think that could work. Sloane keeps me updated on how much shit the guys here will put girls through." Atticus turned away from me. "And I haven't done as much as I should to stop the guys from acting like they have. I can't fully make it up to the girls, but I want to do what I can to help."

"Okay. I guess let me know if you hear anything that seems weird."

"You got it, boss," Atticus joked.

As I watched him leave, I felt like I'd met my first ally outside of the *Warrior Weekly*. I could only hope I wasn't making a mistake by trusting him.

CHAPTER FOURTEEN

After my conversation with Atticus, I went home to finish editing my assigned articles for the week and to finalize college applications. When I entered my house, I was greeted by my mom's
laughter and the warm, comforting scent of *budae jjigae* boiling.

"Hey, sweetie!" Mom greeted me, excited like she always is
when she gets to see me. "How was your day? Anything exciting
happen?"

"Newspaper stuff. School scandal stuff," I said, trying to keep
my tone light, even as exhaustion radiated off me. I dropped
my things onto a pile and placed my phone on the counter, my
head quickly following it. It was hard to believe how much had
happened over the course of one day: Luke, talking to Nick, the
fight. Atticus. It was too much.

"Bad day?" Dad asked.

"Long day."

Mom nodded. "I feel so sorry for the girls. And for the rest of you too. What an odd senior year." She looked at me, visibly concerned. I'd never been great at opening up emotionally, but I was fortunate to have parents who knew how to read me. "Do you want to rewatch a few episodes of *Secret Garden* after dinner? Might make you feel better."

I appreciated the effort; *Secret Garden* was a K-drama I watched with my mom as a kid and it was one of my go-to comfort shows.

"Yeah, I'd love that," I said. But, as if knowing I wanted to think about something other than Nudegate, my phone vibrated on the counter. I groaned.

"Ronnie's calling," Mom said and held my phone over to me.

I accepted it with a small *thanks*, picked my head up, and answered, unsure of why she was calling now. I was too tired to talk Nudegate theories or newspaper logistics.

"Yes?" I answered.

"Did you check your email?"

"No," I said, and from her tone, I assumed it wasn't good. I walked in the direction of the stairs and took them two at a time until I was up in my room and at my computer.

"Tell me when it's up."

I logged on, clicked on the mail icon; there was an email waiting in my inbox from a *Yanick, Rosie.*

"Ms. Greer and Ms. Jeong, I have reviewed your article and have decided that with some editing it should be fine to pub-lish," I read out loud, wondering why Ronnie had seemed so downtrodden over the phone. "I have attached the approved version of my article. Let me know if you have any questions."

Ronnie asked, "Did you open the approved version?"

I clicked on the attachment. "Oh my god."

"There it is," Ronnie said in reference to my shocked response. The attachment in front of me wasn't an article; it was maybe fifty words. All of the quotes had been taken out and instead Principal Yanick had replaced it with a summarized version. The girls barely even had a say in the article.

"Where are the quotes from Alice? And Vera? The only girl from the email referenced is Angela, and her quote was basically trimmed down to 'it wasn't a big deal and it hasn't changed anything in my life.' This is actual bullshit."

"Exactly," Ronnie said. "It's the clean version. The school-approved version."

I sighed, propping my arm up on my desk and put my head into my palm. "This is a joke to her."

"I told you it was," Ronnie said, sounding disappointed. "If anything, I was thinking she might change the headline. But she changed the entirety of it."

"The article isn't even accurate. '*Despite the difficulty of the situation, students have expressed gratitude for the school board's swift response to the incident,*'" I read. "This isn't true. No one said this."

"It's propaganda at this point. She knows I'll refuse to print it, meaning I'll give up my ability to print the story altogether."

"This is . . . ridiculous," I said, unable to find the word to describe how I felt. The entire situation was fucked up, from the actual act of Nudegate to Yanick's expectation that we wouldn't want to print the news. And it still hadn't been addressed that there might not even be criminal charges for Nudegate because there was no legal precedent.

"We could literally figure out who Eros is and the school would probably take the credit for it," Ronnie responded. I could hear a wrapper crinkling on the other line and I knew she was eating chocolate.

"What's the plan?" I asked, already knowing what Ronnie's plan was.

"Throw this shit away and publish the actual news," she said.

"Are you sure you want to? I mean, I get it. But you heard what Yanick said."

"*Rosie* doesn't deserve a modicum of our respect. She has no right to back students into a wall and force them to post bullshit. There's a reason why independent, unfiltered journalism exists. We can't let this happen."

My stomach knotted at the idea. I was angry, too, but the thought of stepping on the toes of the administrators made my palms sweaty.

"There's no scenario where we're going to win this, Eden," Ronnie said, recognizing my silence as hesitation. "We'll have to get creative."

I refrained from groaning. "I know the newspaper is important, but so is *having* the *Weekly*."

"I'd rather have no newspaper than a newspaper that prints this crap," Ronnie said, words that nearly took my breath away. This was the same Ronnie who had been talking about winning a Pulitzer since the day I'd met her. I couldn't imagine her being anything other than an editor in chief.

"Ronnie, are you absolutely sure?" I asked. "What about everyone else on staff?"

"I'm sure," she said. "We have to keep this as much of a secret from everyone else as possible so word doesn't spread to Yanick. I don't want to give her the opportunity to stop us. I'm publishing it."

I thought about everything we stood to lose and wasn't sure I could bring myself to wholeheartedly agree. It seemed drastic. And bold.

But maybe it was what we had to do.

"Before we do anything, we should talk to Ms. Polaski," I said and, after a beat of silence, Ronnie agreed. We would stop by her office tomorrow.

~

I spent most of the night tossing and turning, and when my alarm went off, all I wanted to do was stay in bed. I didn't want to deal with Yanick or Ms. Polaski or having to worry about revenge porn laws. I wanted Nudegate to disappear entirely.

But I also knew it wasn't going anywhere, which was all the more reason to make sure I kept up my energy. I couldn't give up now, both for the sake of the article and the girls.

When I met with Ronnie in the St. Joe's corridor, she was chatty and ready to take on anything thrown at her. We decided to meet early so we'd have enough time to talk to Ms. Polaski before classes started. The hallways took on an eerie, echo-y tone when they were empty, and the school somehow felt smaller without students in it. The only cars in the parking lot belonged to faculty and staff and Warriors for Christ students who prayed together every morning in the chapel.

"I can't wait to see Yanick's face when the article comes out," Ronnie said, forgoing a greeting to jump right into the drama.

There was no second thought on how we should walk into Ms. Polaski's office for the second time. Ronnie saw the door was cracked open, so she walked in and I followed, hoping

Ms. Polaski wouldn't be upset we had entered without permission.

"Principal Yanick edited our article about the email and turned it into straight-up propaganda," Ronnie said. "It's ridiculous. It's absolutely unpublishable."

"Then don't publish it," Ms. Polaski said without missing a beat. "There's no obligation to write about the email."

"But there is," I said, surprising even myself. "It goes beyond the girls who were affected by the email. This is an issue that affects an entire school. It might even be a Greenville issue or a state issue. Whatever it is, it's a big deal that it happened."

Ms. Polaski sighed. "What do you want to do instead?"

"I want to publish the original article as is," Ronnie said. "No edits from Yanick, no St. Joe's changes. Allow the girls to speak for themselves and for the full truth to be shared. I refuse to print a lie about how St. Joe's has been so helpful when they haven't done more than provide free counseling services. There have been no preventive measures, no new steps. They're not keeping anyone updated on anything. They haven't taken an anti-bullying stance of any kind. And did you know revenge porn isn't even illegal here? The police haven't done anything because they legally *can't*."

"I am going to be honest with you, girls. There is no way Principal Yanick is going to let that slide," Ms. Polaski said. "She's not going to agree to it."

"We don't need her to agree to it," Ronnie said. "We'll do it whether she gives us permission or not."

"I can't advise that."

"Did you read the edits she made?" I asked and when Ms. Polaski shook her head, I continued. "You should read it.

The new article has nothing real to say about anything. It's all a blanket statement about the effectiveness of the school's administration with no real information."

Ms. Polaski clicked around on her computer and I watched her eyes skim across the screen, hopefully reading the article like we'd asked her to. Ronnie and I sat silently as she read.

Eventually, she spoke again, pushing her glasses back up her nose while she did it. "If you think publishing is the right call, then go for it. There's a lot on the line to lose here, so I want you to think carefully about what you're doing. Principal Yanick is going to be furious, mostly with me because my job is to stop you from doing exactly this. But she'll also be mad at you for disobeying her. I need you to be prepared for that."

We nodded simultaneously. Having Ms. Polaski's stamp of approval was important since she was the person who reviewed the paper before printing it. She technically had last call, so if she didn't want the original article published, she had the ability to make sure it wouldn't be. But if she believed the article was important enough to be published, she would leave it in.

"Our lips are zipped," Ronnie said, at the same time I thanked Ms. Polaski.

"Be careful, please. I still don't know if I fully agree it's the right call to publish. I just know it's important to both of you that you do."

"Yeah. It is," Ronnie said.

Ms. Polaski waved us out with her hand. "All right, go off to your first class. Go do what students do."

Ronnie and I both said quiet goodbyes as we exited, closing Ms. Polaski's door behind us.

"Should we do it?" I asked, already knowing how Ronnie felt.

"No questions asked. This is the hill I'm willing to die on."

I bit my lip, knowing the cons of publishing probably out-weighed the pros. But all I could think about was how disap-pointed the Slut Squad would be if the only person featured was Angela. And if the only quote from Angela that Yanick kept in was about how Nudegate wasn't a big deal. There was no way any of them would want to talk to me again after that point, and I wouldn't blame them for it.

"I think we have to," I said.

"We do," Ronnie responded. "We have no choice. We're pub-lishing the story as is."

CHAPTER FIFTEEN

Waiting to hear from Principal Yanick was like standing next to a live bomb; we knew the explosion was coming, we just didn't know when to expect it.

As I walked into school the morning of publication, I spotted a stack of newspapers by the front door. On the front page was *Students Respond to Mass Email*. The headline was lackluster, barely capturing how terrible the situation has been, but the body text said what the headline couldn't. Full quotes from victims, details about campus climate. The limited action the school had taken and the lack of legal precedent for revenge porn. It was all there. And Ms. Polaski had left all of it in.

I met Ronnie at her locker, newspaper in hand, feeling as prepared as I could be for our inevitable demise.

"When do you think she's going to call us into her office?" I asked.

"Hopefully never," Ronnie said, "but it'll probably be at

some point today. I can't imagine she'd wait long to hand our asses to us."

We stood in silence for what felt like an eternity. Ronnie knew I wanted to say something, but I had to force myself to say it. "Do you think we did the right thing?"

Ronnie looked away from me for a second, looking at the floor. "We did the right thing for the girls. And the right thing for the girls is the right thing for everyone else."

Oddly enough, I realized I believed that too.

~

It wasn't until close to lunch that we were finally called into the office. My name was called over the loudspeaker to report to Principal Yanick and there was not a doubt in my mind as to why it was happening.

After leaving the classroom and meeting in the hallway, Ronnie and I silently matched each other's steps, ready to walk into the unknown together. Before we entered the office, Ronnie grabbed my hand and squeezed once. It was good to know she was there.

"I don't think I can do this," I said.

"It'll be fine," Ronnie said. "I have a plan."

I didn't know how she could possibly have a plan for this, but I trusted Ronnie. If anyone could get us out of this mess, it would be her.

We entered the office and Mr. Winters barely had to look at us to know who we were and why we were there.

"You can go in," he said, approaching the front counter where we were standing. "Behave yourselves."

Ronnie flattened her plaid uniform skirt and nodded, taking a second to prepare herself for whatever she was about to do. I couldn't imagine her begging for the newspaper to stay, so I had a feeling she was about to start an all-out war with Yanick.

"I am not happy, girls." Yanick skipped over any formalities and went right into berating us before we'd even fully entered the room. Ronnie closed the door behind us, and we sat down in familiar chairs in front of Yanick's desk. "You deliberately ignored my instructions."

"I understand, but I believed it was necessary," Ronnie said. "Look, Principal Yanick, we get that you didn't want it printed, okay? You can skip the lecture. I knew what I was doing when I made the choice to publish the article."

Her choice of pronouns was throwing me off and I wanted to interject to say that it was not a singular decision, but I didn't know how. I was worried it would make Yanick even angrier.

Principal Yanick tossed a newspaper onto her desk, the headline and my name, alongside Julia and Bree's, printed on top. My heart swelled with pride seeing it up there, even given the inopportune circumstances.

"This is not the article I sent to you," she said, tapping a fingernail against the page. Her voice was level, but vehement. "I don't know why you disregarded exactly what I told you to do. The order was simple enough."

"We believed—" I started, Ronnie quickly cutting into my sentence.

"I prioritized the story over anything else," she said. "*I* believed getting the girls' actual voices published was exactly what was needed to be done and at any cost. You and the administration have continued to drop the ball on this story, and I refuse to sit by and watch it happen. We have a *job*. Publishing was a conscious and intentional choice and I am willing to take the heat for it because that's what a journalist does."

Yanick looked at Ronnie, her lips in a thin, pressed line. "I don't know if *you* have the authority to speak on what journalists do and don't do."

If the words were meant to hurt Ronnie, they barely even registered. Ronnie continued on without hesitation. "I've made the decision: I'm willing to step down from my position as editor in chief."

My breath caught in my throat, making me nearly choke, but neither Ronnie nor Principal Yanick seemed to notice.

"Eden will be taking over my position, effective immediately, for the sake of preserving the paper," Ronnie continued. "Lord knows this school needs someone with integrity."

Yanick was silent for a beat, mentally weighing her options. She looked at me for what felt like a century before finally speaking again. "Do you accept this offer?"

"No," I said, turning to Ronnie. "Are you serious? This was your plan?"

"Eden," Ronnie responded, her teeth gritted.

"I—I don't know."

Yanick leaned back in her office chair. When she looked at us, I could practically see the wheels churning in her head. "You taking charge, Eden, is the only way I'll allow the paper to continue running. *Veronica* must step down from her position and is no longer allowed to be on staff." Ronnie shot her a look at the use of her full name; she was practically seething from her seat.

"Why does Ronnie have to leave entirely?" I asked. "She

should still be able to work for the paper. She's been on it for over three full years at this point."

"St. Joseph's has lost trust in the direction in which Ms. Greer is heading. We believe she is not fit to continue to run the *Weekly Warrior*," Yanick said. "Or write and edit for it, for that matter."

Ronnie looked surprisingly at ease, a person entirely in control. She'd said she had a plan and knew this was coming. I just had to have faith in the fact that she was making the right decision.

My mouth felt cottony when I finally decided to respond. "I'll take the position."

"Wonderful," Yanick said, her tone sounding like she thought it was anything but. "You may resume writing, but I expect you have learned your lesson and will not be printing any other stories about this email. If you do, you know the consequences."

"Absolutely," I responded, not feeling as confident as I sounded.

She gave us a final curt head nod and we left the office, my legs so unstable I thought I might actually fall. Ronnie walked easily, her head high.

"Ronnie," I said, and she shrugged.

"I knew. She had told me this morning in an email that my time on the *Weekly* was over." Despite her neutral expression, her voice wavered at *over*.

I knew this was the time for me to offer comforting words, ask her if she was okay, but I struggled to find the right thing to say.

"I'm really sorry, Ronnie. It's so unfair."

Even though I could tell Ronnie's instinct was to deflect and tell me I didn't have to be sorry, she didn't. Instead, her voice was uncharacteristically downtrodden when she said, "I know."

We walked together in silence until I couldn't hold in my concerns any longer. My thoughts were going about a mile a minute, trying to mentally refigure the *Weekly*'s hierarchy and construct a speech for the staff about how I'd be taking over.

"Why didn't you tell me? Warn me?" I asked.

"Because I knew there was no way you would take the position if you weren't put in the hot seat. You're ready for this, Eden. You act like you're not, but you are. You've been doing this forever, like me."

"I don't know what I'm doing."

"You know exactly what you're doing. Keep stirring the pot, Jeong. I believe in you." She went silent for a moment before letting out a long, deep exhale. "Guess we don't have to worry about Yanick anymore. The worst of it is over, I think."

I shook my head. "No, I'm still worried," I said and, to my surprise, Ronnie let out a loud laugh.

Even more surprisingly, I started laughing too. All the built-up tension started to loosen in my chest. It made me realize how ridiculous everything was, how terrible our senior year had shaped up to be. How ready I was to not have to think about any of this anymore. I knew we were far from a resolution, but it helped to remember that there could still be some good even when everything seemed to be falling apart.

"Want to skip class and hang out in the newsroom?" Ronnie asked, and I nodded, feeling my heart rate slow down.

"That would be so nice," I said. As we were walking down the hall, we chatted lightly about the responsibilities of the editor in chief and what the following months would look like for me. I would have to find someone to fill the executive editor position sooner rather than later. And I'd have to alert the staff of the changes, too, something I was dreading. It was hard to know how the staff would respond to any of this.

When we opened the door to the *Warrior Weekly* office, we were startled by someone already waiting in the room.

"Ms. Polaski?" Ronnie asked. "What's up?"

"I got the email from Principal Yanick saying there were some personnel changes," Ms. Polaski said. "Congratulations on your promotion, Eden."

I tried to look excited even though it didn't feel like a promotion as much as it felt like being forced into a new job. I thought about Ronnie and how hard she'd worked to get here, only to deal with the worst of the consequences. It felt like she was being punished for a mistake St. Joe's had made, that they were upset only because someone was holding a mirror up to them. There was nothing to celebrate.

"Is everything okay? What did Yanick say to you about the newspaper?" I asked.

"Once the school board finds someone to replace me, I'm no longer allowed to supervise the *Weekly*," Ms. Polaski said. She sat down on the edge of a table, suddenly looking older while also simultaneously looking less grown up than I remembered. I realized, then, that she was a woman with a job and a family and a home to go back to. She was just a person who'd probably never anticipated this would be an issue she'd have to deal with. She was as out of her element as we were.

"I'm so sorry," I said, knowing it was entirely our fault.

"You don't have to apologize. This was my decision to make and I knew what was on the line when I approved the printer proofs," she said. "I believe in you, girls. You're both doing something important and I'm proud of you."

"But that's not all, is it?" Ronnie asked.

Ms. Polaski chuckled. "No, it's not. I wanted to let you girls know that the story—information from your article—was picked up. Reporters have been waiting for something to bite down on, something that provided a fuller story about what's been going on here, and your article provided exactly that. St. Joseph's has already started receiving requests for quotes and we have news vans from all over the state who have been trying to enter the property."

I looked at Ronnie to see if she seemed equally as nervous, but she looked as confident as ever.

"What does this mean?" I asked.

Ms. Polaski looked at us. "It means this story is about to go big. Really, really big."

~

It was hard to know what Ms. Polaski truly meant by *really, really big*—I didn't think even she knew what that would mean—but I had a feeling it was going to mean chaos for St. Joe's.

Although it was difficult to see if there were actual news vans outside from inside the school building, rumors spread pretty quickly. I tried to focus on class, but all I could think about was what the Nudegate coverage was going to turn into.

What my article was going to turn into.

Knowing that my words were reaching people all around the city, possibly the entire state, was unbelievable to me. I was imagining people in Boston hearing about Nudegate all because Ronnie and I had decided to publish against Principal Yanick's wishes. In a way, I felt a sense of pride about it. But I was also nervous about what this meant for us. And also worried about what would happen to the girls since their names were as attached to the article as mine was.

Already finding it hard to focus on class, I was on my phone looking at updates online when it vibrated with a text.

> Jeremy: What is going on? I keep hearing that local news is on campus? Is this about Nudegate?

> Eden: Yeah, we need to have an emergency staff meeting ASAP.

> Jeremy: 100% agree.

I knew that, realistically, the entire newsroom couldn't be kept in the dark for long. Ronnie and I made the decision to keep the news about the article internal, only keeping it between us and Ms. Polaski so word wouldn't spread. No one else realized how significant the publication of the article was to the fate of the newspaper.

We'd already had a staff meeting this week to prepare for next week's publication, but the news of Ronnie getting fired—I refused to say it happened any differently—in addition to the eventual loss of our advisor, was a big deal. It had to be shared sooner rather than later, especially because it changed the entire editing chain.

Knowing this meeting was going to change the trajectory of the newspaper—as well as, undoubtedly, my relationship with staffers—made me nervous. Having to share one piece of major information was a lot; sharing three pieces was enough to make me want to throw up.

But, at the same time, I was in charge now. I was the lead editor for a newspaper that now had an increasingly popular breaking-news article. This wasn't the time for me to hide.

I clicked on the email app on my phone to start composing a note to the staff, only to see an email from Ms. Polaski.

> Hi Eden. Principal Yanick requested that you and I have a one-on-one meeting to review journalism ethics and responsibilities, as well as the St. Joseph's handbook. I was thinking we could meet today during lunch to get the meeting over with. Let me know. Thanks.

It wasn't at all surprising that Yanick was going to jump down my throat now to try to keep me under control. Maybe she assumed I'd be easier to scare because I wasn't as blunt as Ronnie could be. And maybe she was right to guess that. But I was hoping that, just this once, I wouldn't be. For Ronnie's sake. For the *Weekly*'s sake. For the sake of the Slut Squad.

I responded to Ms. Polaski saying that lunch worked for me, preparing myself for whatever kind of lesson Yanick wanted me to go through. There was something deeply ironic about someone actively limiting student journalism trying to push ethics.

After sending the response to Ms. Polaski, I typed up a quick, informal text to the entire staff about an emergency meeting today after school. I knew there was a good chance some of them would not be able to make it since the notice was so late, but I was feeling optimistic. All I needed was a few people there and the word would spread quickly to everyone else. The only upside was that very few people outside the *Weekly* staff would care about personnel changes, so there was no shot it would become school gossip. I would remain as inconsequential as I was before Nudegate.

I clicked my phone off and glanced outside, trying to see if I could spot any news vans.

CHAPTER SIXTEEN

After getting through two classes that felt excruciatingly long, I was able to go to my meeting with Ms. Polaski. I was nervous about what she was going to say but, at the very least, I'd prefer to hear it from Ms. Polaski than Principal Yanick.

"Hi, Ms. Polaski," I said, knocking on her already-open door to announce my presence.

"Hey, Eden. Come on in." She gestured to the chairs in front of her. "I'm hoping this will be quick so you can go enjoy your lunch."

"It's okay," I said.

Ms. Polaski looked at me. "Like I said this morning, Principal Yanick's not happy. You know you can no longer write about the scandal."

"Yeah, that's basically what she told me and Ronnie during our meeting with her."

"She's worried that you won't listen to her orders again, so spending your time working on an article only to have it trashed would be a waste of time," Ms. Polaski continued. "Her words, not mine. I personally think she's trying to avoid having another 'incident' like what we had."

"Where we have an entire, very important, story written, we just don't have permission to publish?" I asked. "Fair enough."

"I don't agree with her stance, but I am going to have to follow it. You know I'm already in the hot seat. And I don't think Principal Yanick will allow the paper to continue if we keep stepping on her toes. She's threatened to shut down the paper completely or she could easily refuse to appoint a new advisor, which would also mean the end of the *Weekly*."

"Wait, what?" I asked. Telling us we couldn't write about it was one thing but threatening to shut down the entire paper was different. So much larger. "She can't do that!"

"It's in her power to. I don't like it either. I'm just passing the message along. I don't know why she couldn't have told you herself when you had the meeting with her."

I ran my fingers through my hair. "We can't do anything else related to Nudegate?"

Ms. Polaski shook her head. "No, unfortunately. I'm so sorry, Eden. I know you've been working hard on this story. Ronnie said you still had girls you wanted to interview."

"Ronnie?"

"She believes in you, Eden. I do too. I know this is a hard situation to be put in, but I think you will handle the pressure much better than you think. And you'll be able to keep things going even though it won't be me overseeing the paper anymore."

It was as if she knew exactly what I was worried about. I couldn't tell if it was because of everything Ronnie had said about me, or if it was purely a teacher instinct of being able to read the emotions of students.

"Okay, that's all I'm going to talk about today. You already know journalism guidelines and ethics better than anyone on the school board," Ms. Polaski said and waved her hand. "I'm sorry I didn't have anything good to report back to you. I'll keep fighting it, as long as I'm able, but I don't think any administrators are going to budge on this one."

"Thank you, Ms. Polaski," I said.

"We'll figure this out together," Ms. Polaski responded. "Oh! And speaking of together, I hope you have at least one person in mind for executive editor. I trust your instincts, so send me the name of whoever you pick and I'll approve them."

"Okay," I responded, trying to sound casual about it but already feeling my heart rate pick up thinking about it. I didn't know who would want to take over the position right now. Anyone who was promoted would have to find someone else to fill *their* spot. It was an entire chain of events with a lot of moving parts. There was no easy way to handle the person at the top leaving.

After exiting Ms. Polaski's office to go hide in the newsroom for the rest of lunch, I felt my phone vibrate again. This time, it was an email detailing an emergency parent/student/teacher assembly at six that night. It seemed like *Warrior Weekly* wasn't the only staff having issues.

I immediately put it down on my calendar, knowing there was no way I'd miss it.

~

After the final bell rang, I entered the newsroom, put my backpack down, and immediately started pacing. I'd known many of the *Warrior Weekly* editors for at least two years by this point. But having to tell them Principal Yanick fired Ronnie and was threatening to shut down the newspaper made me want to avoid the entire newspaper staff for the rest of the school year.

Once it looked like everyone who was coming had arrived, I walked to the front of the room. "Hi, everyone," I said, my voice quiet. "As you may have noticed, Ronnie isn't here."

I cleared my throat and picked up a dry-erase marker, hoping to ease my nervous energy by giving my hands something to fiddle with.

"Ronnie was fired by Principal Yanick. She's no longer allowed to be our editor in chief or be on the paper at all," I said, refusing to look anyone in the eye.

"Why was she fired?" Jeremy asked.

"We weren't supposed to publish the Nudegate article. Principal Yanick gave Ronnie and me an edited version, but it was basically propaganda and nothing like the original, so we scrapped it." I wanted to add that the newspaper was additionally at risk of being shut down, but even thinking the words made me want to vomit from nerves. It was one thing for Ronnie and me to risk getting fired from our positions, but another thing entirely for us to have put the entire newspaper at risk, especially without asking the rest of the staff. We were lucky Yanick hadn't already given the go-ahead to shut us down.

"So, you'd been warned by Yanick not to publish the original article?" Kolton asked.

"Yes," I said. "But it felt fair at the time to keep the article as it was."

Jenny and Wes, the arts and culture managing editors, looked at me expectantly. Of all of the editors on staff, they were probably the most out of the loop with everything since their section of the newspaper wasn't publishing or editing Nudegate content. I also wasn't as close with them as I was Jeremy since both Jenny and Wes were juniors.

"Well, it sucks that Ronnie got fired but at least it's over now," Jeremy offered, trying his best at a positive spin. "Who's editor in chief?"

"I am," I said. "I'm looking for an executive editor now."

"Cool," Kolton said, his voice dry as usual but still genuine. "Rock on, Eden."

The rest of the staff also looked on, offering smiles and shows of support. I appreciated their attempts at making me feel more at ease.

"It was not a position I willingly took on, I'll be honest."

"You'll do great," Jeremy said. Jenny nodded in agreement, offering her support.

"Since I can no longer be executive editor, we'll need someone to fill in, either permanently or in the interim," I said.

"I'm out as exec editor," Jeremy joked. "We barely have enough people on sports to run the section right now."

At the back of the room, the door opened and Ronnie quietly entered. I looked at her, not sure why she was there, but she waved me off when she caught me staring at her. She propped herself up against a back wall and watched everything unfold.

"We'll also have to prepare for a new supervisor," I said, trying to avoid being distracted by Ronnie's arrival. It made me nervous that she was there; I was half expecting even more bad news. "Even though I know most of you barely know who Ms. Polaski is, her job was also put on the line because of the Nudegate article. She's still our supervisor, but it's not certain how long that'll be for."

The staff nodded, most of them not looking all that interested probably because it didn't seem like it directly affected them. Newspaper supervisors only ever interacted with the editor in chief and the executive editor; even Kolton seemed untouched by the news.

When no one else seemed to have questions, I left the meeting at that, unsure of how to broach the topic of the newspaper's fate. Even though I knew they should be aware, it wouldn't be good for staff morale to know their new leader nearly got the newspaper shut down. It would cause more problems than it would solve, especially because the easy solution was to stop writing about Nudegate for the sake of the paper.

I just didn't know if I could commit to that.

People seemed confused to see Ronnie at the back of the room while they were leaving, but none of them said anything. They struck up small conversations with her, waving and smiling. Eventually, the room was only Ronnie, Jeremy, Kolton, and me.

"Hey." Ronnie stood at the office entrance.

"What's up?" I asked.

"Sorry to hear," Jeremy said, referring to Ronnie being fired.

Ronnie waved it off. "No big deal. Least I could do considering all the trouble I've caused."

"It was just one article and we all wanted to see it published. It sucks that you had to take the fall for it," Kolton said.

"It's bigger than that," Ronnie said. "I want to apologize in person for putting the paper at risk. I never thought Yanick would go as far as threatening to shut the entire paper down."

My heart leaped into my throat and I knew there was no way the news of the *Weekly* almost being shut down would remain a secret. It was stupid to believe something that big could stay under wraps.

"What are you talking about?" Jeremy asked. He looked at me, visibly hurt. "Yanick was going to stop *Warrior Weekly*? Why didn't you say anything during the meeting?"

"I didn't know how to say it. I'm sorry," I said. Ronnie looked at me apologetically, not realizing I hadn't already had this conversation during the staff meeting. "We were warned it would happen before, but Ronnie and I didn't take her seriously. So, now, if we publish anything else about Nudegate, the *Weekly* is over. Ms. Polaski is trying her best to fight it, but it's not clear if she'll be successful."

"So you thought the solution was to not tell us?" Jeremy asked and shook his head. "That's no better than Yanick, Eden. We need *transparency*. It's the least this staff deserves. We should know everything that's going on, especially if it affects us and our sections."

My mouth went dry. It was a low blow to compare me to Yanick, but he wasn't wrong. "I'm sorry, Jeremy. I didn't know how to tell you."

"We believed Nudegate was significant enough to push the boundaries," Ronnie said, stepping in to help me. "I still believe it. We didn't want for there to be casualties, but I also don't feel right continuing on with a newspaper that doesn't report the news."

"But is the story really important enough to justify losing the entire paper? What are the rest of us supposed to do? Sports has nothing to do with Nudegate, and neither does the art and culture section. Why is news the priority here?"

Kolton turned to him. "That's not prioritizing *news*, it's prioritizing the ability to cover school events without student voices being edited out."

"This isn't about a story, it's about the bigger picture," Ronnie said.

"It sure feels like it's about a story," Jeremy said. "And, look, I get that Nudegate is important to cover. This is a huge story and we should write about it and shouldn't be limited, but I don't want to lose my position as an editor over it. I love doing this."

"I loved my position too," Ronnie said. "We're going to do everything that we can to protect this paper."

"That ship sailed when you disobeyed Yanick the first time," Jeremy said. "You're not even on the paper anymore, you can't do anything. You were literally fired for stepping on the toes of the administrators. You have no authority."

"Journalistic integrity is the most important thing to me," Ronnie said. "I don't want to have to give up any part of this paper but know that if any section had a controversial story that we were barred from posting, we would be with you. We all fought for that story about the wrestling team getting kicked out of states last year, remember? We were there for you and the entire sports section, Jeremy. Naira did what had to be done and I did the same."

Naira had spearheaded what had been our most controversial article to date at the time when she'd been editor in chief. The entire staff trusted her wholeheartedly and it seemed like Yanick did too; Naira had gotten away with publishing the wrestling scandal because she hadn't mentioned underage drinking and only focused on the team being out of the championship. It was the perfect loophole. One that the Nudegate story never had.

"I don't want to talk about this right now," Jeremy said, picking up his backpack.

"Jeremy," Ronnie started, "please, we have to be together on this. Let me explain."

"You fucked up," he said. "That's it. That's what there is left to say about this."

Even though I didn't want to get into an argument, I knew I had to say something. If I could look Luke in his face while asking him about Nudegate, I could face Jeremy.

"It wasn't only her," I said. "Ronnie and I both did this."

"Yeah and you both put your own selfish needs first," he said. "The administration has *never* had a reason to enforce any sort of guidelines or censorship on us, but now they have all the ammunition they need to prevent us from ever printing again. Yanick handed you an excuse to explain to the student population why you weren't going to cover Nudegate and instead of accepting it, you covered it anyway."

Jeremy's face was red in a way I had never seen before. I understood where he was coming from, but all I could think about was how necessary the article was. How badly people needed to hear about something like Nudegate. Not writing about it had never been an option.

"We owe it to the school to cover this. We owe it to the girls," Ronnie said, her voice even. Calm. "What would you have wanted us to do if Eros had shared *your* pictures? Continue to ignore your pain like your classmates and teachers, like what is happening to the girls now, or stand up for you, even if it's risky?"

That comment made Jeremy stop.

"I would admit to being wrong if I felt like I was," Ronnie said and stopped to inhale sharply. "But I don't think I am."

I knew, in that moment, I felt the exact same way. I saw where Jeremy was coming from and I'd regret if the newspaper went down because of me and Ronnie. But I also knew if a newspaper was going to be shut down for anything, it might as well be for Nudegate.

"We can figure this out together," I said. "Please, Jeremy."

"I'm in," Kolton said, finally speaking up. "I'll go down with the ship."

"I don't know if I'm ready for that," Jeremy said and left the room without looking back.

I sighed, my body buzzing with nerves and adrenaline. Without Jeremy by my side, I didn't know what I was going to do.

"He'll come around eventually," Ronnie said, recognizing that I was visibly stressed. "I'm proud of you, Eden. Really."

"How are you trusting me with this? I don't think I'm ready."

"You are, Eden."

"But what if I'm not?" I said. "I could barely handle Jeremy, what about anyone else? What about an entire news staff?"

"You're going to do just fine as EIC. And I mean that," Ronnie responded. "You're a leader, Eden. People like you and respect you. You have to learn how to accept it."

"But you're so—"

"What, blunt? Direct? We're two different types of people with two different leadership styles. It's nothing more than that."

I pushed my hair behind my ears. "I was expecting you to fight Yanick for your position."

She weighed her response in her head, tilting it to the side. "I wanted to. But there's only so much that I can do. I could ask over and over again, but she's never been a woman to budge on anything. It would cause more problems than it's worth."

"I guess."

"And I've already sent my applications in for college. I'll be hearing back with, hopefully, early admission from a few schools. I'm kind of over this whole high school thing. I'm over the censorship and the half-assed investigations. I like *Warrior Weekly* but it's hard to feel motivated when you know it's all for a high school paper."

The comment unexpectedly stung, catching me off guard. This was the same girl who had been tripping over her own feet to write *Warrior Weekly* articles, who pushed her way through the hierarchy and found stories in any situation, no matter how minor they seemed. I wasn't sure what to make of her comment.

But, at the same time, maybe she was right. Maybe the best thing any of us could do was think about what would come after graduation.

~

By the time I made it back to my car, I had to actively fight off tears. I knew I still had the assembly to attend and would have to come back later that night, but I needed a lengthy break from St. Joe's.

I drove home in a daze, trying to mentally compose an apology to Jeremy. I knew he had a right to be mad, but I hated knowing that he was upset with me. There was no good way to say *sorry for almost completely shutting down the newspaper*. A sorry didn't feel big enough. And I knew trying to send home the point that the newspaper was technically fine other than Nudegate coverage wasn't going to do me any good; it was the principle of the thing.

I entered my house and my dad's voice bellowed out in greeting. "Eden! You're home!"

"Hey, Dad," I responded, throwing my keys on a side table as I entered the living room. He was propped up on a couch, remote in his hand. "What's up?"

"Perfect timing. Your school is getting a special breaking-news report," he told me and pointed to the TV. "Local news has been teasing it all afternoon."

"What?" I asked. I didn't think news organizations would get anything so soon, especially enough for a report. The chance that they were able to get anything outside of my article was minimal; there was no way Principal Yanick would give the press information. Part of me felt a swell of pride at knowing the *Warrior Weekly* was the only real source for news about Nudegate, but it was also a lot of pressure. Especially considering we weren't allowed to publish anymore.

"There's an assembly going on tonight too," my dad told me.

"That I knew about." I settled into the couch next to him as he muted the TV to hear me. "Are you going?"

"I was assuming you'd go and then report back to me," Dad said. "Ha. Report back. And you're a reporter."

"Hilarious," I responded.

Dad was about to respond when he got distracted by the TV again. "This is what I was talking about." Dad turned the sound up and I directed my attention to it. It was Sloane surrounded by Vera, Danica, and Margot.

"St. Joseph's needs to do more to support us," Sloane said, her voice carrying through the TV. She seemed larger than life and it was surreal to see her on the screen. She was perfectly comfortable on camera, her expression neutral and tone even.

My stomach dropped at the realization that she'd never had an issue with her name being attached to Nudegate; she just didn't want anything to do with me.

"We're disappointed in the lack of resources and even more disappointed in the fact that Massachusetts does not have any laws in place to protect us. We are *victims*. We deserve to be supported. But the only way there can be legal repercussions is if one of the girls was a minor and none of us are. The police have officially dropped the case, so the maximum punishment the person who did this can get is expulsion from St. Joseph's."

The news clip transitioned to a reporter speaking about it, telling us to tune in for more at five. They were going to do a full segment on revenge porn laws in the state, including interviews with legal professionals and victims from other revenge porn cases. This issue was bigger than St. Joe's; it was so, so much bigger.

Eventually, another commercial came on and I felt like I'd been snapped out of a daze.

"Is she a friend from school?" Dad asked. "Are any of them?"

"No, not really. I know Sloane, though," I said. "The one who'd been talking. She didn't want to be interviewed for our article."

"She's a natural," Dad responded. "I'll give her that."

"She is," I admitted, not even a little bit surprised. Sloane was angry, but she was composed and calculating. There was not a doubt in my mind she was the perfect face for the issue and the perfect person to try to take down St. Joe's. Or maybe even the entire state legislature. I doubted she would let anyone stop her.

"Is she going to be speaking at the assembly tonight?"

"I have no idea. But I have a feeling it will at least be brought up."

"Guess we'll have to wait and see."

"Sounds about right," I said, knowing that summed up everything about Nudegate thus far.

CHAPTER SEVENTEEN

St. Joe's looked extraeerie at night, the looming building even more intimidating with a dark sky and a cold whisper of a breeze. As I pulled into the parking lot for the assembly and parked, it required effort to unhook my hands from the steering wheel and unlatch my seatbelt. I watched people wander up in small groups, taking long strides up the front steps and bracing themselves against the biting air.

Eventually, I walked into the building, immediately enveloped by heat and light inside. It didn't make the building feel any more comfortable. The meeting was held in St. Joe's library, with chairs lined up in rows and a microphone positioned up front. Not using the auditorium suggested they either weren't expecting many people or they wanted to keep the number of attendees down by not providing enough chairs.

I spotted both Mr. Winters and Father McGlynn—who was probably there to show allegiance to the school board since he had no role in disciplinary matters—sitting near it, chatting with each other. The large windows provided little light and seemingly little protection; the room felt inappropriately exposed to anyone outside.

Glancing around, I saw mainly adults, some with younger children in tow. I vaguely recognized some of the parents as belonging to fellow seniors. There weren't many St. Joe's students, which logically made sense. It was hard to imagine the average teenager wanting to attend something like this with their parents; even when considering my relationship with mine being fairly open, the thought of talking about nudes with them made my skin itch. I could only imagine the conversations that families were having over Nudegate: parents asking their teenagers if they would ever send a photo, teenagers lying about what they had sent to appease their parents. The endless conversations about trust and making good choices and respecting their bodies and others. The misguided attempts to scare people out of sending photos to willing recipients rather than explain why photos of others shouldn't be shared without permission.

To my surprise, I saw a familiar profile in the back row and walked over in the direction of Atticus. "Is this seat taken?" I gestured to the empty one to his right.

He looked at me, equally as surprised but seeming pleased to see me. "No."

I sat down and he readjusted in his seat to let me pass. "Nice to see another young face here."

"Yeah, not many high schoolers came out," I responded, glancing around. "What made you want to come?"

"Sloane didn't want to come, but she wanted someone to report back to her."

"Fair enough," I responded. "Did you see her feature on the news?"

"Yeah, I'm going to watch the full piece tonight. I only got to see the preview of her speaking."

Yanick was floating around, shaking hands and smiling politely with teachers and parents. Her cautious, conversational tone seemed to say *what a shame this is happening at St. Joe's. I promise I am doing everything that I can.* All I could think about was what Sloane had said about being brushed to the side.

"John," Yanick said, nodding at Atticus. Sloane was the only other person I'd heard call him that. "Eden. Glad to see you both made it."

"Wouldn't miss it," Atticus responded.

She looked us both over again. "And I'm assuming I don't have to say this shouldn't be written about in the *Weekly*?"

I felt my jaw involuntarily tighten. "Absolutely."

She walked up to the front of the room where she gave a nod to both Winters and McGlynn. Atticus turned to me. "What was that all about?"

"We can't print anything related to Nudegate," I said and pulled out my phone to record the meeting anyway, mostly out of spite. "I guess this falls under that category."

If Atticus was surprised to hear it, his face didn't reflect it. "Sounds about right."

Something about his attitude toward the school administration warmed me up to him even more. The more I knew him, the more Sloane's trust in him made sense.

"Hi, everyone," Yanick said into the microphone, making the entire room go quiet. "Firstly, St. Joseph's wants to give a warm welcome and huge thank-you to all of you for coming. We know it was short notice."

She took a moment to clear her throat, surveying the room. "For those who have not been kept in the loop, an email containing inappropriate photos of teenage students was recently sent out to everyone on the school server. However, we have determined that none of the students is under eighteen, which thankfully makes the legal portion less sticky. Regardless, the issue at hand is a difficult one and St. Joseph's has been trying its best to help in every way possible."

"Because my daughter is technically an adult means she is less important?" one parent yelled out. I turned to see if I could place whose mom it was, but it wasn't clear based on appearances. "Eighteen is barely an adult. She's still in high school. She's still entirely dependent on me. She is no different now than she was when she was seventeen, so why is the difference so significant to the legal system?"

"Maybe you shouldn't have raised her to be so tasteless, then you wouldn't have to worry about it," a parent shot back.

"My daughter is not *tasteless*."

More parents started interjecting then. Everyone started speaking over each other, trying to get their voice heard. Atticus and I both sat up straighter, looking around the room to see who was saying what.

"I heard on the news the person who sent the email might get away with not being criminally charged. Is that true?"

"What is St. Joseph's doing to punish the person who sent the email?"

"How about what is St. Joseph's doing to punish the *girls* who sent out such disgusting photos of themselves?"

"How about what is St. Joe's going to do to avoid something like this from happening again in the future?" I heard from the back and saw Margot. She was sitting by herself, making my heart clench. I saw a flash of recognition cross Yanick's face but she didn't say anything.

"I think the girls have learned their lesson and won't be doing it again," one woman said, and I turned to see a woman who looked identical to Claire. There was no mistaking the relation. "As long as we all make it clear that we're disappointed, at least."

I suddenly felt a rush of sympathy for Claire. If she had a loved one willing to be this blunt in a public space, there was no telling what she was dealing with at home. It might explain why she seemed to make such a complete and unexpected turnaround. It also started to suddenly make sense why some St. Joe's students took such a hard, generally unsympathetic stance. They'd gotten that stance from their parents.

Yanick raised her voice into the microphone, the words reverberating against the walls. "Parents, please. St. Joseph's is as appalled as you are at what has been occurring."

Mr. Winters stood up and met with Yanick, the two of them exchanging an unreadable look. The tightness of Yanick's mouth told me she wasn't happy, but I couldn't tell if it was because of the situation or Winters's presence.

Father McGlynn stepped to the front. "We are going to be dedicating at least one part of our monthly mass to praying for the individuals affected by this. It has also been part of St. Joseph's optional morning masses. Anyone is welcome to join. We are all hoping that the girls can find their way."

It was a perfectly vague statement that could either be admonishing the Nudegate Girls or genuinely well-meaning. I knew

St. Joe's tended to not be superprogressive, but I hoped that they were aware enough to know that blatant slut shaming would not be taken sitting down. Especially considering the additional media attention the school had been receiving, thoughts and prayers weren't going to cut it.

I looked around to read the reactions in the room. I saw one parent nodding, another on their phone. Then, out of the corner of my eye, I noticed Violeta peeking through the doorway from the hallway. Before I could stop myself, I stood and my feet started walking me in her direction, my phone left behind on my chair to continue recording the meeting. Atticus let me walk past easily without asking questions.

"I don't want to talk to you," Violeta said as I approached her. We were standing in the hallway, our voices not loud enough to carry and interrupt the assembly. Not that the parents would hear us anyway; the volume in the library was increasing by the second as parents became increasingly fired up. Violeta turned her face away from me.

"Don't listen to them."

"Easier said than done," she responded and crossed her arms even tighter, seemingly in hopes of folding into herself and disappearing.

We stood silently for a beat, the only sound being the voices carrying from the assembly. "I'm sorry about everything you've had to go through this year," I said after a few beats of silence. "I really am."

Violeta's face seemed to change in that moment, and I watched her jaw start to quiver. "I don't know what to do. No one has told me what to do."

I didn't know how to respond. It wasn't even clear if there

was a way to fix what was happening; there might only ever be temporary fixes. The email might never go away completely. But there was no good way to say that to someone.

"Do you know who could've done it?" I asked.

Violeta sniffed and I saw her actively trying to hold back tears. Her voice was low when she said, "Yeah."

"Is it anyone who might've been involved with any of the other girls?" I asked, hoping for a clear path toward the rumored group chat. Even though Atticus had basically confirmed it, Tyson had never gotten back to me. And I was having a difficult time placing Louis in the same circle as guys like Tyson, Luke, and Atticus. Or even the same circle as Nick.

"I know he was," Violeta responded. She looked away from me, but not before I saw her eyes welling up. It was clear how hard the email had been on her. Trying to handle everything, between the scrutiny and the news coverage and the comments in the halls seemed unimaginable, even with the Slut Squad to fall back on.

"Who was it, Violeta?" I asked, keeping my voice quiet.

She looked down, avoiding eye contact with me. I was starting to think she wouldn't tell me when, suddenly, she spoke again. "It was Louis Sanford."

I tried my best to keep my face neutral while Violeta explained the details of her relationship with Louis. Despite everything I knew about him and Alice, Louis was still low on my list of people who could've possibly been behind Nudegate. To know now that he was prime suspect number one was too much to process.

"He and Alice were on break going into this school year," Violeta said. "We'd had a weird on-and-off flirting from freshman year until they started dating, but I'd never fully lost feelings for him. We ran into each other during band camp and kind of hit it off again. I don't know. One thing turned into another. He had my pictures. He and Alice eventually got back together. Suddenly, my pictures turned up on an email for the entire school."

"I'm so sorry," I said, unable to find any other words.

"It was all so stupid. All of it. I regret ever getting involved with him," she said. "He's not even that nice of a guy. Like, he might not look like Luke, but he shares a lot of the same values. And I knew that going in, too, which makes it so much worse."

"It's not your fault," I told her. "The email is not your fault. And the fact that Louis is a dick isn't your fault either."

"That's what Sloane keeps telling me too. She's been helpful at the meetings. I don't know what I'd do without her and Kai."

I racked my brain for any student named Kai, but I couldn't put a face to the name. That almost never happened, considering I was on the newspaper and St. Joe's was so small. Even if I didn't know someone well or know anything about them, I could at least place them in the context of a class or a social group.

"Kai?" I asked.

"Yeah. I can't remember her last name, but she's a victim support advocate Sloane's friends with. I'm not actually sure how they met. But Sloane brings her to some of the Slut Squad meetings, so we know what resources we have, and we have someone to talk to who's, like, trained in this stuff."

It made sense that Sloane would organize support in that way without being public about it. I was genuinely shocked word hadn't spread that there was a Slut Squad to begin with; all of the girls had kept their bonding entirely out of the public eye.

If I hadn't gone to that first meeting, I never would've guessed Sloane and Violeta were commiserating with each other.

"And because I know you're wondering, Alice and I are certain Louis was involved somehow," Violeta told me. "It's too much of a coincidence that we'd both end up in the email. But none of the other girls interacted with Louis outside of class. I don't even think Angela Ainsley knew who Louis was when we were talking about him."

"That is so interesting," I said before I could stop myself. I was also glad to know that Angela was keeping in touch with the other girls. "Sorry. I know *interesting* isn't appropriate for the context."

Violeta's face read more passive and tired than offended. "The whole thing is weird. I don't think there's a good way to describe it."

We were silent for a moment before I spoke again. I could hear the assembly still going on behind us. "Thanks for telling me. It doesn't seem easy to talk about."

Violeta looked at me, meeting my eyes for the first time the entire conversation. "You actually are as good as the girls were saying. Thanks for listening to us."

I wanted to smile, genuinely pleased by the compliment, which surprised me. But instead, I half waved as an awkward goodbye and then made it back to my seat next to Atticus.

"What did I miss?" I asked, checking to see if my phone was still recording.

"Not much, a lot of parents bitching," Atticus said. "Principal Yanick hasn't said anything important."

It was about what I'd expected. It seemed like the assembly had been called to appease parents more than to provide any real answers. "I talked to Violeta. Whole new update."

"Seriously?" Atticus turned to me. His eyes meeting mine made my heart speed up.

"I'll tell you after," I said, and he nodded, turning his attention back to what the parents were saying.

~

Eventually, after what felt like the longest thirty minutes of my life, the assembly ended.

"Thank you all for coming. We will keep you updated on any progress," Yanick said into the microphone. Some parents stuck around to mingle and take advantage of the coffee and snacks provided by St. Joe's, but Atticus and I weren't interested. Instead, we exited the building to get back to the parking lot, where it was safe to divulge part of Violeta's story.

"She said it was Louis Sanford," I said. "Absolutely, without a doubt. It's the same for Alice Huey."

"Really?" Atticus said, and I could practically see his brain trying to put the pieces together. "Do any of the other girls have connections to him?"

"It sounds like they don't. The only two people who definitively do are Violeta and Alice."

"Is there anyone else it could've been? Anyone connected to all of the girls in some way?"

"All I know is there has to be something that connects a wide range of guys who all insist they haven't done anything wrong. But who? Why?"

"You might be onto something with the group chat theory. Just because I don't know any group chats that share nudes extensively doesn't mean it doesn't happen. And since a lot of the guys know I'm good friends with Sloane, they probably wouldn't involve me in a lot of the conversations anyway."

"But Louis isn't connected to any of those groups?"

"No, not even a little bit," Atticus winced. "Sorry, that was harsh. But it's true. If there are people working with him, I don't know how they would've all found each other or why they would be working together. If it was only guys from, like, the soccer team, it would be pretty straightforward. But I don't know where Louis fits into all of this."

"There must be some sort of explanation."

"There has to be. It's just a matter of what it is."

I made a sound of agreement. "I think you're right."

After a beat, Atticus looked at me. "Where's your car?" he asked, and I had trouble forming words.

"Over this way," I finally said, and we walked in that direction. It was stupid to be nervous over a boy when there were so many other things to worry about instead, but I couldn't help it.

"Why are you so okay with helping me?" I asked.

"I owe it to Sloane," he said. "She's known me since I was just going by John. She stood up for me when kids would make fun of me for being this, like, supertall, superskinny kid. She was there for me when all the stuff with my dad first started happening. I don't know. She's a good person, she doesn't deserve this. And by helping Sloane, and helping you, I can help other people too."

"Do you know why she doesn't want to be interviewed by the *Weekly*? By me?" I asked, feeling vulnerable but also a little hurt that Sloane was so blatantly giving me the runaround.

"It's not against you. She doesn't trust anyone at St. Joe's in general."

The answer, albeit genuine, didn't make me feel much better. When we made it to my car, Atticus looked at me. "Do you want to go to a party with me?"

"What?" I asked, caught off guard.

"A party tomorrow night. If I plan it right, I can probably get into some of the conversations and see what people are talking about. People might be more likely to slip up and say something stupid if they're drunk."

"I—" I hesitated, but then realized that, for this party, I'd have a true, determined mission. And someone specifically there to help me. Even if I was a bit disappointed that he wasn't asking me out. "Yeah, I think I can go."

"I was thinking about leaving around ten? Or is that too late?"

"For a party or for me to be leaving the house?" I asked. The second the words left my mouth I realized I was flirting, even if it was badly. "I think it'll be fine if I leave then. I'm usually pretty responsible, so my parents don't usually second-guess where I'm going."

"You're sure?"

"Probably."

"You're probably sure?"

"Yes," I said, and a laugh spilled out my lips before I could stop it.

"Okay, I can send you the address. Would you be able to drive there?"

"You keep asking questions, I feel like I'm being interviewed. And I think I'll be able to figure it out," I said. "Am I picking you up?"

"No, I think we should probably go separately," he said, a comment that stung in another unexpected way. "Not that I don't want to go with you," he quickly backtracked. "I . . . I'll meet you there."

"Okay," I responded, unable to figure out what he was thinking.

"We'll catch up tomorrow, then?"

"Sure," I said, feeling somewhat breathless. I couldn't remember the last time I'd conversed with someone and not wanted it to end.

To avoid embarrassing myself by trying to talk to him more, I unlocked my car and opened the door. "Thanks for walking me out. Goodnight, Atticus."

"'Night," he said, not fully walking away until he saw I was comfortably in my car and driving out of the parking lot.

CHAPTER EIGHTEEN

The following night, when I arrived at the address Atticus sent me, I was about fifteen minutes late, mostly because I wanted to be certain he was already there by the time I showed up. It was another party at another gorgeous house, this one with a private hidden entrance leading up to a stunning house on a hill. Because it was so secluded, people wandered more freely with drinks in their hands and made more noise. I could hear the music from where I parked, picking a spot on the grass next to a few other cars and sending a text to Atticus to let him know I'd arrived.

There was a chill to the air, making me wrap my arms around myself. I had opted for dark jeans and a flattering black blouse, not sure what else I had to wear that was party appropriate, and had pulled my hair away from my face. While I felt cute, it wasn't exactly warm.

Inside the house, I tried my best to not stand at the door with my jaw gaping. The house was stunning. I wasn't sure whose party it was, and the house wasn't much of a giveaway considering the kind of money most St. Joe's students came from. I made my way out to the expansive kitchen where groups of people were huddled. I still couldn't find Atticus and I knew I'd have to try extrahard to fit in. Even though I was sure no one was going to care I was there, it probably seemed odd to be there alone. I didn't want to risk raising any red flags.

I had no intention of drinking alcohol because I had to drive myself home, but I still walked over to the cups and grabbed one off the stack, mostly to keep my hands busy and my profile low. Eventually, my eyes landed on a two-liter bottle of Coke and I poured it out into a cup, taking a long sip and glancing around.

I pulled out my phone again. Atticus still hadn't responded. I considered texting him again, but the situation didn't seem that urgent and I felt embarrassingly shy about double-texting him.

Most of the people here were from St. Joe's, but it looked like there were a fair number of students from other schools, too, since I didn't recognize their faces. I had hoped to see Sloane or at least a familiar face but from where I was standing there was only a sea of rowdy teenagers.

Drunk students stumbled around and groups of friends were hanging out in small huddled circles in every room I checked. But I didn't see Atticus was here yet. And it looked like none of the Slut Squad had come, either, which was odd to me.

I reentered the kitchen, hoping that leaning against the counter alone seemed cooler than sitting on the couch by myself.

"Ricky told me you were here. I didn't believe him, but sure enough." Luke. "How's Nancy Drew?" he asked and stepped closer, making me press myself as far against the counter as I could. "Who invited you?"

A drink was in his hand, a dangerous addition to his already cross attitude with me. "I didn't know this was your party."

Now it made sense why none of the Slut Squad girls had shown up. I had a feeling Sloane and Luke were not reconciling any time soon.

I looked around, hoping Atticus—or anyone at all—would suddenly show up, but no one was paying attention.

"Yeah, nice house, right?" Luke said and took a sip of his drink, his jaw an impeccably sharp line. But unlike Atticus's, Luke's seemed threatening. His entire demeanor told me he was looking for trouble. He took a few steps closer and I tried to look away as he stepped so close I could smell the alcohol in his cup and the cologne on his skin. "So, who invited you?"

"A friend of mine," I said and placed my cup on my counter. "I didn't get the name of who was throwing the party, I swear."

"Where's your friend, then?" Luke snorted. "I would ask why you're here, but I already know why."

"What?" I asked, my heart pounding in my chest.

"You think I've done something wrong and I know you don't like me," he said. "You think I'm the one who sent that email, right? All because I sleep around and have some girls' nudes. But your article made you seem pretty cozy with the Nudegate sluts, so why do you have a problem with me sleeping around? Why are *they* allowed to?"

"I don't have a problem with you sleeping around," I said, the words coming out seemingly before my brain had time to fully process them. "I have a problem with the way you treat the people you sleep with."

Luke let out a short, hard laugh. "So, it's jealousy?"

"What about *that* made you think I'm jealous that we haven't slept together? I'm not interested."

My breath caught in my throat as he stepped closer, moving a hand to my waist. "C'mon Eden. Nick used to tell us at parties what you two kids would get up to. Inside of that quiet shell is a freak waiting to get out."

My mouth went dry at the realization that Nick talking about me was definitely more than a one-off thing. I didn't want to think too much about the specifics of what he'd told people; it made me sick thinking how many personal details were out there about me without permission.

"Luke, please," I said, moving my hands to his chest to push him away. But trying to move him was as fruitless as trying to move a cement wall. "Stop. I'll leave."

"Why are you here, Eden?" Luke asked, his breath hot on my face and strongly smelling of alcohol.

"I told you, a friend invited me."

"I think, maybe, you came to poke around. Maybe see if you could find your next article. Maybe harass me some more. Talk to my boys. Get one of us falsely accused of something."

"I'm not, I didn't know you were going to be here," I said, my voice getting shaky. I didn't want to cry in front of him, but I felt dangerously close to doing it. It was the second time he'd made me feel that way in a relatively short time frame and, even though I wanted to lash back, I didn't think I was capable.

"At my own fucking house?" Luke asked, raising his voice enough to make people look over to us. "I'll ask again, *who invited you?*"

"Chill, dude. I did," Atticus said, forcing his way through

the crowd. At seeing Atticus and Luke together again, the entire room seemed to go quiet and focus on only the three of us.

"Why the fuck would you think it's okay to bring *her* into my house?" Luke asked, walking closer to Atticus. "*You* were barely invited."

Atticus ignored him, physically sidestepping Luke to avoid confrontation and focusing his attention on me instead. Ricky grabbed Luke and moved him to another room, probably hoping to avoid another showdown like in the cafeteria. When the crowd realized there wasn't going to be a fight, they all went back to talking to their friends.

Sloane appeared, surprising me. "Are you okay?" she asked. Despite the humorless moment, there was something funny about me, Sloane, and Atticus all showing up at Luke's house to essentially help each other.

"I'm so sorry, I wouldn't have invited you if I'd known he was going to be like that," Atticus said, his brown eyes meeting mine. "Normally, he's so busy upstairs with a girl he doesn't even realize who's here."

I grabbed my cup with shaking hands, trying my best to take a sip and clear my throat. "Not your fault."

Sloane looked at me sympathetically. "You didn't do anything wrong. People show up here uninvited all the time. I'm pretty sure I'm not invited since Luke and I can barely be in the same room as each other, but I still showed up because most of my friends are here. Name anything more high school than that."

I could tell from her relaxed demeanor that she'd had a least a little bit to drink and I appreciated her attempt at making me feel comfortable. It made it easier to believe what Atticus had told me, that it wasn't personal that she hadn't wanted to be interviewed for the *Weekly*.

"I should've found you sooner," Atticus said. "I found Sloane but we couldn't find you and my phone was so stupidly on Do Not Disturb—"

"I was late arriving," I said. "It's not your fault you couldn't find me at first. But, now, I think it's time for me to go home."

Atticus looked at me. "How much have you had to drink?"

The concern was admittedly sweet. "It's soda."

He nodded, but both he and Sloane walked with me as I pushed my way through the sea of people, out the door, and to my car. They didn't say anything, but it was comforting to have them there.

I pressed the button on my keys to unlock my car doors. Sloane hung back but Atticus walked over to meet me. "I'll hang out and see what's up. I think Sloane is the only Nudegate girl here and she's keeping a low profile, so the guys will probably be more open to talking."

"Thank you," I said, genuinely meaning it.

"Yeah, no problem. I might as well do what I can to figure out who did this." He opened my car door for me. "I'm really sorry, Eden. Again. I should've known better or at least driven over with you. I was just thinking about how Luke's house could provide a good lead, but I didn't want to fumble it by making it clear we were friends."

Warmth spread through my chest at the mention of us being friends. I hadn't thought about it that way until then. Probably a good sign I needed to stop viewing people as only confidantes and sources; as long as I liked and trusted the person, it didn't matter if we'd met because of the newspaper.

"I would've found a way here regardless of your invite," I said, knowing it was at least partially true. A party at Luke's was an excellent lead; he had connections to nearly every athlete and well-known guy on campus, anyone who might be in the group chat. And the whole point of Atticus and I working together was that he was an insider. It'd defeat the purpose if Atticus and I were obviously friendly, which Luke's distrust in me made clear. If Luke thought I was going to falsely accuse him of something, most of his friends probably did too. Atticus was spot-on with how he'd handled the party.

"Drive safe," Atticus said. "Text me if you need anything."

"And you text me if you figure anything out," I said, part of me almost hoping he'd reach out tonight regardless.

"Can do," he said, his hand still firmly on my car door. We looked at each other, obviously wanting to say more but knowing it wasn't the time. It wasn't until my own hands started to go numb with cold that I finally got into my car.

Sloane looked concerned, her arms wrapped around herself for warmth. When I pulled away, she and Atticus were still outside talking to each other, their body language tense.

~

After I got home, I immediately showered, trying not to think about Luke's hand on my waist and the feel of his breath on my skin.

By the time I got out, made myself a late dinner, and climbed into my bed, it was rounding in at around midnight. I still hadn't heard from Atticus. I was about to settle in to watch TV, a half-assed effort to settle myself down after the night's events, when my phone vibrated as if on cue.

Atticus: I think I have something.

I clicked on the attached soundbite and held it close to my ear, uncertain of how clear the audio would be. It was a group laughing and then a distinctively male voice.

"What can I say, girls love sending me nudes." More laughter. "I got some from Sloane earlier this year, before we hooked up at a party."

"Yeah, everyone's gotten some from Sloane," another voice responded. "No big deal."

"It's more than Sloane, though," the first voice continued. "Girls *love* sending me nudes, man. I ask and they send them, no questions asked. I'm like a whore magnet. But it's more fun when the pictures aren't from the easy girls. Shy girls are always the best in bed." Laughter followed, not one person speaking up to say how gross a statement that was.

I closed my eyes, trying to place the voice. I realized I knew exactly who it was. I'd heard that voice at parties and at lunch tables for nearly a full year when I was with Nick. Rolland Pike. Danica's boyfriend.

"Rolland?" I mumbled to no one in particular. It didn't make sense. Rolland getting pictures from Sloane?

Even though it could just be a guy bragging about nudes, a conversation entirely unrelated to Nudegate, my mind jumped to the email. Maybe the pictures of Sloane's that were in the email were from Rolland. But that would mean, somehow, Rolland and Louis had to be connected. But since they weren't in the same circle, it was difficult to imagine them suddenly forming an alliance to do something like Nudegate. Going from barely speaking to committing what was a crime in other states seemed like a huge leap.

I texted Atticus, asking if he was able to talk. He responded back almost immediately that he was going to leave in the next few minutes and he'd call once he was in his car.

I tried my best to be patient, but I was also getting restless. I wanted to talk through theories.

There was no doubt in my mind that I had to keep working on Nudegate. The more I learned and saw, the more I realized how necessary it was for me to keep compiling notes about it. Even if I couldn't publish anything for *Warrior Weekly*, I was optimistic this story could go places. If anything, maybe one of the local newspapers would be interested in hearing what I had to say.

It was more than the article—it always had been, in a way; I wanted to solve the case. Atticus then called, interrupting my train of thought.

"Hey," I said, leaning into my bed.

"I don't know if that recording came out at all, but it was Rolland Pike talking."

"Yeah, I recognized him. He's still dating Danica, right?"

"They're rocky at best," Atticus admitted. "They've always had kind of a weird relationship. It doesn't seem like they liked each other that much as people, but I guess they're in love. That's what they like to say, anyway."

"Do you think she knows that Sloane and Rolland had something going on at one point?"

Atticus was quiet for a beat. "I'm not sure. It's hard to tell with Danica. She's kind of a reserved person."

"I wonder if he's behind Nudegate or if he's just benefiting from the clout that comes with nudes."

"It's weird, he's never struck me as a malicious guy, so if he did do it, I don't think he meant for it to be anything. I can't see him meaning badly."

"At this point, I think it goes a lot further than intent. If it hurt people, it means something," I said. "And, to be fair, we should be cautious about assumptions. I don't think there's anyone at St. Joe's who *seems* like the kind of person who'd send an email like that. It's kind of the point that there's no single type."

"Yeah, true."

"Except maybe whatever Luke is," I responded, hoping it could clear the air of what had happened at the party. It'd hang in the air between us until we openly addressed it.

"Are you okay?" he asked quietly. "I am sorry about not telling you it was Luke's house. I didn't want to scare you away and I didn't think it'd be a big deal. But I should've at least texted you to figure out where you were. Or warned you Luke would be there."

"It's fine. Seriously, Atticus. He would've been a dick about it regardless of when you found me."

Atticus exhaled on the other end. "Do you think he sent the email? Genuinely."

"I don't think so," I said. "I'm still wary of him, but I don't think he could be behind it. Something about it doesn't feel right. And having two different girls connected to Louis . . . I think Louis might be more of a suspect than Luke."

"Yeah, maybe," Atticus responded, but I could tell he didn't fully buy in. "At the very least, I could imagine Luke and Rolland working together. That pair makes sense to me more than Rolland and Louis."

"I can't figure out what either of them would gain from it," I said and then realized I might've been handed a piece of the puzzle without realizing. "Wait, Luke did say that he doesn't understand how girls can be sluts, but guys can't. It's ridiculous, but he said it to me at the party and actually believes it."

"He thinks guys can't sleep around without criticism, but girls can?" Atticus snorted. "Imagine being that disconnected from reality."

"He was mad about the article because he thought I was supporting the Slut Squad while chastising him for what he saw as doing the same thing," I said. "I mean, he was right about me supporting the Slut Squad. But he missed the mark on why I don't like him."

"Maybe it's a motive?"

"Maybe," I said and pulled my comforter tighter around me. "There are so many moving parts to this, it's hard to believe it's all happening. All of the stuff with Louis and Luke, and now Rolland."

"Yeah," Atticus responded. He paused for a moment like he had something else to say but didn't know if he wanted to. There wasn't anything else we urgently needed to talk about, which kind of disappointed me. But I didn't want to hold him on the phone for essentially no reason.

"All right, I'm going to go to bed. I'll talk to you soon," I said, mostly out of habit. I didn't know if he had any intention of talking to me ever again, but I found myself hoping he did. "Get home safe."

"Goodnight, Eden," Atticus said, and I felt my heart flutter in my chest involuntarily. I hung up the phone before I could embarrass myself.

After readjusting in bed to get more comfortable, I quickly clicked through social media apps to see if anything new had come up. I didn't see anything at first, but when I went on Facebook, a post from Sloane was the first thing on my feed.

It'd been posted much earlier in the day, during school hours, but a fairly large number of people had responded to it. There were comments and reactions of all variety. It was a relatively brief post, but the point was clear.

> Since students at St. Joe's seem to believe that people's sex lives are not private information, we're being forced to have a long overdue conversation about sexuality. To Eros and any of his cronies—I'm not scared of you. I know what I've done. But the real question is if you're able to face yourselves knowing what you've done.

Some of the comments were of an appreciative nature, giving their blessing to Sloane for speaking out. Most of the names were of alumni that I'd forgotten about, or people I'd never met. Vera commented with a heart.

Then there were, expectedly, a few comments telling her that the best way to get Eros off her back was by not sleeping with so many people.

Clicking on a few names, I realized most of the more positive posts were college students currently attending Greenville Community College. The fact that most of the people standing with Sloane didn't currently attend St. Joe's stood out to me as a relatively appropriate representation of our high school; even the more sex-positive students didn't want to get wrapped up in her situation.

But seeing the names attached to colleges brought me a strong sense of relief too. It often felt like high school was everything, but realistically, after graduation, most of us wouldn't think about what had happened in the past four years. There was potential that even Eros would soon forget about it, seeing it as a stupid prank he'd pulled in high school. Or just a small mistake, something with little to no effect on his day-to-day adult life.

But it was inevitable that the victims would never forget. It wouldn't surprise me if they'd face constant situational fear for years spanning past high school. It didn't sit well with me that the women who'd sent the pictures were demonized while those who requested them, and later shared them, were not. It put the girls in the situation of second-guessing and believing that they had made a mistake not only in sending the picture but in trusting the person to whom they'd sent the picture.

And the pictures were not going to go away. Even if the girls were able to move past it, the internet could still hold on. All it would take was someone reposting their pictures with the girls' full names attached and anyone could find it. Colleges, jobs, friends. Anyone.

The thought made me nauseous.

As I was reading through, I realized I did recognize one of the names. Kai Sharma. That had to have been the same Kai Violeta told me about. She'd posted a comment.

> If anyone involved needs someone to talk to, the hotline
> is always available. We won't be able to provide high
> school–specific resources, but we're here to talk.

A phone number followed the post.

I clicked on Kai's profile, unable to fight my curiosity. Under her profile picture, it listed that she worked as a victim advocate for Greenville College. A quick internet search told me she was trained to work on a hotline and assisted victims of specifically sex-related offenses.

Even though I knew Yanick had explicitly said *Warrior Weekly* couldn't pursue Nudegate and would be furious if I contacted a source from outside St. Joe's, I couldn't help myself. If anything, this conversation would be for me and not part of the larger article. I wanted to know how Kai fit into the Slut Squad, and I wanted to see if she could shed some light on Massachusetts laws and the next steps for the Slut Squad.

I didn't know if it was curiosity or stupidity or irrationality, or maybe all three, but it seemed like a next step and I wanted to take it.

I sent her a friend request, adding an additional message about wanting to talk to her about revenge porn. I didn't specifically mention *Warrior Weekly*, but I mentioned that I was a student journalist with hopes that might give me some credibility.

And, to my surprise, the first thing I woke up to the next morning was a message from Kai.

> Hey Eden. Sad circumstances but I'm glad to hear from you. If you're close to campus we can meet somewhere, maybe the Greenville Student Wellness building. I'll be free Monday starting around four.

She attached an address to a building conveniently not far, probably only a fifteen-minute walk from the school.

I responded with a *sounds great* and something in me, a small part, felt better for not letting the story go completely. Even if this wasn't going to be published, I could at least know I'd done something.

CHAPTER NINETEEN

After school got out on Monday, I met with Kai.

As I walked up to the Student Wellness building that she'd told me about, I wasn't sure what my plan was. I didn't know what I was hoping to get out of the conversation, especially since I wouldn't be able to use her information in an article. And she was already helping the Slut Squad, which meant I was no use in being a liaison there. But she was a source who was close to, but not directly affected by, the email. And she knew Sloane, which might provide some insight into whether or not Sloane was going to do more with the Slut Squad in the future.

The building was small and built as a separate entity away from the rest of campus. From what I'd gathered before I'd arrived, Student Wellness was the place students went to when they needed help with mental, as opposed to solely physical, health. It was mostly staffed with counselors rather than nurses.

I entered and found a woman sitting at a desk surrounded by pamphlets, snacks, and condoms all neatly lined up in baskets. "Hi! Can I help you?"

"I'm here to see Kai?" I said, my voice rising at the end as if I was unsure.

"I'll tell her you're here!" the woman said cheerily. I sat down on a couch, hugging my backpack to my chest while I waited.

Eventually, the person whom I assumed was Kai rounded the corner and approached me. She was as young, probably in her early twenties, and as pretty as she looked in her profile picture. She had tan skin with thick, dark hair and round brown eyes. "Hey, I'm Kai."

"Eden," I said and stood up.

"We can go back to Ashleigh's office," Kai said and started walking. "Ashleigh is one of our on-location counselors who specifically helps out with DV, but she's out sick today and said I could use her office."

"DV?"

"Domestic violence." She led me into a small office, barely larger than a closet. "Door open or closed?"

"Closed is fine," I said, and Kai quietly closed it, shutting out noises from around the building and making the room practically silent. There were two chairs facing each other from across a desk. Kai took the chair behind and I sat down in the other.

"What did you want to talk about?" Kai asked, looking at me. She took a swig from the water bottle next to her, giving me a second to think. I tried to formulate any kind of purpose but was coming up short. I decided to stick with what I knew.

"I think you've heard about everything that's been happening at St. Joe's?" I asked. "From Sloane?"

"Somewhat," she said, "but people can experience the same situation differently."

"I'm not one of the girls who got their pictures leaked," I said, and Kai nodded. "But I know some people who have. And I'm a reporter at St. Joe's who's trying to cover the story."

I had a feeling she'd already gathered that from my Facebook message, but I was nervous. This was the first time I'd ever interviewed someone who wasn't directly connected to St. Joe's. "And mostly I'm trying to figure out what's going on. Because everything has been weird lately and none of the faculty seems to care about what happens. And it sounds like the police can't do anything?"

"That sounds like a lot to deal with."

"And I've also heard you're helping with the Slut Squad?" I asked, hoping the question wasn't too up front. "One of the girls told me about it."

"Yeah, I've gone by twice to chat. I think it's important there's a support system in place, especially for anyone who might not have one at home or day-to-day at school." Kai looked at me, reading my face. "Do you want to talk about what you've seen?"

The question caught me off guard. "I was thinking I'd focus on talking about the story."

"That's okay too," Kai said. "Was there anything in particular you wanted to ask about?"

We sat in silence until it became uncomfortable and I felt like I had to speak. "Why do people do this? Why would they?"

"Every case is its own beast, but it's usually related to power or revenge. Someone trying to prove a point of some kind."

"Revenge porn," I said.

Kai nodded. "Revenge porn *is* when people share explicit

photos of others for some sort of gain, usually to embarrass the other person. But revenge isn't the only motivation. Sometimes the pictures will be shared because a person wants to say *look at the nudes someone sent me* and they don't have the malicious intent of trying to actively harm someone. We've started using the term *nonconsensual pornography* instead, at least in this office. There's still a lot of uncertainty around what can be done about it since a digital footprint is as close to permanent as can be."

I looked at her. "Doesn't it seem pretty obvious, though? If someone posts a picture like that without permission, it's wrong. The person should be punished."

"Agreed."

"And it seems like St. Joe's isn't even trying to find the perpetrator at this point. Unless there's a minor involved, they don't care," I said.

"It's an unfortunate reality. The laws haven't caught up to the crimes yet. In some places, at least."

"I just don't get it," I said. I recognized Kai's tactic as one I'd used during interviews; she was letting me fill in the space, carry the conversation. But even knowing what she was doing, I couldn't stop the words coming out of my mouth. "Why people aren't taking it seriously, I mean. The day the pictures were first released this girl Margot ran from the classroom. I found her crying in the bathroom and she was saying how it was all her fault and how she deserved what had happened to her."

"As unfortunate as it is, self-blame is something a lot of people go through," Kai explained. "They keep telling themselves if they hadn't done this *one thing* that they wouldn't be where they are, which is unfair to themselves, but a natural response."

"And the guys at school don't get it either. I talked to my

ex—" I cut myself off, realizing I was treating this as a vent session rather than an actual interview. But, maybe, in a way, that was what I'd wanted from Kai all along. Someone to talk to.

"It's okay, Eden. You can talk about what's going on if you need to. Even professional, full-time journalists will seek help after they've covered something traumatic or emotionally draining."

I picked at my fingernails, the skin permanently tender after the stressful two weeks. "I never thought something like this would happen. I sent pictures to my ex, admittedly before I even turned eighteen, which I'm now learning is illegal, and never thought he'd do anything with them. But he'd talked to his friends about it. People who weren't even his friends. And it feels stupid to be upset about it considering how much worse it is for the Slut Squad, but it still sucks."

"You're allowed to be upset," Kai said. "Your trust was betrayed. You're feeling hurt. It's a natural human reaction. And at least some of this pain you're experiencing is similar to what the girls are going through. If anything, that's a strength. It means you can sympathize with them. Maybe even empathize on a certain level. That's powerful."

"What if I'm not able to help them?" I asked, and when I saw Kai's expression, I elaborated. "St. Joe's won't let us write about the story anymore. I feel like I have *nothing* to contribute."

Kai raised her eyebrows. "Really?"

"Yeah, our principal is threatening to shut down the paper completely if I publish anything else about the email."

"I'm sure the secrecy and bureaucracy of schools aren't helping with that at all," she said and shook her head. "Unfortunately, I can't help that much. I'm sure if we had a student-run newspaper here, they'd love to help you out, but we don't."

"I'm still trying to figure out if writing about this is even worth the effort or not. It seems like it might dig up more dirt than it's worth."

Kai leaned over and I watched as she pulled a copy of *Warrior Weekly* out of her bag, catching me off guard. She laid it out on her desk, pointing at the front page where my article about Nudegate was printed. "This is why you do it. You do it for them."

"But doesn't this put them in a weird situation?"

"It's because of them that a difficult conversation about a difficult topic can be had," Kai explained. "If we didn't have people speaking out and fighting like this, we wouldn't have progress. You gave these girls what they needed at the time and you did it because you felt like you should, not only because it was an assignment."

"Who told you that?"

"Sloane. She and I have been good family friends for a while, predating the email, and I think she trusts you. She's the one who brought me a copy of the newspaper because she appreciated the coverage so much. She probably doesn't show it all that well, but I think she'll come around eventually. She needs time."

Kai continued, "I'm not going to push you to do anything, especially if there's a risk you'll get into trouble, but these girls need you. They didn't have a choice in the matter, but you do."

I looked at the newspaper again. The entire story, the obstacles, the number of interviews, its local and state relevance, all felt absurd and out of my league. But I knew we could, and should, still try all the same.

I thought about the girls, too, on a personal level. By giving the Slut Squad a voice, we might be able to help other girls in the future. And we could maybe stop people like Nick and Luke and Rolland from so openly talking about and sexualizing women without their consent.

"Thank you," I said, meaning it.

"Of course," Kai responded. "If you need anything, don't hesitate to call. We're technically for Greenville students, but our office is willing to make exceptions for those who need it."

My phone vibrated multiple times in my pocket, signaling a call. "I'm so sorry," I said and checked the screen. It wasn't a number I had saved, but it was a local number.

"Go ahead." Kai waved her hand in goodbye. "It was lovely to meet you, Eden. Take care."

I waved and then exited the room quickly, pressing the green button on my phone to answer the call. "Hello?"

"Eden?"

I didn't recognize the voice. "Who is this?"

"It's Sloane. I got your number from John, I hope you don't mind. I think it's time to do the interview." My heart involuntarily fluttered at the mention of Atticus.

"Oh! Okay. Glad to hear it." But Sloane was quiet on the other end, making me nervous. "What's up?"

"Have you checked your email?"

"No," I said. "Give me a sec."

I clicked out of the call and refreshed my email. A new email from Eros popped up at the top. It was fairly straightforward. The message at the top declared *four days* and below that was a new picture of Sloane, different from the one in the Nudegate email. In this one, she was proudly displaying a bare chest, a finger in her mouth.

"Four days until what?" I asked, mostly to myself until I

realized Sloane could still hear me on the phone. It was hard to believe that, two weeks after Nudegate, things could somehow get worse.

"I'm not sure but I'm not looking forward to finding out," Sloane responded, her voice tinny through the phone speaker. "Are you able to do the interview tonight? I want to get this over with sooner rather than later."

"I think so," I said, glancing at the clock on the wall. Even though I still couldn't publish, I knew I couldn't let the opportunity pass. If I turned Sloane down now, the chance might never come up again. "Do you want to meet at the *Warrior Weekly* office?"

"I was thinking we could use one of the study rooms in the library."

"There are no study rooms at the library."

"I mean the study rooms at the local library."

I wanted to ask her why she wasn't interested in meeting on campus, but part of me understood without needing confirmation. There was something safe about doing the interview away from St. Joe's. No one could listen in or see her.

"Okay," I said. "Give me twenty."

~

Sloane met me in a small study room toward the back of the library, her backpack in the chair next to her and her phone in front of her on the table. It looked like an interrogation scene, which wasn't an inaccurate comparison to what it felt like I was about to do.

Despite her offering, I wasn't sure how much of this was

her wanting to talk versus feeling like she should. Despite her appearance on the news, it would make sense for her to be cautious about being quoted in a newspaper run by the same school blatantly hurting her. There was nothing desirable about being interviewed by someone deemed untrustworthy. I understood, even though it was, in a way, me that she'd deemed untrustworthy.

I opened the glass door and stepped into the room, trying to keep the shaking in my hands to a minimum.

"Hey," I said, letting the door close behind me as I took the three steps required to be in front of the table. I put my backpack down, feeling the need to move as quietly as possible. The acts of unzipping my jacket and pulling out my phone were all too loud for the room.

She looked at me, her eyes focused on each action that I took, each slight tremble of my hand. I felt like an animal being preyed on, locked away in the tiger's cage with nowhere to run.

"Are you able to get this printed this week?" Sloane asked.

"I understand the urgency, but we'd most likely have to include your interview with other information," I said. I made the intentional choice to not mention that we probably wouldn't be able to print it at all, at least anytime soon. "Our rule is we need at least three sources in an article."

"What about a profile?" Sloane asked. "A profile with the slut who started the Slut Squad."

"You're okay with me writing about the Slut Squad?"

"I can't let this Eros dickhead think he can get to me. I can't let him think I'm alone in this," Sloane said. "Even if Eros has a vendetta against specifically me."

Despite the inopportune circumstances, it was an amazing story and too good to pass up. Ronnie and Kolton would be thrilled. I placed my phone in plain sight on the table. "Is it okay if I record?"

"Please do," Sloane said. "I was thinking we could start with how royally St. Joe's fucked up this investigation."

I looked down at the notepad in my hand and then glanced back at her. "You know we can't print that."

She let out a half sigh and then spent time constructing the next words out of her mouth. "I do not know what Eros's plan is, but let it be known that we're—meaning, the Slut Squad—not going to sit back and take it silently. Whoever this dickhead is deserves to know what he's done is wrong." I tried to keep my voice level as I told her, again, that profanity couldn't be printed in the paper, but she didn't give me a second thought. "We're going to fight back."

"Can you talk about what your plan is? For the Slut Squad, I mean."

"As if Eros ever did." She said the name with a spiteful indignation I had never heard from anyone before. Her lips turned up with each word she said. "We're here to stay. That's all that matters."

"What made you want to start the Slut Squad?"

"I feel like that's pretty clear."

I breathed out of my nose, trying not to get irritated that she wasn't providing anything substantial. "What are you hoping to do with the Slut Squad?"

"Make a statement."

I waited for her to elaborate but she didn't. "Is that all you had to say?" I asked, the words slipping out of my mouth before I could stop them.

To my surprise, Sloane looked amused. "Yes, that's my

statement. Slut Squad has a plan and we won't take this sitting down. This should've been done a long time ago and we'll be here as long as we need to be."

"You don't want to talk about what it's been like to be a victim of Nudegate? How your friends have been impacted? What you think this countdown means?" I asked. That was barely anything enough to be featured in a full-length article; it definitely wasn't enough to be a featured piece focused on Sloane. "You told me you were ready for an interview."

"This is still technically an interview. I don't know why I have to bare my soul to you for it to count."

"You don't have to bare your soul to me."

"Is that not what you asked me to do? Did you not want me to tell you how I've been feeling so you can print it and everyone can read about how hurt I am by all of this? About how I have real feelings and years of name-calling and harassment fueling me?"

I stumbled over my words, unsure of what to say in response to that. "I—"

"I'm not interested in talking about my feelings. None of them are particularly good or flattering, and frankly, talking about them is embarrassing."

"If it makes you feel better, I don't even know if what you tell me will be able to be printed," I said, and Sloane looked at me curiously. "We got in trouble with the St. Joe's administration. We can't print anything related to Nudegate."

"You couldn't have told me that before you agreed to the interview?"

"I'm looking for things to print. I was hoping with enough source material I'd be able to at least write something and figure out publishing later."

"Maybe try to run your own newspaper and find more than one source, then," she said, and I grabbed my phone to turn off the recording. I had very little interest in picking a fight with Sloane; if she wanted to provide a general, and somewhat useless, statement, then so be it.

As I was about to stand up, she placed her hand over my own. "You want to know how I feel? You want to know what this has been like for me?" She moved her hand and glanced at my phone again, verifying that I turned it off. "This is the worst thing that has *ever* fucking happened to me. I'm miserable."

I was, again, at a loss for words, but it didn't seem like Sloane needed a response from me. "You know they call us St. Hoes now? All of the schools in the area call us St. Hoes." She let out a humorless laugh. "I've been getting propositioned by everyone within a twenty-five-mile radius about hooking up with them. People are offering to buy more nudes from me. There's a fucking *Reddit* thread dedicated to me.

"And I know you're probably like, *oh, that sounds like a compliment*," Sloane continued, the inflection in her voice changing as she imitated another person speaking to her. "I know people are thinking it. Danica fucking said that shit to my face. But it doesn't feel that way. And what's incredible is that these people will go and call me a slut for doing exactly what they wanted me to do in the first place. Like, I'll be flirting with a cute guy, we'll have something going on, he'll ask me for a picture and I'll send it because why not, you know? And then he'll be talking to his friends later like he's some huge player and he's a real lady's man, as if us hooking up wasn't a mutual act. Like we didn't have consensual sex because we both *wanted* to. It's like sex is something they do *to* us so they can brag about it later. I'm not a conquest to feed someone's ego, I want to get laid. And now I can't even have that."

There were spite and venom in each word, the turn of her lips emphasized by her lipstick. The more she spoke, the more I realized maybe she'd just been looking for someone to talk to, like I had with Kai. I looked at her. "So, you never second-guessed sending the pictures?"

Sloane let out another sharp, singular laugh. "No. Why the fuck should I? What kind of person shares photos like that with a third party? What kind of person sends an email like that to *anyone*, much less the entire student body of a school? There's always talk about trust when we're sending photos and I get it. We should do private things only with people we trust to keep it private. But why should I have to *demand* privacy when it should be the natural human response?

"And now there's all of this media coverage and so much stuff happening. I didn't want to be on the fucking news but I had to be because Eros gave me no other choice. Like, more than anything, I want to be able to tell St. Joe's to fuck off. And I want to see real criminal prosecution instead of this civil suit bullshit we're being told is the only option. I want so much more. But I also can't keep doing this. I'm tired and I'm angry and I'm lonely. I feel like I'm fighting this ridiculous uphill battle against people who don't think I deserve to be treated like a real person because I enjoy casual sex."

Sloane stopped and took a deep breath as she sat up straighter in her chair. Silence settled over the room, but I knew she wasn't done talking yet.

"I'm not sure where I'm going to go from here, but I have to hope that the pictures don't follow me around forever. I know people all over the world have probably seen them because of Reddit and I know they've been sent to other people at other schools. And I don't even think there are real steps to be able to take down the photos at this point, which is so fucking ridiculous. No one other than myself is looking out for me.

"I want to say that it's all going to be over soon, but it's never going to be over. I'm going to have to worry about this forever. And did you know I asked Principal Yanick if she could delete the email from the servers and she basically put me on hold? She was worried about invasion of privacy since the email 'technically belongs to the recipients.'" She scoffed. "Couldn't even imagine what it feels like to be a victim of *that*."

I sat up straighter. "You spoke to Yanick?"

"Three days after it happened." Sloane shook her head. "Basically brushed me off and said she'd let me know what she planned to do."

"Can I get *that* on record at least?" I asked, pulling open the front of my notebook.

"Yeah, whatever. Let everyone know what a terrible job St. Joe's is doing with this whole thing. Their internal 'investigation' was barely anything. I guess they weren't able to get any easy answers, so the entire administration gave up," she explained. "It was too much for them to deal with, having seven girls where fewer than half were cooperative with the school. And all different suspects. And all different social circles. It's like *no criminal charges, no effort*, you know what I mean?"

"The choice to feature the seven of you specifically seemed weird to me too," I said, and Sloane looked at me, waiting for elaboration. "I've been doing my job as a reporter. Violeta told me about Louis. But it seems like the only common denominator is all of you being eighteen, either from early fall birthdays or, in Angela's case, being held back."

"Yeah, both Violeta and Alice," Sloane said. "Angela's was Tyson Post. Claire's was some guy in theater. Vera's pretty sure hers was some guy on the lacrosse team. I'm not totally confident since I'd sometimes send repeats, but I think mine might've been that guy Derek."

"Derek French?" I asked. He was a stoner type who pretty much only showed up to school to sell weed. "Really?"

Sloane shrugged. "He's charming, I don't know. I get bored of the generic pretty boys. It's nice to talk to people who have things to say."

"No Luke?" I asked, realizing not one of the descriptors would match him.

"No, not one. I thought it was surprising too," Sloane said. I thought about Luke's anger toward Sloane. Was he targeting girls who'd rejected him?

I mentally thought through everyone and realized there was still a name missing. "What about Margot?"

Sloane thought about it for a second, mouth partially open. "I'm not sure, actually. I don't know if she ever said, now that I'm thinking about it."

"Maybe there's a clue in there?" I asked. "In whoever she sent it to? Maybe it's Luke?"

"I doubt it," Sloane said. "I'm assuming it's some guy she's met through all of her art stuff. Or maybe debate."

"None of the guys here make sense," I responded. "It seems like they're all from different groups and have no reason to interact. Lacrosse team and Tyson make sense. But Louis? And a guy from the theater group? How would they have found each other?

And why would they do something like Nudegate together? It seems risky."

Sloane shrugged. "Same thing I've been thinking for days."

"Who do you think is behind the countdown?" I asked.

"Point blank. Who's the first name that pops into your mind? Do you think it could be Derek?"

Sloane was at a loss for words. "I—I don't know. I can't think of a reason why Derek would do this. He must've been involved somehow, but orchestrating something like this? Creating a countdown? I don't know who would have a personal vendetta against me to that degree."

I felt like I couldn't make sense of any of it. "So, what is there to do? If we've run out of leads and it doesn't seem like there's a real investigation happening anymore?"

"I don't know," Sloane said. "I genuinely don't know."

We sat there in silence, together, the two of us, both equally confused and upset. But, if anything, hearing that the Slut Squad and St. Joe's were no closer to finding Eros made me even more determined to find him. Someone had to.

CHAPTER TWENTY

After my conversation with Sloane, I was feeling less certain we would ever find a resolution for Nudegate. There were no clear next steps.

I decided to spend lunch the next day in the newsroom so I could work on editing and homework, and hopefully keep my mind off Nudegate. I was also worried I wasn't going to be welcome at the *Warrior Weekly* table. I'd maintained professional contact with the staff about editing and deadlines, but I knew Jeremy was still upset and word had spread quickly about the near shutdown. I wasn't sure anyone on staff wanted to see me in a casual, friendly capacity. And since we'd never been in a situation where the paper had almost been completely shattered, I wasn't sure what the turnaround forgiveness period for that was, if there was one.

As I was finishing my reading for my world religions class, I was startled by my phone vibrating on the table. Sloane.

Sloane: If you're not already going to opening night
tonight, you should come to Oklahoma

Eden: Why?

Sloane didn't reply but I had a feeling it was going to be something Slut Squad related. She was inevitably about to get herself into trouble. And Claire would be furious; she already seemed to have separated herself completely from the Slut Squad and their goals. Losing her show to the Slut Squad, too, would lead to conflict.

I hadn't been planning on going to see *Oklahoma!* but I suddenly felt like I had to. I pulled out my phone to text Atticus.

Eden: Sloane is planning something
for during the musical tonight.

Atticus: I'm in. I can pick you up at 6.

I caught myself smiling and placed my phone down before I could think about it too much.

The first musical of the school year was a big deal, like most plays at St. Joe's were. The theater program thrived due to the consistent inflow of donor money, all from parents who believed their child was the next and brightest rising star.

Claire, the indisputable queen of everything theater at St. Joe's, was not going to be patient with any sort of disruption. Part of me couldn't help but think that might've been part of Sloane's plan. Thinking about the blowup they'd had at the Halloween party, I wouldn't have been surprised if Sloane saw this as the perfect opportunity to screw Claire over as an individual and St. Joe's as an institution. Either way, I'd have a few hours to mull over it.

Kolton decided to hang out in the office after the bell rang, so I left alone to head to my next class. As I turned the corner to go to ethics, I spotted Ronnie. She was talking to a short, curvy girl with dark skin, the two of them genuinely laughing. It was nice to see her happy, so much more relaxed than she'd ever been in the newsroom.

"Eden!" Ronnie said. She excused herself from the other girl, throwing out the phrase *newspaper business*, which made me think she was close enough with the other girl that she would understand. It made me sad to think that she had an entire life outside of the office that didn't get spoken about, friends we didn't mention and things we never brought up to each other. But I also realized that it wasn't too late to change my relationship with her or anyone else on staff. There was still time in the semester. No one said I couldn't get to know Ronnie, or anyone else on staff, in that way.

"Hey," I said, pausing so she could catch up with me.

"How is everything going?"

"Business as usual," I said, "It's not as difficult as I thought it would be to adjust to the new job, even though I don't have an executive editor yet."

"Okay, good, good," she said. "What's been going on with Nudegate? It sucks being out of the loop."

"Oh! It's fine," I said. "I finally got my interview with Sloane."

"You're kidding."

"No, she went all out." I knew I couldn't quote most of what she'd said, but her commentary still stuck with me. I'd never seen someone so angry. "She's been part of this group called the Slut Squad, made up of all the Nudegate Girls. I think she's planning something big in response to the countdown."

"Eden, that's nuts! That's literally incredible," Ronnie said and punched me lightly in the arm. In all the time I'd known Ronnie, I'd never known her to be chipper, but she seemed genuinely enthusiastic. Maybe being away from the *Weekly* was the best thing for her. And from Ronnie's supportive tone, it sounded like she believed it was good for me too.

"We still can't print anything, which sucks."

"Maybe it's not the end," Ronnie said, hugging her books tighter to her chest. "Now that I'm not Yanick's biggest concern, I might be able to pull something together."

"What are you thinking?"

I waited for a response, but I could tell from Ronnie's distant expression that she was already miles away, formulating some great save for the *Weekly*. "You'll know when I have it."

And I believed it.

~

Later that night, I changed out of my school uniform to get ready for my outing with Atticus. For just a second, I allowed myself to fret over what I was going to wear, not wanting to look sloppy but also not wanting to overdress and scare him away.

But, after I'd settled on a casual long-sleeve dress and tights, my mind wandered back to Nudegate. Between the countdown and what Sloane had told me, in addition to Ronnie refusing to give up on the Nudegate article, I knew something had to give soon. We had to be close to finding Eros. It just didn't seem to be happening quickly enough.

I glanced at my phone, waiting for Atticus to arrive. After the incident with Luke, we realized arriving separately at events was more dangerous than inconspicuous. It also seemed like Atticus was starting to have little to no interest in hanging out with any of the guys anymore, whether it be for the sake of our snooping or not.

While mindlessly clicking through apps, an email notification popped up from Eros that reminded us the countdown was at three days. I clicked on it, already knowing what to expect. No new clues leading to Eros, only a picture of Sloane, this time in deep-purple lingerie, and *three days*.

I deleted it immediately, knowing there was nothing to gain from it and having the email on my phone felt like a violation of Sloane's privacy. As I was about to check to see if Atticus texted, there was a knock at my door. "Come in!"

My dad appeared in the doorway. "There's a very tall gentleman waiting for you downstairs."

I tried to play it cool, even though the thought of Atticus and my dad interacting made me want to throw up. "Great, thanks."

Atticus was standing in the entryway, looking somewhat uncomfortable but still cute in his casual navy-blue button-down shirt. "Hey."

I turned to my dad to wave goodbye and he waved in return. I wouldn't be surprised if he was going to text my mom the minute I left, telling her all about how he was pretty sure I was going on a date. The thought made me feel surprisingly warm, like maybe there still was time for me to have a normal senior year. Maybe, eventually, I could spend all my time worrying about whether Atticus was going to ask me to prom or what bedsheets I'd get for my dorm room without it feeling childish and lacking urgency.

"Ready?" I asked, and Atticus nodded, opening my front door. "I'm not sure what the deal is or what to expect, but I have a feeling it'll be something."

"How do you know?" he said as we walked to his car.

"Sloane texted me," I said, and he let a small chuckle slip. "I'm surprised she didn't update you about it individually."

"She did," he confessed. "But I wanted to let you have this since you're technically the investigator here. I just have connections."

It was a nice comment, one that invited something cute or overly friendly in response, but I couldn't bring myself to do it. I'd never been that kind of person. Instead, I stuck with the familiar.

"Can you think of anyone who might have something against her? Maybe like a shitty ex? She couldn't come up with anyone, but she might be too close to the person to see it," I said and then winced, taking a step back in my approach. We both climbed into his car, a surprisingly clean Lincoln. "Sorry to turn you into a source. But I guess maybe if you noticed anything as a general concern for her."

"I've been thinking about the same thing and I keep coming up empty. She doesn't talk about her dating life much, even with me, but I don't think any of the guys she's seen could be considered exes. It's, like, some guys here and there but nothing superserious."

That made sense. It probably would've been easier to narrow down if she'd been the type to have clearly identified partners, but Atticus was right—the more I thought about it, the more I realized Sloane tended to keep everything low-key. It was well known around St. Joe's that she was sexually active, but the guys she was rumored to be hooking up with were rarely mentioned by name.

"Do you know anything about Derek French?"

"Yeah, dude's pretty chill. I think he and Sloane had a thing for a bit, but I don't know if they're still talking."

"Do you think he'd have connections to any of the girls involved in Nudegate? Or any of the other guys?"

"I can't imagine the connection would be that strong if there was one," he said. I appreciated how honestly he would answer my questions; he treated what was essentially an interrogation as if it was a normal conversation. "He keeps to himself a lot, spends more time hanging out with the people at Greenville High than St. Joe's. I only know him because he sells to Luke and hangs out with us sometimes."

"But none of the girls sent photos to Luke, which is the weird part," I said. "The best lead we have is Louis and this group chat, so they must be connected somehow, but I can't figure out how or why."

Atticus pulled into the St. Joe's parking lot, the building eerily vacant against the backdrop of a dark, empty sky. The unforgiving northeast wind helped set the scene.

Warm air from a heater was the first thing that greeted us as we entered the lobby of St. Joe's. It felt less abandoned than when I'd come for the assembly, but the long dark hallways still felt intensely grim. I couldn't help but think St. Joe's would never feel like a home away from home, or even a place I was comfortable being in, despite spending close to forty hours a week there. It would always be associated with Nick, Margot crying in the bathroom, Luke making derogatory digs at people, a mysterious and anonymous Eros spilling secrets. Nothing I was sure I wanted to remember.

We approached the table where tickets were being sold. Two people, probably mothers of theater kids, were sitting at a table with flyers and playbills with Claire's and Jason's faces on them. There was a man standing beside the table, talking to one of the women.

"How many?" the ticket woman asked, but my attention was drawn to the first woman; I recognized her. Claire's mom.

"Yes, thank you. We're very proud of her. We're hoping we can get her into a good acting program somewhere, maybe in New York. I want her to try TV, but I think she already has her eye on a Tony."

They both laughed politely, but I knew it wasn't really a joke.

"How is she with, you know, all of this additional attention?" the man asked, and the woman's million-dollar smile wavered.

"It's good she doesn't want to be a politician," she responded, her voice tight. "At least now producers will know she won't be shy about showing off in front of a camera."

I felt another wave of sympathy for Claire. I could only imagine what the conversations were like at home for her.

"You good?" Atticus asked, and I nodded as we entered the auditorium for the first time since the first day of Nudegate. I suddenly ached for some semblance of normalcy or simplicity; I ached for the senior year that I knew we would never truly have.

We found two empty seats in the middle section toward an aisle and I braced myself for Sloane's main event, whatever it might be. The thought that maybe it had fallen through crossed my mind, but I doubted Sloane would let the opportunity pass. The school administration would probably have to threaten to expel her to keep her off school grounds. She wouldn't take the Eros countdown quietly.

"When do you think it'll happen?" I asked, keeping my voice low.

"I have no idea," Atticus responded, glancing around the auditorium to see if anything was out of place. Yanick was there with a pale-skinned, smartly dressed man who was tenderly holding her hand, most likely her husband. Father McGlynn was there, too, greeting parents and chatting animatedly. Unsurprisingly, it didn't look like Mr. Winters was going to make an appearance. He could barely make it through the school day without looking like he was ready to up and quit at any given moment.

The crowd was mostly composed of family members and familiar faces that I knew both from St. Joe's parent conference days as well as from pictures in the *Greenville Gazette*. In addition to educating the children of some of the wealthiest and most accomplished people in the region, St. Joe's attracted the friends and colleagues of those people to their events as well. I spotted the mayor alongside a campaign organizer, and St. Joe's alumnus, who was recognizable from helping on previous mayoral campaigns. St Joe's administrators and members of the board of trustees floated around, talking it up in hopes of earning a worthwhile donation at the end of the night.

"I always forget what kind of crowd St. Joe's is made up of until I see it all in person," I said, using the noise level of the room as an excuse to lean closer to Atticus.

"No kidding," Atticus responded. "The St. Joe's administration is probably working double-time to keep Nudegate and the countdown under wraps for the sake of fundraising. Can't be easy after Sloane's appearance on the news."

The lights flickered, signaling that it was time to find seats, and I braced myself for whatever it was that was about to come. Mrs. Thompson, who to my surprise was also the theater program director, introduced the show. She looked happier than she ever did in class. I hoped for Mrs. Thompson's sake that Sloane had warned her the play would be interrupted, but I knew how risky it would've been to tip off a staff member that she was planning something.

The musical began and despite the tension in my shoulders, I found myself starting to enjoy it. Claire looked great, practically glowing under the harsh stage lights. Time passed quickly, and surprisingly easily, as musical numbers flew by with no interruption. Maybe Sloane was going to wait until intermission, or at least until the end of the play.

But I knew, the second I thought it, that she wouldn't.

But, as Claire got into the swing of a song about starting over after a relationship gone wrong, the theater doors flew open and slammed into the wall with a loud bang. Immediately, the air in the auditorium changed. I grabbed Atticus's hand, lightly and only for a fleeting moment without thinking, an effort to slow my heart rate down.

Claire continued on, unaffected by the interruption, but the rest of the cast members were thrown off their steps. Uncertain about what was happening, the crowd turned to face the door and low chatter echoed off the walls. If I didn't know better, I would've assumed it was part of the show.

"We're the Slut Squad," a voice echoed through the auditorium, unmistakably Sloane's, marking her transition from reluctant, quiet leader to the face of the movement. She stood in the backlight from the hallway, her frame the only thing visible. "It's been a *long* senior year and the fact that we, the actual victims, are not being heard is not making it any easier."

"We're taking a stand," Vera yelled, her voice strong and clear. "You can't ignore us anymore."

At this point, Claire stopped singing.

"We are sluts," Sloane yelled, and the crowd to let out gasps and uncomfortable chuckles before she continued, "and sluts don't give a fuck."

All the girls chanted the slogan *We are sluts and sluts don't give a fuck* as they made their way down the aisles. They were all wearing tight, revealing clothes. It was a protest, launched right in the middle of a school event that had brought in some of the most notable figures from the region.

"We *demand* St. Joseph's do more to protect its students than telling us to not send photos! Support us! Investigate! Find out who did this and punish them!" Sloane shouted, now standing in front of the stage and facing the crowd. "In three days whoever is doing this will strike again. I'm being intentionally targeted and St. Joseph's hasn't done *anything* about it. I refuse to be pushed to the side and forgotten. Something has to change."

As I watched Sloane parade down the aisle near Atticus and me, I was proud of her, that this was the reaction I'd anticipated from her all along. The girls' yelling was magnified by the structure of the room and the microphones set up over the stage. Alice, Vera, Sloane, Margot were all there. Angela had joined, which I thought was surprising considering her place in the social hierarchy and her seemingly passive attitude toward

Nudegate. But maybe the countdown had made her realize how serious this was.

Violeta showed up from the other side of the theater, joining hands with Sloane, both of them still chanting. All of the girls were now there, linked together, only missing Claire. There weren't many of them, only six compared to the hundreds in their seats, but people were listening. The responses were mixed, some angry and telling the girls to be quiet and sit down, but there were also light cheers.

Yanick had risen out of her seat, but she looked small next to the group of girls. Other administrators started to sprint to the front, but I think they knew that a forceful exit was exactly what Sloane needed to further create buzz. Phones were taken out and flashing as people took pictures, illuminating the girls.

During all of this, Claire was still on stage. In the lights, I noticed the glisten of tears. Sloane approached her and I prepared myself for a snide comment, maybe something physical, but instead Claire fell to her knees at the edge of the stage and hugged Sloane. Claire propped her chin on Sloane's head while Sloane chanted, still facing the crowd. As I watched the scene unfold, confusion nipped at me, the scene of the two of them in a showdown at the Halloween party flashing before my eyes. But there was a sign of allegiance in the gentleness of Claire's arms around Sloane, the way Sloane had placed a hand over Claire's forearm.

Claire let go of Sloane and, in that moment, I watched Claire's face change. With tears still falling down her cheeks, she smiled. The mounting feelings of hostility had finally, or at least seemingly, reached their peak. I'd been anticipating a blowup but, instead, was witnessing solidarity.

St. Joe's staff tried to get the girls out of the auditorium. The lights turned on and people shuffled around, unsure if they should leave. The staff quickly took the girls out of the auditorium, each of the Slut Squad members proudly marching away without an ounce of shame. Finally, after all this time, they were able to show off that they were unified. All seven of them.

It was obvious Yanick wasn't going to let them off easily, a thought that made me genuinely angry. They were protesting how they'd been treated by the school and the administration; it seemed unfair to punish them for revealing how miserable the situation was.

And knowing that St. Joe's was only further punishing the Slut Squad by not allowing the *Warrior Weekly* to write about them, or the email in general, made me even angrier. The school was setting up all of the girls to fail. It was punishment with no trial, no jury.

Most of the parents were still in their seats, but there were some who had gotten up. They exchanged side-eyed glances, probably saying *I'm glad my child was smart enough to not get involved in this.*

Claire was the last one removed from the auditorium, but she barely needed to be asked. Boldly, she walked out, still in full costume, chin high, as Yanick trailed behind her. The fact that she hadn't been chanting along with them or holding any signs wasn't going to matter; what counted was that she hadn't expressed any outrage toward the girls. She'd looked almost relieved that Sloane had come. I thought about how she'd shown up to the first Slut Squad meeting, and realized she most likely had always been standing alongside the rest of the Slut Squad, but was torn between pleasing her parents and standing up for herself.

After the girls were escorted from the auditorium, flashes from cameras still following them like amateur paparazzi, Yanick walked up the steps to the stage. She took the microphone that Mrs. Thompson had been using earlier. "The show is over for the night, unfortunately. We will be refunding tickets. We hope to see you at another performance in the near future."

Mrs. Thompson looked upset, but not entirely surprised, as she walked toward Yanick. They spoke quickly and quietly, their words tumbling out so quickly I couldn't decipher what they were saying.

"Wow," Atticus said, making me jump. I'd been so distracted by the rest of the auditorium I'd almost forgotten he was there. But hearing him speak again reminded me that I'd held his hand just moments earlier, albeit briefly. I was a little embarrassed, but unapologetic, to be so forward. "I had a feeling it was going to be something like this, but I still wasn't prepared."

"This school is going to burn to the ground," I responded, watching the faces of the parents as they exited. "Do you think we'll be able to talk to Sloane?"

"She's probably going to be in the principal's office for a long, long time after this," he responded. "I don't think any of us are going to be talking to her for a while, at least not on school grounds."

"And the drama's not even over yet. We still have to wait for whatever is at the end of Eros's countdown."

"I don't think the school can handle another blow like that." Atticus looked around at the slim crowd remaining in the auditorium.

Yanick would most likely not hear the end of it anytime soon. This was the kind of horrific year that led to firings and changed leadership and early retirements. Even with everything that had happened between the *Weekly* and Yanick, I still felt a nagging sensation of sadness for her, knowing that this was how it would all most likely end for her. She'd made shitty decisions, but she wasn't the only one making them. It wasn't like she was the person who'd chosen to have such a significant scandal occur during her time at St. Joe's. She was dealing with furious parents and probably had the school board breathing down her neck about budgets and keeping the scandal under control. It couldn't be easy.

"Maybe the end of the countdown will be Eros admitting who he is," I responded dryly.

"We can only hope."

Students had their phones out, their mouths and fingers moving as they spoke to each other and texted their friends who weren't there. Maybe the events would be enough to overshadow Eros's countdown, at least temporarily. A small reprieve for the girls.

"Want to head out?" I asked.

We left the auditorium and slipped through the crowd, brushing past parents who were all speaking to each other at a furious pace. I spotted Ms. Polaski, who had her two sons—it looked like twins, around first or second grade—and her husband with her.

"I'll be right back," I said to Atticus and walked toward her while Ms. Polaski waved.

"Hey, Eden. Interesting addition to the show, right?" she asked good-naturedly. "I always thought 'Many a New Day' needed some spice."

I appreciated her casual tone. She was probably the only

person on the St. Joe's payroll who seemed unfazed by the Slut Squad's performance. "Do you think we'll get permission to write about this?"

"I doubt it, but I think we should," Ms. Polaski said, sending a wave of appreciation through me. "Get your quotes and keep writing. Ronnie and I have been talking over some ideas for publication."

I hesitated, knowing how much she was putting on the line by supporting me. "Are you sure?"

"Yes. I might not know much about journalism, but I have learned a thing or two by watching you and Ronnie. You have to take the leap sometimes," Ms. Polaski said, a cautious smile at her lips. "Have a good night, Eden."

I said the same to her and she and her husband collected their sons to leave. We waved goodbye and I rejoined Atticus.

"I think the article is back on," I said.

"Nice," Atticus responded.

It was obvious to both of us what that meant. Progress.

CHAPTER TWENTY-ONE

After the musical, I had too much stored-up nervous energy to sleep. All I could think about was what Ms. Polaski's—and Ronnie's—plan would be. I trusted her and I hoped she knew what she was doing, but I also wasn't sure I wanted her putting her job on the line for us. Ronnie being kicked off the staff was one thing; Ms. Polaski getting fired from full-time employment was something completely different.

First thing the next morning, I returned to Ms. Polaski's office. I'd spent more time there in the last three or so weeks than I had in the entirety of my high school career.

Ms. Polaski greeted me and waved me in. I sat down in a chair in front of her. "Ronnie reached out to me and it's gotten me thinking we should find an alternative route for you. She didn't know exactly what she wanted to do, but I've been trying to come up with something. After last night's events, I think it's more than worth it to try. And the thought of having to scrap all of this work as it's picking up momentum is a waste of your effort."

I realized she was the first, if not the only, teacher who had praised the work that had gone into the Nudegate articles. The content matter was one thing, but it was nice to be recognized for the amount of effort that went into finding sources, interviewing, transcribing, and writing.

"Thanks, Ms. Polaski. I really appreciate that."

"Of course." Ms. Polaski took a sip of her coffee. "This is going to sound a little ridiculous and I'm not sure how the technicalities would work, but my husband proposed it. What if you published using a third-party website? The article wouldn't be on the *Weekly* website and it wouldn't be published in the newspaper, but it would still be accessible to the students. All of the quotes, all of the information, the reality of the situation. Links to the information could be shared with local newspapers and parents and students. I think this could be a workaround. It would be an independent publisher but with the accessibility of a funded student newspaper."

The option sounded like the best we had, but I was feeling cautious about getting too excited. "Can we still get in trouble for it? Since I'm still technically representing *Warrior Weekly*?"

"I can't promise you as an individual that you wouldn't face any consequences," Ms. Polaski said. "And I'm sorry about that. But this would be a way of protecting the paper, since it would be your individual action instead of the paper as a whole. You would be a kind of whistleblower."

My heart thudded in my chest at the realization of what this could possibly mean. "People would still be able to read about Nudegate."

Ms. Polaski nodded. "The implications here are pretty huge, especially since the story has already picked up major attention. People want more. And I think, if cards are played right, it could go national. I don't say that to scare you; I say that as an indication of how unique this situation is. You could spark a dialogue, Eden. I've already learned a lot from you and Ronnie about the significance of this email. I think others could benefit from it too."

"Oh," I said, feeling somewhat unprepared and inadequate for the role. I knew the story was important and I knew, in a way, I'd wanted it to mean something. Local news was scary enough; trying to take it national was an entirely different ball game. I'd lose control of the story entirely.

But, then again, I'd never had control of the story in the first place.

"I'll talk to the rest of the staff."

"Okay," Ms. Polaski responded. As I was gathering my things, she spoke again. "Thank you for staying invested in this. Your work is so, so important. I hope you understand that and know that despite what might happen, I appreciate what you've done. My *husband* of all people is engaging in conversations with me about masculinity and how to raise our boys. That's because of you."

It was surprising to hear. In a way, I'd always imagined adults as stuck, never able to change. No adult had ever told me I'd taught them something. It seemed like by the time people had kids, they stopped picking up new hobbies and spent most of their time doing what they'd always done. My parents had become creatures of habit as they'd aged; I assumed the same of everyone, including my teachers. But maybe it was more complicated than that.

"Thank you for supporting us," I said before leaving. Before I'd even fully left the classroom, I texted the editor's group chat, bypassing email this time to be more efficient.

> Eden: New update on how to write about Nudegate without getting the newspaper shut down. Emergency editors meeting during lunch?

I also followed up with a similar text to Julia and Bree since they were the reporters who'd helped me with the Nudegate story since the beginning.

I was nervous that the editors—Jeremy especially—wouldn't be willing to listen to me or take me seriously after the trouble Ronnie and I had caused but responses came in almost immediately. I texted Ronnie, too, appreciative of how hard she was still fighting for the *Weekly* despite being sidelined.

We were finally going to get the real and full Nudegate story out there. I could only hope St. Joe's wouldn't implode before then.

But, as I walked into my first class of the morning and saw stacks of printouts in Mrs. Thompson's hands, I knew it was going to be a difficult day.

"Good morning, everyone," Mrs. Thompson greeted us. We all settled into our usual seats, watching her with tired eyes. "We have a slight addendum to our lecture today. Principal Yanick has asked that all first-period teachers review St. Joseph's antibullying policy." Groans echoed through the room, but Mrs. Thompson went on, ignoring them. "I'm handing out scanned copies of the student code of conduct."

Starting at the front of each row, Mrs. Thompson passed

down stapled papers, about four sheets thick, that provided definitions of bullying, cyberbullying, and harassment. A write-up of examples of the acts and forms of punishment for the acts were listed below those. There was also a list of state-level legal references, explaining why each policy had been put into place and how the school board had decided on the definitions. I noticed there was nothing specific to sexting or privacy laws.

"Michael, can you start off by reading the definition of intimidation?" Mrs. Thompson said. Even though I knew I should listen, I immediately zoned out, more focused on what was happening outside the window than what was being read.

It was a cop-out for policies to be reviewed now. It was proof that the Slut Squad's protest had worked, but it was also proof that St. Joe's had always had the means of helping the girls—they had just chosen not to.

My phone vibrated with a response about the emergency editorial meeting.

> Ronnie: You can fill me in after the meeting. I don't want to step on your toes. This is about you and the girls!

At the mention of the girls, Margot popped into my mind and I remembered that she was in my economics class. But I didn't see her in the chair she always sat in. Considering the events from the night before, I believed it was probably because Margot had been suspended rather than Margot intentionally choosing not to come in. Yet another misstep on the part of the St. Joe's administration.

Mrs. Thompson called on other people, asking them to

read definitions without elaborating on the terms or what they meant, or even why this was important. There was no mention of Nudegate or the countdown, or even the protest the night before. It was a pointless exercise since the words clearly didn't have any meaning to anyone; students were bored, peeking at their phones under their desks or exchanging looks with their friends.

And it was unlikely that reviewing school policy was going to stop Eros or help the Slut Squad, anyway. By starting the countdown, Eros had asserted that he was out for some kind of revenge or that he wanted to prove some kind of intentional point. Since no one seemed to actively be looking for him, there was no point in hiding. The countdown was going to continue and whatever Eros had in mind for the big reveal was going to be shared.

The only way it wouldn't be was, realistically, if someone figured out who Eros was. And since Atticus and I were seemingly the only people on Eros's tail, it wasn't likely it'd pan out well.

I looked at Margot's empty seat and wondered, not for the first time, when exactly all of this would be over.

~

Later that afternoon, after otherwise uneventful classes, I met with the editors in the newsroom to talk out Ms. Polaski's proposal.

"Hi, everyone," I greeted the editors as they walked in. I was trying to put on an optimistic front, but the reality was that my heart was beating so quickly I thought it might burst. Again, I hid the tremble in my hands by fidgeting with a dry erase marker.

"Hey," Kolton said and took a seat. A few other editors filed in, some with lunches from the cafeteria and others with snacks they'd purchased from the vending machines. I noticed Jeremy walk in and felt a wave of relief. I knew, in a way, we weren't best friends or even that close, but I didn't realize how much I'd enjoyed his company until I didn't have it anymore.

Once all of the editors were in, I couldn't stall any longer. I leaned against the whiteboard. On the wall to my left were the original notes we'd written about Nudegate on the very first day it happened. It felt like years ago, instead of just over two weeks.

"Ms. Polaski pitched one idea about how to still write about Nudegate but keep the newspaper going too," I said. "We'd use some sort of blog or personal website and operate as a whistle-blower. Everyone will know it's us still, but it won't be technically published in *Warrior Weekly*, which means the newspaper itself will most likely be fine. But I can't promise that I'll be able to keep my job or avoid getting in trouble."

Multiple pairs of eyes stared at me, all trying to process what I was proposing.

"That is so *cool*, Eden!" Julia said and, to my surprise, a few of the editors in the room chuckled. It helped break the ice.

"Would the paper absolutely be fine? Guaranteed?" Jeremy asked.

"I can't guarantee anything with Yanick," I said honestly. "But I know she made it clear we couldn't publish in *Warrior Weekly*. She didn't want it in the newspaper or on the *Warrior Weekly* website since it would be associated directly with the school."

"I feel like we're past the point of worrying about association," Jeremy said. "Considering everyone in the area knows what happened and that it happened at St. Joe's."

"Fair enough," I responded, relieved he seemed to see where I was coming from. "I'm willing to take the fall for this. The feature can be all me. You guys can keep running the newspaper, business as usual, and I'll still complete all of my *Warrior Weekly* duties. The only difference is I'll be working on the Nudegate special with the intention of publishing."

"Do you need help with the website?" Jenny asked. Wes nodded too. "I would be happy to help create it. I feel like presentation is going to be a big part of proving legitimacy here."

"That would be great," I said, becoming calmer with every sound of agreement.

"I'll help with editing," Kolton said. "I'm cool with being on this project. I'm a senior, Yanick can do whatever she wants with me. I don't care."

"I don't know what I can help with, but I'm here for you on this," Jeremy added. I knew he genuinely meant it; he'd never been a bullshitter.

"And we'll keep giving you interview content if you need it," Bree offered, gesturing to Julia and herself.

"Thanks, everyone," I said. My phone vibrated in my jacket pocket, but I ignored it. "I know this is uncharted territory and the process is going to be a little weird, but I'm excited about this. I think it could be something."

"I'll see if layout is interested in helping out at all too," Jenny said. Layout referred to what was, arguably, one of the most important parts of running *Warrior Weekly*. Without them, we would have a bunch of unorganized articles and not the aesthetically pleasing final product the reporters, and the St. Joe's students, were accustomed to.

"This is kind of sick," Kolton said. "I'm hype. Cool idea, Eden."

"Ms. Polaski was the one who offered it to me," I said. "And Ronnie was the one who pushed Ms. Polaski to find a loophole. I didn't come up with any part of it."

"You kept fighting for Nudegate, though, which means something," Jeremy responded, making me blush. "No, really. This is cool. I'm glad you're standing by it."

I exhaled for what felt like the first time in days. "Thank you, guys. I'll keep you updated on next steps. I'd like to get this article polished and out as soon as possible."

"I think I have a solid new addition to the article," Kolton said and held up his phone screen to face me. "Check your email."

I pulled my phone out of my pocket and spotted a new email from an unfamiliar address. I was hesitant to click on it, but I knew I had to.

"Can someone read it out loud? I don't have my email hooked up to my phone," Wes asked, and I looked up, half expecting someone else to do it, until I realized as the assumed group leader it was my job.

I read, "We're the Slut Squad. We've already appeared in the news and during the opening night of *Oklahoma!* but we're not done yet. Because the investigations into the big email and countdown have slowed down, and there seems to be no easy answers to who is behind so-called Nudegate, we've decided to make our own contribution to the cause." I paused, unsure if I wanted to know what their next plans were. "We're offering the Slut Squad Watch List. This is the list of male St. Joe's students who we believe have, in particular, made our lives miserable. We want other students to avoid the same fate. Approach them with caution. Best of luck. Signed, Slut Squad."

"Jesus," Kolton said, practically snorting. "The hits keep coming."

Jeremy said, "Holy shit."

I looked through the list of names and realized it was pretty much everyone I'd talked about with Sloane. I recognized Jason McDonough, the guy from theater who Claire must've sent photos to. Tyson Post from the lacrosse team. Freddy Ulrich, one of Nick's teammates from football. Louis. Luke was on the list, too, even though none of the Nudegate Girls had sent photos to him.

"I guess there won't be any shortage of content for this investigative series," Kolton responded. "We should start setting up interviews as soon as possible."

"No kidding." I scanned over the list, unsure of what I was looking for. One of these guys could have easily been behind Nudegate. Maybe more than one of them. Maybe all of them. It was hard to know. I spent a few more moments gaping at the list before realizing I could end the meeting. "Are there any questions or concerns about the article? I know it's early on so there are a lot of logistics to figure out, but I'm feeling optimistic. I'll text if anything else comes up."

When no one raised their hand or spoke up, I dismissed the meeting. I was already trying to piece together how the Watch List would tie in to the article. I could interview at least a few of the guys on the list to gauge how they're feeling; maybe this would make Tyson more likely to talk to me. Bree and Julia could talk to other students to see how they felt about the Slut Squad's decision to release a list like this. This added an entirely new dimension to the article.

It added an entirely new dimension to the Nudegate situation in general.

I was drafting an email to each guy featured on the list, including a follow-up with Tyson, hoping at least one would respond. I had a bad feeling none of them were going to get back to me.

"Hey, Eden?" Kolton interrupted my brainstorming.

"Yeah?"

"Have you figured out who's going to be your executive editor?"

"No, not yet. I've been waiting for someone to step up so I wouldn't have to force anyone into the position."

"I'm interested," Kolton said. "I think I've figured out the logistics of moving everyone around to make news operate without me."

"That would be amazing, Kolton. Seriously. I think you'd be a great fit for the position."

"Cool," he said, as modest and casual as ever. "I guess we'll have to see how long we last in these new positions after we publish this Nudegate article."

I wanted to laugh, but I also recognized he wasn't too far off base.

CHAPTER TWENTY-TWO

Despite the rest of the day going relatively smoothly, I was tired and stressed by the time I made it home. I'd spent the entire day on edge, waiting for another bomb to drop, but it hadn't happened. Yet, at least. I was too much of a skeptic to believe that the email would be the end of it. The countdown had only one day to go and I knew something big was coming; I just didn't know exactly what.

My mom was home, which I didn't realize I'd wanted until I saw her. I was scared about pushing Yanick too far, scared I'd disappoint the Slut Squad, scared the article would be poorly received while also being scared that it'd cause a tidal wave entirely out of my control. I was also scared for Sloane and what was waiting for her at the end of the countdown.

I dropped my things at the door and immediately walked over to hug her.

"Hey." Mom put down the academic journal she'd been

reading and hugged me. "What's going on? How is everything at school?"

"Not great, if I'm being honest." None of the guys on the list had gotten back to me except Freddy, who'd responded with a straightforward and eloquent *fuck off.*

Mom looked at me, her smiling fading as she went into concerned-mom mode. "We're always here if you need someone to talk to."

"Yeah," I said, feeling like there was too much to ever be able to properly articulate.

"Just remember that college isn't that far away," she said. "Have you started getting your applications together yet?"

"Sort of," I said. I didn't have any schools to which I wanted to apply for early admission, so I'd lied to myself in saying I had plenty of time to apply and worry about it later. But they'd need to be submitted soon. I couldn't think about what was going to happen two days from now, let alone next year. It seemed so far away.

My dad looked up from his laptop. "Don't put it off for too long."

"I know, Dad," I said, smiling a little. Usually, their nagging frustrated me, but it was a welcome change to what had been happening at school. Getting home felt like my only real break from reality and even then, I still had to do homework and answer emails when I was here. "I don't think I can worry about that right now on top of everything else."

Dad frowned. "School isn't doing much?"

"No. Their response has been pretty lackluster," I said.

"St. Joseph's said it held an investigation," Mom offered.

"Yeah, but they've barely done anything," I said. "The girls were basically asked to describe their experience and say who they think sent the email. They still haven't found who did it, even with this countdown going on. I don't know if they ever will."

"Wow, sour attitude, kid," Dad responded. "Where'd you get that from?"

"She got it from you," Mom said, raising her eyebrows.

"Hey, I provide good food and jokes," he said, putting his hands up in front of him defensively.

"Bad jokes," I said. My mom and I laughed. It was all so normal for a second that a weight lifted off my shoulders. I hoped that, maybe, the countdown would signal the end of Nudegate so we could all go back to our normal lives. At least as much as we all could.

~

I woke up the next morning to my phone ringing instead of my alarm.

"Hello?" I answered, not bothering to check the caller ID.

"Eden," Atticus's voice greeted me on the other end. "I've got some weird news for you and I'm not sure how you're going to take it."

I moved the phone away from my face so he wouldn't hear me let out a small groan. "What else could've possibly happened?"

"Luke was arrested this morning." That woke me up. "Have you checked your email?"

I felt like, for someone who usually checked my email constantly, I had been missing a lot of key updates lately. "Give me a sec." I clicked on the email app on my phone and found an email from Principal Yanick.

This morning, there was an arrest related to a crime
that occurred on campus. We will not be disclosing the
student's name, but St. Joseph's would like to make it
clear that the incident is being dealt with by the Greenville
Police Department. If you have any questions or concerns,
do not be afraid to reach out to us.

Below the email was a bunch of information related to reporting crime on campus and assuring parents that criminal offenses at St. Joe's were not common occurrences.

"I think it's Luke," Atticus said.

"But what was the criminal offense? Did they find a loophole for Nudegate? This is so infuriatingly vague."

"I don't know, but the team will sometimes get together for early morning practices the week of a big game and Luke wasn't here. Coach didn't even say anything about it, which is weird considering Luke's the other team captain."

"Have you spoken to Luke at all?"

"Not directly. He sent some stuff in the team group chat about the game yesterday morning, but there hasn't been anything from him since."

I weighed my options. On the one hand, I wasn't particularly thrilled about fact-checking to see if Luke had been arrested for a valid reason. But on the other, I knew an arrest at St. Joe's amplified the entire Nudegate case—whether it was directly related or not—by a hundred. I couldn't ignore it.

"I think we're going to have to talk to Luke," I said, even though the words made me want to throw up.

"I can talk to him alone if you want me to," Atticus offered. "I don't want to put you in another situation with him after what happened last time."

"I'm worried about *you*. Are you guys . . . civil?" I asked. "It seems like it's been kind of tense between you two."

"It's always been like that between us," Atticus said, which wasn't reassuring. "But I'd bet he's willing to overlook any tension for the sake of clearing his name. Soccer means everything to him, even if he is an ass. He wouldn't want to let the team down like this."

"That checks out." I allowed myself an eye roll to get it out of my system before I was face to face with Luke.

"I'll pick you up in thirty," Atticus said, and I responded with a nervous *okay*.

Even though I'd never been keen on blatantly skipping school, there was something exhilarating about the opportunity. I usually justified any missed assignments or skipped class by working on *Warrior Weekly* assignments—even though I knew the excuse wasn't particularly good—and this sort of fell under that umbrella. At the very least, it could probably be a piece of the puzzle.

I got dressed as quickly as I could, deciding to wear my St. Joe's uniform since there would still be time to make it to school after talking to Luke. Realistically, we would probably miss only the first class of the day.

When I spotted Atticus's car outside, I walked outside to meet him. I gripped my jacket closer to me, trying not to think about how my legs were already going numb from the cold.

"Hey," I said after opening the car door and sliding into the passenger seat.

"Hey. Luke is so pissed about what's going on that he said he'd talk to anyone right now. He knows we're both coming."

"I'm supposed to talk to him knowing that he's already mad and that he doesn't really want to talk to me?"

Atticus sighed. "I think he's desperate, Eden. His dad called in a lawyer already. Something is going down related to Vera's car."

"Seems kind of late to be making the arrest."

Atticus shrugged. "I guess they finally got around to looking at the camera footage."

"Camera footage?"

"There are cameras in the parking lot."

"There have been cameras this entire time and no one was caught sooner?" I asked, not entirely surprised but still cling- ing to some skepticism. The school might be going about this poorly, but why would they have passed up such an easy victory?

"I will only say that I know from experience that there are cameras in certain parts of the parking lot and keep it at that," Atticus said, his cheeks turning pink. "Luke's stupid, but I doubt he's stupid enough to do something like that without disguising himself first. It might've taken a while to identify him."

"Does it seem like they're trying to make a case that he was involved in Nudegate too?"

"I'm not sure. Maybe. But they'd be pushing it, I think. And Sloane has talked about how there are no criminal charges for revenge porn, so they'd have to get creative to charge him for anything."

"Yeah. I don't think they're there yet, for some reason. There's still something missing," I said. It was a pessimistic view, but the arrest seemed like a Hail Mary of the worst variety. There was no proof that Eros was also the person who'd graffitied Vera's car. It was an arrest made solely because of desperation instead of based on true guilt. No matter how disgusting Luke was, he at least deserved fairness in law.

But the looming threat of whatever Eros was going to do at the end of his countdown hadn't escaped my mind. I couldn't shake the realization that we had roughly twenty-four hours until Eros's countdown was completed. It was inching closer and I wanted to beat the clock and find Eros before then as much as anyone else, but I wasn't sure arresting Luke was the answer to that. And getting Luke while letting the actual Eros slip away—and allowing Eros to complete his countdown—was something that didn't sit well with me.

"What do you think Eros has in store for the end of the countdown?" I asked.

"I have no idea. I don't want to have to see it."

We sat quietly for a moment, but I was feeling too nervous to sit still. My heart rate was rapidly increasing with every second we drove. I channeled my energy into wringing my hands.

"What do you think Luke's going to say?" I asked as we pulled down a road that looked somewhat familiar. It felt different during the day, but I recognized some of the landmarks, like the sprawling yards, the stunning houses, the quiet roads with little to no one driving.

"I might have known Luke for roughly the past four years, but I can easily say that I have never been able to predict what he would do next," Atticus said, sounding terse.

"I'm sorry," I responded, not knowing why I was apologizing but doing it as easily as a reflex. "I know this isn't—"

"I don't want to think of him as anything more than the asshole who messed with all of these girls' lives, you know? I can't see it that way after everything he's done. Especially to Sloane."

"We don't know if he's guilty yet," I said.

"It's more than just Nudegate," he responded, and I let the

comment bring our conversation to an end. He was right; Luke was, undeniably, one of the worst people I'd ever met, and I hoped that he would get what he deserved in the future. But I also couldn't comfortably sit and let him be punished for something someone else had done.

Atticus pulled into the circular driveway in front of Luke's house. It was even more stunning in the daytime—huge windows, and a gorgeous, tall front entrance—but I couldn't shake the bad feeling I got looking at it. Despite never really being someone who cracked jokes, I felt a sudden desire to say something to help lighten the mood and take some of the weight off my chest.

But, despite my nerves, I knew we had to commit. I took a deep breath and unbuckled my seat belt, as ready as I could be for whatever Luke had in store for us.

We walked up the front steps to the door, but neither of us made an immediate move to ring the doorbell or knock. I moved my hand to the doorbell, hoping that this would be worth the trip. I felt Atticus's hand briefly and lightly envelop my other hand, a touch so light that it barely registered but still felt meaningful all the same. I took a deep breath and rang the doorbell. The faint sound of the ringing echoed through the inside of the house.

After a few long beats, the door was unlocked and opened, revealing a Luke that was like a ghost of his former self. He was wearing a worn sweatshirt that said *DUKE* on the front in bold letters and had what looked like paint stains on it. It fit loosely on his frame and his hair was messy in a way that looked unintentional, more like a cry for help than tousled. But the most surprising part of the whole display was Luke's tired and puffy face, accented with rough, patchy stubble. He was, in other words, not at all the Luke I'd seen over the past few years.

But then again, I wasn't sure what else I had been expecting.

"Hey, man," Atticus said, sounding casual, like we had all gotten together to hang out. There was no lightness to his tone and the forced straight line of his jaw was clearly visible.

"Come in. My parents aren't here right now, but we can't talk for very long," Luke said and turned to start walking through his house. "I don't want them to know you were here. My attorney and my parents would have my ass if they knew I'd spoken to you."

"Yeah, no problem," I responded, my voice sounding small. The word *attorney* took the wind out of me.

Internally, my immediate response was a snappy *not that we were planning on being here for more than a few minutes*, but it felt inappropriate to say. No matter what kind of state Luke was in, he was still Luke and I had no intention of getting into it with him while I was at his house. The fearlessness I'd been trying to embrace recently seemed to evaporate instantly in his presence.

He gave a vague and halfhearted motion to his couch before nearly throwing himself into an armchair across from it. He slouched in his seat, his knees going out so far they nearly hit the coffee table in front of him.

"All right," I said and pulled out my phone to record. "So we have it on record, can you say and spell your name for me?"

"Are you serious?" Luke asked, reverting back into his usual form so quickly it nearly gave me whiplash. When I didn't respond, he sighed and said his name, taking the time to spell it out clearly despite looking pained the entire time.

"Do you have a statement you want to make about the arrest?"

"Yeah, that I'm innocent," he said. "I didn't touch Vera's car.

And I know they're trying to use this a setup to get me to confess to the whole email thing. It's all such bullshit, man. I check my email maybe once a month. I don't even know how to send an email to the entire student body."

I didn't tell him that all it required was using the student directory and basic knowledge of a LISTSERV. It didn't require a tech wizard to figure out.

"Do you genuinely believe St. Joe's is going to try to use the car as the basis of a Nudegate accusation?" I asked. "Does it really seem like that's the direction they're going? Or is it only a guess that they're going to do that?"

"My attorney seems pretty set. I'm the only person who has done anything slightly suspicious, so I'm public enemy number one," Luke said. I decided not to tell him that he'd basically just confessed to vandalizing Vera's car.

"Do you expect people to believe that you didn't send the email?" Atticus asked, surprising both Luke and me in equal measure.

"I mean, yeah. Telling everyone that I'm innocent should be enough."

"Everyone says they're innocent; it doesn't matter if they actually are or not," Atticus insisted.

"Wait, okay," I said, putting my hands up in front of my chest. "I think what Atticus is trying to say is, how would you respond to people who doubt your innocence?"

"I'd tell them they're wrong. Sure, I've fucked up in the past, but just because I've done some bad stuff doesn't mean I'd do something like this. Like, I'd be pissed if someone sent a naked picture of me around."

"Don't act like you haven't shown pictures of girls in the

locker room before," Atticus said, leaning forward in his seat. His jaw was tight and I could sense the direction the conversation was going in.

"Atticus," I said, my tone quiet but forceful. He looked embarrassed about being scolded, but I knew he meant well. He'd spent years hearing about how Luke had treated Sloane, years listening to the way his friends and teammates talked about girls. He knew who guys like Luke turned into and how they treated women—Atticus saw it in his own father.

Atticus sat back in his seat and I looked at him, my eyes tracing his side profile. He looked at me, brown eyes meeting my own, and I knew he wouldn't say anything else during the interview. He'd just be there with me, which was the extent of what I needed.

I paused, collecting my thoughts. I was nervous but, as I took long breaths, I realized Luke was a person. He was an asshole and he made me viscerally uncomfortable, but he was also a high school student who made stupid, irrational decisions. I could entirely handle him.

I decided to go back to my original plan of talking to him the way he talked to everyone else. "Look, I think you're innocent."

"Thank—"

"Not about the vandalism," I said, cutting him off to avoid inflating his ego. "I know you still did *something* and you deserve to be taken down for that. But I can feel that there's something wrong in all of this. There are people who are more likely to have done this." I thought about Louis, and the list of guys the Slut Squad mentioned that they'd each sent photos to. Luke might've played a role in campus climate, he might've encouraged Nick to talk about his sex life with him, but it didn't mean Luke was Eros. My gut told me it wasn't him.

He looked at me and nodded, turning his head down to look at his hands in his lap. "Never thought you'd be the one person who'd think I wasn't guilty."

"Yeah, believe me, I didn't exactly think this would be happening either," I responded dryly. "None of this is based on character, though. Don't get too cocky. I still think you're a bad person."

He shrugged, taking my candor with ease. "I'll take anything I can get right now."

I hated that I felt a tug of sympathy, but I couldn't deny that I felt it. I wasn't sure what that said about me or my character to feel any form of sadness on behalf of Luke Anderson. I wasn't sure I wanted to think about it too much.

"Do you think someone could be setting you up? Or is this a wrong place/wrong time scenario?"

"I think I did this to myself," he said, sounding so authentic —so entirely not like Luke—that it caught me off guard. "I've done some shitty stuff. It's not that far-reaching to assume that I could've been behind Nudegate."

"Do you have anything you want to say to the victims?"

"I'm sorry it happened to you," he said. "And if you ever want to send nudes, I'll more than happily accept them."

My stomach coiled, immediately reminding me of why I'd never gotten along with him in the first place. There was nothing like his ability to turn what could've been something good into a play on someone else's trauma.

I turned off the recorder, deciding I'd spent as much time with Luke in the last few weeks as I could handle in one lifetime.

As I stood up, I couldn't resist asking another question. "What charges are being brought against you, anyway?" I asked.

"Malicious destruction, vehicle damage," Luke said.

"Something like that. It's only vandalism at this point. The punishments can be pretty harsh, but since it's a first-time offense I might get off light."

Of course he would.

"Why did you do it, Luke?" I asked. "Off the record."

Luke scratched at his patchy beard, averting his eyes. "I didn't think people would take it so seriously. The paint wasn't even permanent. And Vera and I mess with each other all the time."

"The same way you mess with Sloane?" I asked, and Luke refused to look at me. He was ashamed now, but I remembered how he reacted, how cavalier he was about everything, the day Vera's car was vandalized. All of the slut shaming, the email, the vandalism would always be a joke to him. He didn't get it. Not then, and probably not ever.

I said a quiet goodbye to Luke, but Atticus didn't say anything as we exited Luke's house. It wasn't until we were back in Atticus's car that I felt like I could breathe again.

"No official charge for Nudegate yet," I said, mostly to myself.

"Yanick basically lied to the entire school," Atticus said. "She's playing off the fact that most students have forgotten a vandalism occurred in the first place."

"Don't sound so surprised, this isn't the first time," I responded. "And technically, she didn't *lie*, she just didn't explicitly tell us what the arrest was for. We all assumed."

"Your cynicism is admirable."

"I've decided to skip right to that stage of being a journalist," I said. "But it sounds like his attorney is pretty confident they'll try to turn the Nudegate thing on Luke. I don't think they'll have enough evidence to pursue that, though. I also don't even know what charges could be made against him for it."

"I can't even tell if I agree with that decision or not," Atticus said, and he suddenly turned his attention to my phone screen. It was lit up with an email notification. "Please tell me that isn't what I think it is."

I was feeling a similar way, but I tried to brush it off and pretend like it could be from anything; it could be junk mail from a store, or maybe an email from a teacher. Anything. I unlocked my phone and let out a sigh of relief. "Just an email from my English teacher about senior projects."

"God, I totally forgot about all of the usual senior year stuff," Atticus said. "I would do anything to go back to when senior projects were my biggest concern."

"Imagine how the girls in the email feel," I said and immediately bit my tongue. "I'm so sorry, I didn't mean that."

"No, no, that was a totally valid point," Atticus said. "It's not bad to have some perspective on the situation. They've got it a lot worse. It all-around sucks."

"I think that about sums it up," I said, thinking about my experience as a senior so far at St. Joe's. I knew it was probably going to get worse before it got better, and I wasn't ready for that.

"The countdown will be over tomorrow," I said, making a sad attempt at a positive spin.

"At least Sloane won't be in school for it," Atticus responded. "She was suspended after the whole rally thing. I think all of the girls were, but Sloane got the worst of it. Sounds like St. Joe's is trying to figure out what to do with that whole Watch List thing too."

I put my head in my hands. "When will this year end? I'm going to lose my mind."

Atticus placed a hand gently on my thigh. It was comforting, in a way. "You're not the only one feeling that way."

I checked the dashboard clock, impatiently waiting for the seconds to count down but also feeling like I might throw up at any moment.

CHAPTER TWENTY-THREE

Being forced to wait for whatever Eros was going to do was nothing short of a nightmare. By lunch the next day, all of St. Joe's knew that Luke had been arrested but only for vandalizing Vera's car. Eros was still out there and, if the email he sent late the night before was any indication—one that simply said, *TOMORROW*—he wasn't backing down.

By the time our all-staff *Warrior Weekly* meeting came around, organized last minute by the editors and me to prepare for incoming breaking news, I could barely handle waiting anymore. I almost wanted Eros to get it over with so we could start dealing with the consequences. But he knew what he was doing. Everyone had been talking about it, barely able to focus on anything else except for what was going to happen at some point before midnight.

I walked into the empty office, trying to shake off the feeling of dread so I could be at least somewhat effective as the editor in chief. It was arguably one of the most important staff meetings we would ever have; we had to deal with Luke's arrest, the end of the countdown, telling the staff about going rogue for publication. It was almost overwhelming, but I knew we could handle it.

Despite everything that had happened, I still got the same feeling every time I walked into the newsroom. There was a buzz of excitement, of potential. I could visualize where I'd made my initial pitches for stories, where I'd finished writing my first article, where I'd gone through training to become the executive editor. If I tried hard enough to picture it, I could see myself walking into newsrooms for the rest of my life.

I placed my backpack on the desk at the front of the room and waited for people to arrive. They always came in a trickle and then a flood; one or two people strolling in individually, and then groups of people wandering in, talking loudly with their friends.

I stood up in the front of the room and suddenly ached for Ronnie's excited chatter and the drive she had. She made this feel like a real newsroom for me and never let me think that what we were doing was useless.

We finally had a chance to make all of this effort matter, beyond just the walls of St. Joe's. People wanted information; I saw the posts online demanding St. Joe's be more open with the city of Greenville, the occasional updates from local news stations. I had to share the full Nudegate story for the sake of the girls, for the sake of transparency and free information. For the sake of knowing that this should never happen again.

"Hi, everyone," I said, allowing for the appropriate amount of time between the last bell and speaking. Usually by ten minutes after, everyone who was coming was already there. "Thanks for coming on such short notice. I know having a meeting on Fridays after class isn't customary, but nothing about this year has been so far."

A hand shot up from near the back of the room: Ivy, a freshman from the news section. "Can we write about the email from Yanick? Or the Watch List? I know we can't talk about Nudegate but so much has happened since then."

"I'm honestly more interested in the Slut Squad protest," Jeremy said. "The backlash from that must've been hefty."

"The girls were suspended for it," I said, but then hesitated, not wanting to completely confirm yet. I trusted Atticus, but I knew the risk of overexaggerating the confirmed accuracy of source information. Taking a note from Ronnie, I toned it down. "At the very least, Sloane was."

"I really thought she'd be expelled by now," Julie said, her face immediately flushed into a deep red. "No, I meant with Yanick being on a warpath and all. To do that in front of so many important people is . . . crazy. It was crazy."

"It was brave," I heard from the door frame and saw Ronnie hovering near the back wall. On instinct, I smiled broadly when I saw her. "The kind of big move that student press should be able to cover without repercussions."

"What's the deal with this countdown? Has anyone done anything about it?" Bree asked from her seat next to Julia.

"It's hard to say. Luke Anderson was arrested earlier, but that was in relation to vandalizing Vera Porfirio's car," I said. I knew I could talk about it openly since it was public record. St. Joe's most likely didn't release his name to the student body directly because they knew his dad would do everything he could to file some sort of lawsuit against the school for it. But the rumor had spread around school pretty quickly thanks to the soccer team, and it was reported by the police, so I didn't have to keep it a secret. I also felt a small thrill at saying *Luke Anderson was arrested* and knowing it was for something he'd done.

I heard murmurs throughout the room, some from people who'd heard about it and others who seemed to have not known. Since it seemed like everyone had moved on to other topics, I knew we could call the meeting.

Ronnie waved at me from the back of the room, making it clear she had something important to say. I turned my attention to the rest of the staff. "I need five minutes. Everyone talk to your editors, make sure you're on track for publication. I'll be back in a second."

As soon as staffers started talking to each other, I speed-walked to the back of the office to meet Ronnie.

"Sorry to interrupt," Ronnie said, sounding more like she was saying it to be polite rather than genuinely meaning it. "Yanick would have an aneurysm if she saw me in here, but I couldn't resist talking to you about it. I have to help you with publishing this Nudegate article."

"You want to be on the investigative team?" I asked, knowing that was how it should have been all along. From the very first day, Nudegate should have been a combined effort by Ronnie and me. It was only right.

"If you're okay with me helping. I know I pushed the article onto you and I'm sorry for doing it. It was a lot of pressure. I want to make sure you have support now, especially since this publishing third-party thing is kind of a big deal. And if anything, if we get caught and in trouble, it can still be blamed, at least in part, on me."

I snorted. "You know I'd take the fall with you. But your help would be wonderful. I think we're going to need all hands on deck for it."

Ronnie looked pleased. "Okay. Great."

The Nudegate story would be the perfect farewell after spending the entirety of our high school career doing all things *Warrior Weekly* together. Having the support of both the editors and Ronnie made me comfortable with green-lighting the project and opening it to the entire staff. It was the perfect time to tell them. I'd never been so sure of anything.

"Hey," I said, trying to get the attention of the room. "Guys. Hey." The room quieted and looked at me with a few glances being tossed at Ronnie, probably trying to figure out what was happening. "This is something that has to remain in the newsroom so word doesn't get back to Yanick. The editors, Ronnie, and I have been talking about publishing a Nudegate article independently, using a website that isn't funded by St. Joe's to protect the newspaper from getting shut down." Some comments get tossed out or mumbled, but I continued on. "I know this sounds ridiculous, but you have to believe me when I say that I feel like this is what we have to do. This story needs to be told, even if it's through drastic measures.

"If you want to help by cowriting the article, come and speak with me. Julia and Bree have a ton of information, too, that they might need help with sorting. We have interviews to transcribe, major events to write about within Nudegate. This is a big project and we need as much help as possible. I know we usually don't work with deadlines this tight, but I believe we can do it."

The room remained still, but I caught Jeremy's eye in the back of the room and he gave me one small nod.

"I'll order pizza," Ronnie said and placed a hand lightly on my arm before slipping to the back of the room again.

The energy in the room changed immediately. Reporters began asking for assignments, trying to figure out how best they can help. Bree and Julia offered input of what they knew and some quotes they'd recorded from underclassmen. Everything moved quickly—chairs were pulled around the room, conversations were heated, keyboards clicked. Hours passed by without us noticing. It was electric.

"That quote should be earlier," Kolton said, pointing at the desktop screen in front of us. "It provides context."

"But it doesn't transition well," I said and looked at Ronnie. "Where should quotes from Danica go in?"

"Wherever it seems like they logically fit," she responded from the couch, a paper plate with pizza on it propped up on her crossed legs.

"Thank you for the sage advice," Kolton mumbled. It felt like how our newsroom used to run, before all of the Nudegate drama. "Jeremy, how's the section about Luke going?"

"It's okay, about as good as it can be when we know jack shit about the situation," Jeremy said and ran a hand through his hair.

"Have you tried Luke's attorney? He might have a comment," I said and pointed at a sentence on the screen. "Kolton, can you keep working on this part? I don't think the wording is right."

"Yeah, sure," he said and put his pizza down.

The work was done in small steps, but progress was still progress. It was a monster of a feature story and while we had most of the pieces, there was still a lot to be done.

"So, for timeline," Ronnie clarified, "we so far have the

beginning, the first few days and immediate aftershock of Nudegate. Then we follow up with the car incident, formation of the Slut Squad . . ."

". . . the protest from the Slut Squad, and then the Watch List," I said and sat on the arm of a couch.

"The lead up to the countdown, the fact that the police can't charge anyone for anything except vandalism," Ronnie said. "All of these stupid walls and limitations, especially from St. Joe's."

Kolton shrugged. "Lack of transparency isn't exactly something new. We'd probably be dealing with it at any high school in any part of the country."

"Realistically, any newspaper in the country, high school or not," I offered.

"Yeah, but you'd hope it wouldn't basically help someone get away with a mass virtual sexual offense." Ronnie yawned. "All right, I vote we wrap this up for the night, at least in the office. I'm tired and my brain hurts and if I have to spend another second thinking about Luke Anderson I'm going to hurt someone."

We all agreed. Work would resume tomorrow.

~

Later that night, I was wrapped up in my comforter after a shower and working on my homework when I heard the familiar email notification ping from my laptop. I clicked on the pop-up notification without giving it a second thought and realized almost immediately what a big mistake that had been. It was the kind of email I needed to be prepared for. I'd been so distracted with my homework that I'd forgotten it was the last day of the countdown.

My phone rang, making me jump, and I answered it after reading the name on the screen. "Holy shit," I said.

"Things somehow got even uglier," Atticus responded.

The email was from Eros, a brief couple of sentences with a video attached.

"*It's time for the main event,*" Atticus read from the screen and I was appreciative since I had so many thoughts running around in my head that I couldn't make sense of the words on the screen. "*Here's what you've all been waiting for.*"

"Are you going to click on it?" I asked, tentatively hovering over the attachment icon. It could be anything, literally anything, and I didn't know how to prepare myself for something like that.

"How about we click on it together and then watch only as far as we need to," Atticus said.

"Okay," I responded and took a deep breath. I clicked on the attachment and a video popped up in a different window. It revealed what looked like an everyday, traditional kind of family kitchen. It was dark outside the windows and there were Solo cups and bottles scattered everywhere, implying it was most likely during, or after, a party. The camera focused on two people, a woman sitting on the counter with her legs spread, her dress up to her waist, and a guy with his shirt unbuttoned pressed to the woman's front. Loud, clearly sexual moans exploded from my computer speakers and I turned it down, praying that my parents hadn't heard it.

"Oh my god, it's a sex tape," I said. "Are you watching this?"

"Yeah," Atticus responded, sounding hesitant. "Who is it?"

There was something immediately surreal about basically watching homemade amateur porn while on the phone with Atticus and having him so calmly ask me questions. I felt like I was having an out-of-body experience.

"Give me a second to see if I can enlarge this," I said and clicked on the button to make the video full screen. I immediately knew who it was; I would recognize that hair anywhere.

"It's Sloane," I said, "the video is of Sloane."

Atticus went silent on the other end, so quiet that I would've thought he'd hung up if I didn't know better.

"I'm sorry," I said, not knowing why I was saying it but feeling like it was appropriate. "God. Poor Sloane."

Atticus was still quiet, and it was making me nervous; I couldn't tell what he was thinking or how he was feeling without hearing his tone, seeing his face. "It looks like the video was taken by someone who was uninvolved," I said. "The camera angle is superweird, and it keeps shifting." I hoped that the change of topic would keep Atticus on the line with me. The video felt inherently sinister and I felt dirty watching something so exploitative. I needed his presence to ground me, even if it was through a phone line.

"Do you think someone random caught them and decided to take the video?" Atticus said, finally breaking his silence.

"I'm thinking it might've been someone who knew them. Or at least one of them," I said. "This feels personal. People hook up all the time at parties and sometimes things get more physical in public than people mean it to. Jokes will be made and whatever else, but I like to believe people wouldn't . . . record something like this. Especially while trying to not be seen."

"Can you see who the guy is?"

"No, I'm struggling to figure it out. We can only see the back of his head," I said and tried to find something familiar in him, but it was difficult since everyone wore uniforms at St. Joe's. This guy's jeans, casual button-down, and Nikes didn't mean anything to me. The clothes people wore outside of the classroom were unfamiliar; this guy might as well be two separate people inside and outside St. Joe's.

"Does he fit any of the guys that we've talked about?"

"Definitely not Luke," I said. "Hair color doesn't match. This guy also looks like he's on the shorter side based on where his waist is in relation to the counter."

"What about Louis?"

"No, I don't think this is him either. This guy is pretty thin and muscular based on his arms," I said, but I heard a certain tone to his voice that made me realize he was thinking about something. "What's your train of thought?"

"Maybe the guy in the video is someone who has a girlfriend or bitter ex-girlfriend who saw him having sex with Sloane. She could've taken a video," he said.

"You think . . . Eros is a *female* St. Joe's student?" I asked and then, suddenly, the theorizing started to make sense. Maybe that's why we couldn't figure it out sooner. We hadn't considered a different type of revenge.

"Yeah, maybe."

"Or Eros could also be the guy in the video. It would be ridiculously stupid, but maybe he's ready to be caught, he wanted to have his last big moment before getting turned in," I said, finding comfort in the idea. Having Eros turn himself in might not be as satisfying as cracking the code ourselves and being able to forcefully bring him in, but it was still something.

"I feel like there's definitely an answer in this video. Some sort of big clue that we're missing." As he said it, I could almost picture what Atticus would look like while he was thinking; the way his brow would slightly furrow, the focused look he'd get on his face.

"Maybe we're not supposed to know the answers. Maybe this is a clue for Sloane," I said, looking at the video one more time for some big glowing sign that said *this is Eros*. "We have to talk to her."

"I'll text her," Atticus said.

I'd been thinking that this was all about Sloane from the beginning. Maybe this would give it away; maybe the answer would be obvious to her. I could only hope it would be.

~

Within an hour of the email being sent out, the three of us met up. I was tired, but Atticus insisted Sloane wanted me there, and I knew I had to do it for her.

I knocked on the door and Atticus appeared, wearing a plain T-shirt that fit admittedly well across his broad shoulders. "Hey," he greeted me. "She's inside."

"You're sure she's okay with me being here?" I asked, needing it to be confirmed for me for the fourth time that night.

"She wants you here," Atticus said, and I couldn't help but believe him, mostly because I wanted to. I brushed past him to walk inside the house, which seemed emptier and colder since the last time I'd been here for the Slut Squad meeting.

We walked down the hall and turned into what looked like a family room, with comfortable and more well-used couches than what was in the front room. Sloane was sitting on the couch with her legs up to her chest, looking tired like I had never seen her. For the first time in the years that I'd known her, even with all the pictures and the suspension and the words being used against her, Sloane had never looked like this. She looked utterly defeated.

"Hey, Sloane," I said, using a soft, even voice similar to what a doctor might use when informing a patient they were going to die soon. I walked farther into the room and Atticus placed himself on a couch perpendicular to Sloane's.

"Hey," she said, her voice taking on a fake chipper tone. "I look great, don't I? Probably look about as great as I feel."

Her face was truly bare. She looked tired and her cheeks were red and puffy from crying. The most jarring thing was seeing her hair up; I didn't think I'd ever seen it up, even in gym class. And her signature lip color was entirely gone. She wasn't the Sloane I knew; she wasn't even Sloane at all. It reminded me of Margot that very first day of Nudegate, seemingly so long ago.

"I'm so sorry, Sloane. You don't deserve this," I told her, unsure of what else to say. It felt like there were so many things to potentially go with—a *fuck that guy* or maybe a gentle joke— but I was never that kind of person. I wanted to ask her how she was, but that felt clearly inappropriate since the answer was an obvious *not well*. I didn't do the comforting role well.

"No one really deserves it," Sloane responded.

"I mean it, Sloane. The way people have talked about you has always been mean and the photos were terrible, to say the least. But this is cruel," I said.

"Yeah," she said, not seeming to know what else to say.

"Do you know who the guy in the video is?" I asked, keeping my voice gentle and hoping it sounded conversational.

Sloane let out a harsh bark of a laugh. "You never let up, do you? You're always a journalist. Can't let a lead go. But no, I don't remember. It wasn't up there on the things I cared about that night. Embarrassing, right? School slut can't even remember the name of the guy she had sex with, even after seeing the sex tape."

The rush of guilt and sympathy rushed through me so quickly that it almost knocked me off my feet. I fought off the desire to cry, knowing this wasn't my time to do it.

Atticus looked at me and when he realized I was out of things to say, he tried. "Do you remember anything at all from that night?"

"Nothing important. I remember it was a house party hosted by one of the guys on the football team just after school started."

"Any idea who might've taken the video? Or anyone you might've told about this party?" Atticus tried, feeling the same drive I had to at least get a name to go off.

"No. The night wasn't all that important to me if I'm being honest. It was another boring party that Rolland had invited me to. The guy in the video might not even be from St. Joe's. Over the summer people will invite all their old friends over who have gone on to college. He could go to Greenville or maybe he's a college student in like, I don't know, Boston or something. Or he could go to one of the other high schools in the area. I don't know," Sloane said and closed her eyes for a second, turning her head away from me. "God, I really don't know."

"Is there anything we can do for you? To help?" I asked, feeling a desperate need to do something.

"No, there's absolutely nothing anyone can do. The only thing at this point is erasing everything that has happened," Sloane said and when she looked back at me, her eyes were red. No tears were on her cheeks, but it was clearly taking a toll on her to have to hold them back.

I walked over to her and fell to a squatting position. "Sloane, you have changed the lives of so many people at St. Joe's. There are girls who were able to find solace in the Nudegate incident only because of you. You brought them together. You made them protest. You made them realize that no one had the right to speak to them in the ways they've been spoken to. And that no one has the right to make them feel guilty for having sex. What you have done is huge and it is important, and I know it doesn't cancel out the bad, but it's still something."

She looked at me for a second, every bit of her tired, pale, and tear-stained face exposed to me. For a second, I thought I might've said too much until she leaned forward and wrapped her arms around my shoulders in a gentle but firm hug.

"Thank you," she whispered so quietly I could barely hear her, but it was significant all the same.

I allowed myself to hug her too. The moment was brief, and the second Sloane pulled away, it felt like things were back to normal. In a way, however, I knew they weren't going to be exactly the same between us.

"I'm sorry I can't put this together." Sloane sighed and put her head in her hands. "I know this *should* make sense to me. It seems like a message directly aimed at me, but I can't figure it out. There's something I'm missing."

"It's okay, it shouldn't be your responsibility to figure out who's harassing you," I said.

"Is there anyone you can think of? At all? An old friend? Old hookup? Think beyond the last few months," Atticus said in a tone that was more helpful than pushy. "Or think about someone so obvious you wouldn't even consider them."

Sloane paused for a moment but shook her head, her face crumpling together to fight back tears. "I'm sorry."

"Maybe a woman," I offered, thinking about Atticus's suggestion. "A current friend. A past friend. Someone who'd have a reason to be upset with you but hasn't been explicit."

Something about that seemed to trigger a thought. Sloane looked down, suddenly refocused. "I—"

"Do you have someone in mind?" Atticus asked and glanced at me.

"I—" Sloane shook her head. "I don't want it to be true. But I think. . ."

Sloane refused to say more to us in the moment. She disappeared upstairs, leaving me and Atticus in her family room, wondering what to do.

"Are we supposed to leave? Wait for her?" I asked. Atticus shrugged. I paced around the room, trying to gauge if this was something Sloane planned on dealing with alone or if she was going to report it somewhere or do something else entirely.

Eventually, she appeared around the corner fully dressed and ready to go out. Her face was still pink and swollen, and it was obvious there was something still troubling her, but her lipstick was back on. She seemed more like Sloane.

"Cole Hartman's birthday party is tonight. Can you drive me to his house?" Sloane tossed Atticus's keys to him.

I looked at Sloane and then Atticus, wondering who Cole Hartman was and what his connection to Nudegate was. The name didn't ring a bell at all.

"Man, I haven't seen him in years," Atticus said. "But sure."

They started walking toward the door when Sloane turned back to me. "You're coming too. Don't think you can get out of this."

We piled into Atticus's car and I tried to save myself from being snapped at by Sloane by not asking any questions. Curiosity was digging at me, but I didn't want to push it. She sounded like she knew what she was doing, and I could only tag along for it.

The drive to Cole's house was only about fifteen minutes. It was a colonial style with a driveway that went along the side of the house. Based on the number of cars, it was a pretty big birthday party.

Atticus parked at a spot near the end and Sloane hopped out of the car before he'd even come to a full stop. Once she was out of earshot, I looked at Atticus. "Who's Cole Hartman?"

"Some guy we went to middle school with. We played basketball together," he said. "He goes to Greenville High, though. I have genuinely no idea what connection he'd have to Nudegate."

I appreciated Atticus's willingness to go along with Sloane even though it wasn't clear what she was thinking or what she'd hoped to achieve.

The serene exterior of the house didn't match the interior; there were a ton of people crammed into each room. The house felt like it was upwards of eighty degrees.

The number of people made it impossible to spot Sloane in the crowd. Never at ease at a party, still, after the last few weeks, I was at least growing comfortable with the fact that I'd never recognize half the kids crammed into the crowded living spaces. There were a few people from St. Joe's here and there from various sports teams, but otherwise, I didn't know anyone. The muffled music and vibrations in the floor told me everything was happening in the basement, though, so maybe there were even more people here than I'd thought.

Atticus and I slipped into the dining room where it was a little quieter and we could avoid the path of the front door, making us a little less obvious.

"Should we wait in the car?" I looked at Atticus and then back at the party. I wasn't dressed to be out—I'd put on joggers and an old *Warrior Weekly* T-shirt to meet Sloane—and crashing a party wasn't my scene.

"I think Sloane has something she wants to do," Atticus responded, somewhat unhelpfully.

We stood there for what felt like years before our phones vibrated at the same time. Sloane had created a group chat. *Come meet me in the upstairs bathroom in the first bedroom to your left. Be quick.*

Without hesitation, Atticus and I walked as quickly as we could without concerning the people around us. I'd assumed it would be difficult to figure out which door she meant, but the bedroom door was open, revealing a room with décor that screamed *grown up*. We walked in and spotted a closed door with the light on.

I knocked on the door. "Sloane?"

The lock turned and the door opened, revealing Sloane with a phone in each hand.

"Did you take someone's phone?" I asked. She shushed me and rushed me and Atticus into the bathroom, locking the door again. "Whose phone is that?"

"It's Rolland's," Sloane said. "Look at it." She tossed the phone in our direction and, thankfully, Atticus had enough hand-eye coordination to catch it before it fell on the floor. We stood next to each other and looked at the screen.

On the camera roll were all of the photos from the email. The video was there too. I felt my stomach drop, but I wasn't ready to fully accept what I was looking at. "Maybe he saved them from the email?"

"Check his email. He was the one who sent it."

Atticus exited the camera roll and went onto her email, going into the Sent folder. "Oh my god," I said. The only messages in the Sent folder were the ones we'd all received from Eros. There were upwards of 150 unopened email responses to the Eros account from students, faculty and parents alike, but a quick check revealed the notifications for the app hadn't been on. Unless someone clicked directly on it, they would have no idea an email had been connected.

"This can't possibly be true," I said.

"Rolland?" Atticus asked and looked at Sloane. "Why?"

"How would he have gotten all of those pictures?" I asked. "It doesn't make sense. What's the motive?" Even though I knew what I was looking at, I couldn't comprehend it. Something about it felt off; there was still a piece missing.

"Group chat," Sloane said, confirming my earlier beliefs. "Probably a combination of a few of them."

"It seems weird for him to have all of this on his phone like that," I said. "It's like he's not even trying to be subtle. Was there a password on his phone?"

"No," Sloane said.

"All of the photos seemed to be saved next to each other," I said. "It's either the only photos he has from the last few months are saved nudes from girls, or he saved them all on his phone in one go."

"They're all from before the email," Atticus offered. "Based on the time stamp. So, he must've had them before the email went out."

"It would make sense they'd all have to be on here since it seems like the email was sent from his phone," I said. "It's odd he'd waited to save all of the photos onto his phone until he had them all. Like he waited to save them until he knew he was going to send the email."

I reached for the phone. Atticus handed it to me and watched as I clicked through and checked the messages, trying to figure out where the photos were coming from. "Okay, here's one. Some photos sent in here, which explains a few of them."

Atticus looked at the screen, trying to see which of the Slut Squad's photos were in the group chat. "Angela, Vera, Sloane." He checked the names involved. "Louis isn't part of the chat. How would Louis be related to this? Or some of the other guys?"

I barely had to think of an answer. It'd been right in front of me all along. "He got suckered into it. They did the same thing to my ex. Guys will talk about girls and the photos the girls have sent and the girls they've had sex with. And the guys who want to fit in play along with it."

I clicked through his messages, looking for some sort of connection that explained the rest of the guys. Jason McDonough, unknown to me, had a cousin on the St. Joe's basketball team who was good friends with Rolland. Derek sold weed to a few athletes on campus, like Atticus mentioned, which connected him to Rolland. It was all there, clearly laid out in his messages. The only guy still missing was Louis.

If anyone had done an even partially effective investigation it all would've been found. I relayed the information to Atticus and Sloane as I found it.

"There's something else still missing," Sloane said. "Why is Margot's photo so far up? It's saved on here twice."

I glanced at the screen and, separate from the rest of the photos, was Margot's. She was saved in the chunk of Nudegate photos, but also saved as one solo shot a few months earlier. Both were the same exact picture of Margot, but there were at least forty pictures of various social events and football practices and class notes between the two saved versions. The only reason why that could be was he would've saved it twice, but at two separate times.

Margot sending her pictures to Rolland would explain why she never openly talked about who she'd sent her nudes to. She was probably worried Danica would come after her for it.

"Why would he have done that?" I asked.

"Maybe he wasn't the one who did it," Sloane said. "Maybe he didn't realize what was happening."

"But it's his phone," I responded.

"Danica would drop hints sometimes that made it sound like she'd go through Rolland's phone," Sloane said, her voice catching on Danica's name. "I don't think she trusts him. I don't think she ever has."

"What are you saying?" Atticus asked.

"I think Danica did this," Sloane said, her voice suddenly sounding stronger and more certain. "I think she went through his phone, realized he'd been flirting with other girls, got upset, and did the most vengeful thing she could think of."

As confident as Sloane sounded, I couldn't fit the pieces together. Danica had been by Sloane's and Vera's side the entire time. She had helped them start the Slut Squad. And those were only the things I knew; she had also been friends with Sloane for years before Nudegate. They probably had memories and inside jokes and shared secrets. They'd probably been through so much together. The thought of Danica betraying Sloane like that seemed impossible.

"Why would it be directed at you?" I asked and then thought about the conversation Atticus had recorded and sent to me from Luke's party. "You hooked up with Rolland too."

"Before they were dating. But yeah."

"Oh god," I said.

"Oh god," Sloane echoed.

Unsure of what to do next, I did the only thing I could think of: gathered information. I took photos of the screen so we'd have time-stamped evidence that these photos were on Rolland's phone. I was worried that, somewhere between now and the time we reported it, the evidence might disappear. But that made me think of something else.

"Who are we supposed to report this to?" I asked. "What do we do with this information?"

Atticus considered it for a minute. "St. Joe's might be a good starting point."

"But who at St. Joe's would listen to this?" Sloane asked. "Who's going to listen to me? Or to any of us, for that matter, considering none of us have had clear records the last few weeks?"

"Ms. Polaski," I said. "My journalism teacher. She'd listen to us, I think. At the very least, she'd take us seriously. I'll send an email with the screenshots and a quick explanation and we'll see what happens from there."

"So, do we wait then?" Atticus asked. "Like, wait until tomorrow for Ms. Polaski to do something?"

Sloane scoffed. "No fucking way."

"This is the only—" I started, but I knew Sloane wasn't going to have the patience to be talked down.

"I am not waiting for this to get back to the administration. I can't possibly wait for them to get their shit together," Sloane said. We all stood there for a moment, in the bathroom of a house belonging to a person I'd never met, talking about one of Sloane's best friends betraying her in a horrible, very public way. I had never felt so out of my depth. "She has ruined my life. Everything that has happened in the past few weeks has been unforgivable. The thought of her having peace of mind for even another second is too much for me."

"Maybe we should approach this—" I wasn't able to finish my sentence. Sloane grabbed the phone from my hand and pushed through the bathroom door to leave.

I could feel my stomach knotting up and everything in me told me to leave the party as quickly as possible.

"We should stop her," I said.

Atticus looked at me. "I think she's got it."

He grabbed my hand and started walking me out of the bathroom, leading me downstairs to go find Sloane and see what she had in store.

~

We found her in the living room, openly handing Rolland's phone back to him. There was a small group of St. Joe's students who had gathered near the fireplace to drink together and pass around a blunt. I spotted Rolland, Danica, Vera, and then a few other guys from the football team. Thankfully, Nick wasn't there.

I tried to walk toward Sloane, but Atticus tugged me back, keeping us at a comfortable distance. We could still see and hear everything, but we didn't have to be involved. This was Sloane's moment; she deserved to have it.

"Hey, Rolland," Sloane said. "Thanks for letting me use it. I can't believe I was stupid enough to leave the house without charging my phone." That explained how she'd gotten Rolland's phone; she'd lied and told him hers was dead. She refocused her attention on Danica. "Hey, Dan."

Danica watched her cautiously, placing a hand tighter on Rolland's arm. "Hey, Sloane."

"How's everything been? I've missed you guys," Sloane said. "Being suspended sucks. A girl can watch only so many episodes of *Scandal* before needing a break."

"Rolland heard from University of Alabama again this afternoon," Danica said. "I guess they're interested in recruiting him."

"Oh, how fun. You're thinking about going there, too, right?"

"Just like my parents," Danica responded.

"Yeah, yeah," Sloane said.

"What's up, Sloane?" Vera asked, looking at her. "You're acting weird."

"I was wondering how Alabama would feel about accepting people who'd committed what some might call a criminal act," Sloane said. "Or people expelled from their high school."

Danica's face twitched. It was subtle, but I noticed it. Atticus tensed up next to me and I knew it was really starting.

"What?" Danica asked.

"You know, sending out pictures of people might not be illegal here, but it sure is in other states."

"What are you saying?" Vera said and took a step forward. "Chill, Sloane."

"No, let her talk," Atticus said.

"Who asked you?" Danica shot at Atticus and then she turned her attention back to Sloane. "What does that even mean?"

"You think I don't know what went down here? You really think I'm that stupid?" Sloane asked. "You were the only person I brought to that party with me where I fucked some dude in a kitchen. Remember? Vera was in Cancun for her sister's wedding. But what's interesting is that, now I think about it, you didn't seem at all surprised when I'd told you about it later that night. It was like you already knew it'd happened."

"Okay? So that means I sent out a video of you and him doing it? Are you serious?" Danica asked and looked at her.

"Not necessarily," Sloane continued. "The actual proof appears to be on Rolland's phone. Rolland, did you know you're Eros?"

Rolland looked between Sloane and Danica, unable to follow the game they were playing. Either he was an exceptional actor or he truly had no idea that Danica had been using his phone as a cover.

Danica's face grew visibly paler. I tightly crossed my arms against myself.

"There's this fun little group chat where it seems like people share other people's nudes," Sloane said. "How cool is that? A quirky thing the guys like to do as a form of bonding. And what's weird about that is it makes nudes superaccessible. So all you have to do is know the group chat exists and save the photos, and then you can do whatever you want with them after that."

"I don't know what you're—" Danica said.

"Yeah, of course you don't," Sloane said. "I will say, this was slick. I couldn't piece this one together until I realized, of course, you are *still* upset that I hooked up with your current boyfriend before you were even dating. Even after you told me it was all fine."

"God, shut up!" Danica said, raising her voice so loudly that it visibly caught Sloane off guard and caught the attention of everyone else in the room. Even Vera had started to move backward away from the scene. "You knew how I felt about it. You knew how I felt about him and you still slept with him."

"Danica, please. You mentioned him, like, twice. You didn't have a crush on him. You're just mad your boyfriend had a hard-on for me. Maybe he still does."

"Oh my god, *enough*," Danica said, clearly getting worked up. "I cannot stand you. I can't stand your stupid drama or the guys you hook up with or the way that you carry yourself. You are absolutely *infuriating*."

"Excuse me?" Sloane asked.

"You heard me. You are *so* self-possessed. And all everybody ever says is how much they admire you, how hot you are, how much they want to be with you. Rolland was talking about it before he and I started dating. Did you know he still has all of those nudes saved from when you were hooking up? He never deleted them, even after he asked me to be his girlfriend."

"Wait—" Rolland interjected, but everyone ignored him.

"Danica," Vera said, clearly trying to calm Danica down before she said more that she regretted, but Danica put a hand up to stop her.

"Do you know how that makes me feel?" Danica asked. "Knowing I'm being compared to people? Knowing that my boyfriend still thinks about you?"

"Then bring it up with him," Sloane said. "It really is that simple. Why would you bring other girls into it?"

"Because other girls are constantly around! That group chat is filled with girls willing to put themselves out there. Girls who want to fuck my boyfriend, fuck his friends, whatever. And I found photos saved on his phone that he'd somehow gotten during the, like, week-long breaks we'd take. Who moves that quickly? Who claims to be in love and then fucks someone else when you're on *break*?"

"So, that gives you permission to send out a bunch of girls' nudes?" Sloane asked. "What the fuck is wrong with you?"

"Everyone is so fucking casual all the time. What happened to commitment? What happened to people waiting to have sex with someone they're in love with?" Danica asked. "I needed to have sex to keep Rolland interested."

"But that's still not the fault of the girls. It's not *my* fault."

"You perpetuate it! You are part of this mentality that sex doesn't mean anything and that it should be casual and fun. But I can't do that."

"And you don't have to!" Sloane said. "No one is forcing you to!"

"But they are! I've always felt like I needed to. I get asked for nudes like it's no big deal. Rolland asked me to send him photos before we were even dating and I didn't want to, but he didn't seem interested in me until I did. Otherwise, boring. Vanilla."

"That's on him, Danica. That's entirely on him. No one else."

"He's not the only one," Danica said. "He never has been. And you know that." Danica pushed past Sloane to leave. "Rolland, let's go."

"No," Rolland said. I could tell by his expression that he was a few steps behind but slowly piecing it together. Everyone else in the group was too. "I don't think I ever want to talk to you again."

Danica was nearly vibrating with anger, but after a few seconds, she turned on her heel and disappeared through the crowd. I was so in shock that I could hardly move, but Sloane looked surprisingly calm, as if she'd been having a pleasant lunch with a group of friends rather than a public fight during a party. Sloane walked over to meet me and Atticus as my phone vibrated in my pocket. I'd received an email from Sloane.

"What's this?" I asked, opening it.

"It's the soundbite. You think I'd bait her like that and not record it? I learned it from the best."

I could hardly hide my smile despite how inappropriate it felt in that moment. "I can't believe you did it."

Sloane smiled. "I can."

EPILOGUE
TWO MONTHS LATER

"Yo, check out this comment! '*Proud of the reporters at St. Joseph's High School in Massachusetts for breaking this story open. Excellent read and even better promise. Looking forward to what these students achieve in the future,*'" Kolton read off the computer screen. "That's a reporter from the fucking *Washington Post*. Can you believe that?"

We were in the middle of hosting a very G-rated party at the *Warrior Weekly* office, featuring soda, chips, and all of us wearing our school uniforms. Our article about Nudegate was finally finished and published in the physical *Warrior Weekly* newspaper. No more secrecy, no more hiding.

It'd created a major buzz already; journalists from all over the country—some from other countries, too—were commenting on the work we had done on the Nudegate story. They were proud of us for doing what we could to get the story published, including risking punishment from the school and the loss of our newspaper.

The article was particularly meaningful because it featured an ending, with Danica facing charges of harassment and cyberbullying. Between my photos of Rolland's time-stamped phone screen, Rolland's statement, and Danica's recorded confession, it was obvious something had to be done. The charges were pretty minimal and didn't give the full picture of the harm caused by Nudegate, but since Vera's dad was on a warpath, we were hopeful something harsher would come up. At the very least, Danica had been expelled from St. Joe's without question. Ms. Polaski pushed hard to make that happen; she made sure the email Sloane, Atticus, and I had sent her went directly to the school board.

She also made sure to report Principal Yanick's behavior to the board. They weren't thrilled about how she'd handled the issue, and definitely weren't happy that we'd openly bashed St. Joe's in the latest issue for trying to keep the newspaper quiet. Even though they hadn't done anything to help us at the time, they were pretending that—all along—they'd been supporting student journalists and couldn't believe Principal Yanick would threaten to shut us down. They'd also still tried to claim they couldn't believe Yanick didn't offer more direct support to the Slut Squad.

The charade was laughable, mostly because none of the male students who were involved had gotten into any real trouble. The boys involved in the group chats were scolded about cyberbullying, but there was nothing on public or school records. They could return to their normal lives, unscathed and unconcerned about how this would affect them.

The only guy who expressed any guilt was Louis. It turned out Danica had gotten into his unlocked phone during a group project and sent herself the pictures of Alice for the email. In a way, it turned out neither Louis nor Alice was at fault. Louis, however, had shown Alice's pictures to his friends, a guilt that seemed to consume him only once Eros had been found. Alice, reasonably, was unable to forgive him for the way he'd treated her.

But, even with disappointments from the school board, the article led to some real changes. Sloane started to make a name for herself as an advocate; she'd already been contacted by a few groups working against revenge porn and expressed interest in trying to update Massachusetts laws to reflect virtual sex crimes, something we all fully supported her in. She still couldn't remember who the guy from the video was, but in a way, it didn't seem like his identity was at all important to her story.

Luke also ended up fading pretty quickly into the background. He finally started leaving everyone alone after he was fined for vandalizing Vera's car, and St. Joe's told his parents it was for the best he finished his education elsewhere. I can't say that I missed him. Or Nick, either, for that matter; I hadn't thought about him once since Sloane had unmasked Eros.

"The papers are printed!" Jeremy said as he walked into the office. He was carrying a stack of newspapers. "The school was not happy about having to print advanced copies, but I wanted everyone to see it while we were all together."

Ronnie walked over and grabbed one, then ran over to me. "We got it printed! We got Yanick out of here *and* we got to keep our article as is. Name a more powerful duo."

After all the drama with the school board, Yanick—and a few

other administrators—were forced out of their positions with the ultimatum of quitting or being fired. Yanick was given the option of early retirement. Once she was gone, the acting principal told us we were allowed to print the article we'd posted online in the actual *Warrior Weekly* newspaper. All it took was sharing our article far and wide on social media until someone listened to us. It seemed like overnight Nudegate had gone from local Greenville news to every major outlet in the country.

Ronnie had gotten her time in the sun from the story, too, despite Yanick removing her from staff. Undergraduate journalism programs and working journalists were practically drooling over Ronnie and loved her willingness to fight for a story even if they risked getting fired. Once Yanick was gone, I was more than happy to offer Ronnie her position as editor in chief again, but she'd already secured a part-time internship with the *Boston Globe* by then. The position was perfect for her, indicated by the seemingly endless stream of all-caps texts and exclamation marks I received whenever she was in the office. I missed working with her and seeing her all the time, but we considered it practice for when we'd have to do long distance in college.

"It came out great," Atticus said to Ronnie and me. Something about the resolution of Nudegate made Atticus and I realize we liked spending time together, and we didn't need to use solving a mystery as an excuse to hang out. I thought, if all went well, I might have a prom date later that year.

I looked over the Nudegate article on the front page of the paper, unable to stop admiring it. The email, and Eros, had been a dark cloud over the school for over two weeks, and the fallout stretched for a few more. It was freeing to have finally reached the end.

All of the editorial staff shared a byline, something that made my heart swell. The photo was perfect: it was the Slut Squad standing together with their backs against a row of lockers. We'd managed to talk everyone into it, including Violeta, Angela, and Claire.

Claire became more vocal about her Nudegate experience, directly against her mother's wishes. After the Halloween party, Claire reached out to Sloane, feeling guilty about the way she'd talked to her and admitted she didn't know what to do. She'd been working closely—but secretly—with the Slut Squad since then, and had helped plan the protest, right down to which song the girls would interrupt.

Even more surprisingly, Claire joined forces with Sloane, Vera, and Margot and had become a face for the issue. Violeta, Alice, and Angela expressed how proud they were of the other girls but did not have the same desire to do TV interviews and deal with backlash online, which made sense. There was a lot of positive support for the Slut Squad, but there was also a lot of expected hate and slut shaming still happening.

"We found Eros," Sloane said, walking over to me. The Slut Squad was invited to join the party, too, since the newspaper issue had been basically dedicated to them. I was glad to see all of them there, genuinely laughing and seeming somewhat more relaxed. Angela and Jeremy were cracking jokes; Violeta was chatting with Kolton. Vera was talking to Margot and Alice, casually, with a cup of soda in her hand. Claire was talking to the reporters who'd written a review of *Oklahoma!* after the show had finally opened for real and had a successful run. The understudy for Jason McDonough was unexpectedly allowed to have his shining moment, too, after Claire refused to be on stage with

Jason. Jason was since banned from all St. Joe's theater involve-ment, a decision made and enforced by students in solidarity with Claire.

It was hard to believe looking at them that, not that long ago, most of these girls had never had a reason to interact. They'd never had a reason to believe any form of tragedy would bring them together. Maybe after graduation they'd keep in touch, brought together by a nightmarish high school experience. Or maybe after this point, they'd have no reason to keep in touch and would decide not to. Either way, it was their decision where they would go next.

It was the kind of peace and autonomy the girls had deserved from the get-go. Even though some of their parents were still upset with them and they were still hurting and afraid of how the Reddit threads and internet hate and having their name attached to a school scandal would catch up to them one day, they seemed to be doing okay. At least, as okay as they could be considering the circumstances.

Everything about Nudegate had been avoidable and unneces-sary and painful, and it would never go away completely, but it seemed like, maybe, there could still be a happy ending.

"*You* found Eros," I offered, and Sloane raised her cup to me.

Sloane then smiled at me, that single expression saying more than words could ever express.

ACKNOWLEDGMENTS

I've been dreaming about writing an acknowledgments page for a book since I was seven years old, and to actually be writing one now is nothing short of surreal.

First, I absolutely must thank the team at Wattpad Books for all of the support they've offered. They saw something special in *Revenge of the Sluts* and, despite having written an entire novel, I still don't have the words to articulate how thankful I am. To Deanna, Monica, Samantha, Jen, Robyn, and everyone else behind the scenes, I owe this all to you.

Also a huge thank you to my parents, my brothers, my family, for being just as excited about this book as I am. And also for not being too openly shocked by the title. Sorry I didn't mention I was writing a novel until I got a book deal.

Additional love to my friends and girlfriend who have supported me, listened to me, carried me through this. I literally cannot thank you enough. Your patience is worth everything. Maddie, Matt, Aidan, Anna, Brian, Ian, Trainor, so many other people who I told about this book (and took me out for drinks to celebrate the publication announcement): I love you. Moth Manor lives on in our hearts.

I also literally owe this novel to Ivey, my Wattpad wife, the first and best friend I met through Wattpad, and one of my actual, real-life best friends. You've stuck with me from the very beginning. I don't know if you actually believed ROTS would get somewhere or not, but you supported me regardless and it means so much to me. Thank you for reading all of my frantic texts, for being my first reader, for boosting ROTS so much and making me feel like I could do this.

To my very first editors, Jenn and Olivia, who read through the earliest drafts of this book (edits that almost definitely helped me win a 2018 Watty), even with classwork and article editing and real life happening: thank you.

To my Wattpad readers who followed me here: thank you. One of my favorite things about Wattpad is watching readers engage with the material in live time and I read all of your feedback, all of your comments theorizing over who Eros is, all of your debating in the comments. Thank you for supporting ROTS and for all of the kindness in announcing publication. I hope all of the changes to the original (and there have been a lot—I won't lie) are good changes.

And, additionally, because I wrote (and edited and prepared to publish) this book while I was still an undergraduate, I owe huge thank-yous to the University of Delaware faculty, staff, and coworkers who have supported me through so much:

Kristin B, it was because of you that I gained the courage to actually talk about ROTS to people offline. Your support and genuine belief in what I'm capable of means so much.

Santhi, thank you for being a driving force in figuring out what I want to do. I have learned so much from you already, both in and out of classrooms. ROTS would not have been so bold, so self-aware, and so big, had it not been for you. An additional thanks for advising me and being so understanding during the absolutely ridiculous endeavor of editing this book while working on my senior thesis.

Ellen, you always lumped ROTS in with all of the other academically-focused work I was doing and I'm really appreciative of that. It was never seen as a burden to have to work around publishing deadlines. Thank you for believing in me from the first class I took with you.

To my Special Collections family: I love you all so much. I'm sorry for spending so many hours clocked-in editing ROTS. Looking forward to donating a copy so I can get it added to the collection, just for the sake of saying I did it.

To *The Review* staff, past, present, and future: you are the driving force behind this novel. My two years on staff inspired so much of this book. I hope I did it justice.

To my fellow SOS advocates: I learned everything I know from you. My four years spent with you were heartbreaking and challenging and life changing and empowering. I wouldn't trade it for anything. I'm so proud of everything that you have all done and accomplished, and thank you for making me, me.

And, because I'm a girl connected to her hometown and I'm writing this down the street from my old elementary school, thank you to the teachers who supported me as a kid. I still have all of your notes. I still remember being individually introduced to a visiting author because you all saw how much time I spent writing in my notebooks. I think of you all fondly and still remember you by name and face.

And to the loved ones who aren't here to see this, I love you. I miss you. Rest easy.

To the people who are reading this, who relate in ways to the Nudegate Girls that might be too painful to admit—you are brave. You are loved. Your stories are the momentum for change.

To the journalists, either aspiring or currently working in a newsroom, reading this: you fucking rock. Journalism, and the public, needs you. Keep going, keep fighting. Whether you are a Ronnie or Eden or Kolton or Jeremy or Bree or Julia or whomever else you relate to, your voice is so important.

There are also places of significance that I feel like I should thank, considering I've emotionally bonded this novel to them: the second floor of Smith Hall, the Writing Center in Morris Library, where I finished the first ever draft of ROTS, the offices of Special Collections (specifically, the desk near the typewriter), *The Review* office, the bedroom floor of my campus housing where I got the call confirming Wattpad Books was publishing ROTS, the big Moth Manor couch, my childhood bedroom.

To the music of significance to this book, Tchaikovsky, Harry Styles, Leonard Cohen, Nina Simone, the *Funny Girl* soundtrack, Fiona Apple who helped write the Slut Squad, and so many others for keeping me company during lonely periods of writing and editing.

I also have to shout out *Veronica Mars*, the show that made me realize I didn't have to choose between writing a social commentary and a mystery, and that teen girls are so, so badass. I still have your early seasons on DVD so I can do my yearly rewatch. So much of my teen angst was given a voice through you. Thank you.

And, finally, to the reader who has so patiently read through my ramblings—thank you for reading *Revenge of the Sluts*. Thank you for believing in me enough to give this book a chance. *Revenge of the Sluts* has been cathartic for me to write and edit, and I hope reading it had the same effect on you.

ABOUT THE AUTHOR

Natalie Walton has been writing for as long as she can remember, completing her first "book" in second grade. She began posting her stories on Wattpad at the age of fourteen and has since amassed over eighteen million reads on her works. Natalie is a Delaware resident and wrote *Revenge of the Sluts* while being a full-time student at the University of Delaware, working toward her degree in sociology and criminal justice.

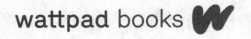

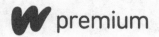